Merrill's English Texts

SILAS MARNER
THE WEAVER OF RAVELOE

BY
GEORGE ELIOT

EDITED WITH AN INTRODUCTION AND NOTES
BY CORNELIA BEARE, INSTRUCTOR IN ENGLISH,
WADLEIGH HIGH SCHOOL, NEW YORK CITY

NEW YORK
CHARLES E. MERRILL CO.
44–60 EAST TWENTY–THIRD STREET

CONTENTS

PUBLISHERS' NOTE

Merrill's English Texts

THIS series of books will include in complete editions those masterpieces of English Literature that are best adapted for the use of schools and colleges. The editors of the several volumes will be chosen for their special qualifications in connection with the texts to be issued under their individual supervision, but familiarity with the practical needs of the classroom, no less than sound scholarship, will characterize the editing of every book in the series.

In connection with each text, a critical and historical introduction, including a sketch of the life of the author and his relation to the thought of his time, critical opinions of the work in question chosen from the great body of English criticism, and, where possible, a portrait of the author, will be given. Ample explanatory notes of such passages in the text as call for special attention will be supplied, but irrelevant annotation and explanations of the obvious will be rigidly excluded.

CHARLES E. MERRILL CO.

INTRODUCTION

BIOGRAPHICAL SKETCH

Marian Evans ("George Eliot") was born November 22, 1819, at Arbury Farm, near Nuneaton, in Warwickshire. Her father, Robert Evans, is described in the characters of Adam Bede and Caleb Garth, the two manliest of all George Eliot's men. Touches of his personality also appear in the old violin-maker of the poem *Stradivarius*. Like Adam, he rose from carpenter to surveyor and land-agent, and Arbury Hall, the home of his principal employer, appears in *Mr. Gilfil's Love Story* as the charming Cheverel Manor. He possessed Adam Bede's stalwart figure and Caleb Garth's sincerity and love of good work for its own sake. Mrs. Evans was a woman of indefatigable industry and epigrammatic, pungent speech, and her portrait is given in the characters of Mrs. Hackit and Mrs. Poyser. There was an older sister, whose picture is partly sketched in the character of Celia, in *Middlemarch*, and a brother, whom all know as Tom Tulliver, in *The Mill on the Floss*.

She first attended school at a little village near Griff House, the "Shepperton" of her first story. At seven she was sent to Nuneaton, and at twelve to a girls' boarding-school at Coventry, where she astonished her companions with her learning, her music, and her strange manners. A neighbor described her as a "queer, three-cornered, awkward gel." She lacked beauty and grace, was dreamy, serious, and wise beyond her years, and lived almost without child-companionship because of the intellectual distance between herself and others of the same age. Her schooldays ended at sixteen.

7

The death of her mother, and the marriage soon after of her sister, brought upon her the burden of her father's housekeeping. For the next six years a double education was carried on, for with persistent diligence she continued her studies, while acquiring a practical knowledge of domestic arts, especially the art of butter-making. It was this experience that gave us the delightful description of the dairy in *Adam Bede* and many other such idyllic scenes in the early stories.

George Eliot brought to her novel-writing an intellectual equipment probably unsurpassed, if equaled, by any writer since Shakespeare. To natural endowments of the highest order she added a store of acquired knowledge that is truly marvelous. One reads her books with perpetual astonishment at the richness and fullness of her wisdom. With Bacon's ambition, but without his egotism, she seems to have " chosen all knowledge for her province." She learned French, German, Italian, Spanish, Latin, Greek, and Hebrew mainly without an instructor; was an accomplished musician, and, as a student of literature, language, science, and philosophy, could have taken rank with the first scholars. Moreover, the insatiable desire of the student remained through all her years. Late in life she said in a letter: " I enjoy all subjects, all study, more than I ever did in my life before. I learned Spanish last year but one, and see new vistas everywhere. I could enjoy everything, from arithmetic to antiquarianism, if I had large spaces of life before me. But instead of that I have a very small space. Unfeigned, unselfish, cheerful resignation is difficult; but I strive to get it."

In 1841 Mr. Evans removed to Foleshill, on the outskirts of Coventry, leaving Griff House to his son Isaac. This was an epoch-making event for Marian Evans, for it brought her suddenly under influences that determined her lifework. She loved her father and brother, but she found no intellectual companionship in their narrow, practical lives. Her eager aspiring mind yearned for sympathy and expression. What had been long lacking in her life she

found at Foleshill in the friendship of Mr. and Mrs.
Charles Bray and a sister, Miss Sara Hennell, people of
wealth, culture, and learning, and engaged in broad intellectual pursuits. In this congenial society she remained nine
years, studiously attending to the discipline of her mind.
But the most important effect of the change was upon her
religious life. Hitherto she had ordered her conduct and
thinking by the most rigid principles of Calvinism, being at
one time strongly influenced by an aunt, Mrs. Elizabeth
Evans, who was a Methodist preacher, and the original of
Dinah Morris. Her new friends had accepted some of the
most advanced ideas of modern science and philosophy, and,
with the broadening of her own knowledge and the developing of that introspective and analytical tendency which became her fixed habit of mind, doubts and questionings crowded
in upon her spiritual perceptions that carried her rapidly into
agnosticism. It cost her a severe struggle to renounce her
early faith — a struggle rendered more painful for a time
by the alienation of her father, who could not endure the
scandal of " unbelief " in his house. One of the most conspicuous elements of her character, as revealed in her writings, is intense religiousness. The spirit of religion pervades
all her books, and it is pretty certain that the spiritual impulses of her youth continued throughout life to urge their
protest against the materialistic conclusions forced upon her
by positive science. But her studies were always inspired
by a conscientious devotion to truth. " My only desire," she
says, " is to know the truth; my only fear, to cling to error."
The mental and spiritual struggles of this period, as well
as many events of her early life, are faithfully described in
The Mill on the Floss, in the character of Maggie Tulliver.

George Eliot's literary career began with the translation of
Strauss's *Life of Jesus*, which appeared in 1846. Her
next work was a translation of Feuerbach's *Essence of
Christianity*, which was published in 1854, with her name
upon the title-page, the first and only time her real name

appeared in print. She also left in manuscript a complete translation of Spinoza's *Ethics*, executed about this time. These translations won for her little beyond a reputation among her immediate friends for profound scholarship.

In 1849 the death of her father occurred, bringing upon her a long and almost inconsolable grief. Her friends, the Brays, always tenderly watchful of her, arranged a trip to the continent, where she remained one year, mainly in quiet study at Geneva. Upon her return she was invited to become the assistant editor of the *Westminster Review*. The next six years were occupied with editorial work, writing critical essays, and with study. She was intimately associated with some of the greatest thinkers of the age — Thomas Carlyle, John Stuart Mill, Herbert Spencer, and, more important than all, George Henry Lewes, with whose life her own was linked for twenty-four years. Her first story, *The Sad Fortunes of the Reverend Amos Barton*, appeared in *Blackwood's Magazine* in 1857. Two other short stories were written during the year, and the three appeared in 1858 as the *Scenes of Clerical Life*. With the appearance of *Adam Bede*, in 1859, the unknown "George Eliot" was acknowledged to be one of the greatest writers of the age. *The Mill on the Floss* followed in 1860, and in 1861, *Silas Marner*, which many critics maintain is the most perfect novel in the language, in respect to artistic qualities. *Romola*, a study of Florentine life in the time of Savonarola, was published in 1863, and *Felix Holt* in 1866. She now turned her attention for a time to poetry. *The Spanish Gypsy*, her most important achievement in verse, appeared in 1868, and *The Legend of Jubal, and Other Poems*, in 1874. But the restraints of verse were ill suited to her genius, and the finest work of her imagination is found in her prose. *Middlemarch*, generally regarded as her greatest novel, appeared in 1871, and *Daniel Deronda* in 1876. Her last published work was *The Impressions of Theophrastus*

Such, an anomalous mixture of fiction and didactic criticism that added nothing to her reputation.

Mr. Lewes died in 1878. On May 7, 1880, George Eliot was married to John Walter Cross, and the surprise of this event had hardly passed away when, in December of the same year, the news of her death spread sorrow and regret throughout the world. Her life was one of noble aims and grand achievement. She is the one woman in literature who has been worthily compared with Shakespeare, and in her writings she has reached that immortality which "makes undying music in the world."

DEVELOPMENT OF THE NOVEL TO
GEORGE ELIOT

The love of story telling is as old as the human race. In the early days bards and minstrels sang the great deeds of the heroes, weaving them, little by little, into epics such as the *Iliad* and the *Odyssey* of Greece. Naturally, since the tale was sung, it was in verse, deemed the only proper medium for expressing what was great, noble, inspiring.

As civilization advanced and the power of introspection deepened, the epic tale was crystallized in the single incident which is represented in the drama; with this stage literary art in plot construction may be said to begin. Previous to this the narrator had merely told the deed as it happened, with no attempt to subordinate parts or emphasize climax; but in the drama attention is centered on form — the Greek drama, in particular, laid stress upon this so-called unity of action, which selected the crisis for presentation upon the stage and so completely subordinated all other parts that the merest hint of them was given to enable the spectators to comprehend the causes and the significance of the climax.

In the later days of Greece and Rome, epic and narrative poetry gave place to philosophical work, to the study of humanity — perhaps a sort of preparation for the character analysis of the modern novelists; but for the time being, men gave themselves to the study of causes and effects of the philosophy of life; and the art of the story teller seemed almost lost.

During the dark ages, men were too much occupied with the struggle for existence to pay any attention to literature. Only in the monasteries was there any attempt at culture beyond the merest rudiments of education; but naturally, the literature produced here all centered about the church, or the disputes of the school-men; and it was not until the fourteenth century that the art of story-telling was again resumed.

In this century lived the first great story teller of England, Chaucer, "the morning star of English poetry," and the father of English fiction. The *Canterbury Tales*, though with one exception in verse, are the direct ancestors of the modern novel. They present carefully studied characters, they analyze motives and follow out results, and, above all, each one moves from a definite beginning to a carefully wrought out climax. Moreover, the men and women who move across the pages of Chaucer are not mere lay figures, but living, breathing human beings, so much so, in fact, that our interest in them is even keener than in the incidents of the stories, a condition which brings Chaucer close to the realistic writers of to-day.

To this same era belongs Sir Thomas Malory's *Morte d' Arthur,* "first, and in many ways, greatest of prose romances; with its dignified simplicity and its wealth of legend " that proved such a treasure store for later writers who tell of Arthur and his knights.

About this time, too, that engaging fabricator, Sir John Mandeville, visited strange realms, as fabulous as those islands where Captain Gulliver stopped; and in his *Travels,* he tells of what he saw and heard with such an air of simple belief in what he says that the reader forgets for the moment that the highest art in fiction is the making of the unreal real, and believes with Sir John. But neither Malory nor Mandeville pay any attention to plot — they are mere narrators of incidents and events; and so, while their work is fiction, it does not stand, as Chaucer's does, in the direct line of development of the novel.

The age of Queen Elizabeth saw the full development of the literary spirit of the Renaissance — a spirit of exuberant life, and of desire to describe that life which found its favorite expression in the drama, the form of literature most closely allied to the novel. The age was one which loved stories, especially romances. The "new learning" opened up the treasure houses of Greek and Roman myths; the new world, so recently discovered, offered vast fields for the imagination to roam at will, and gave rise to the narratives of voyagers. With such material as this to draw upon for subjects, prose fiction became possible for England. Hakluyt's *Voyages* (1589), a compilation of the great deeds of the English on the seas, has been the source of many a story, since then, in prose and verse.

To this age belong Lily's *Euphues* (1579) and Sir Philip Sidney's *Arcadia* (1580), prose romances both, very crude, it is true, but important in that they show that men were beginning to realize the possibilities of prose and its fitness as a medium for story telling. Both have a plot, though the merest skeleton, serving chiefly as an occasion for introducing episodes in themselves short stories; both pay some attention to character sketching, and both have an aim — three characteristics which mark them as in the class of novels. Both, however, are written in a prose which shows clearly the influence of poetry — the wording is that of poetry, and all sorts of poetical devices are used which seem out of place to our modern conception of prose.

With the close of the Elizabethan age, fiction passed out of fashion, for a time, not to reappear until the close of the Puritan era. The Puritan frowned upon anything which had for its aim mere pleasure; his literature was strictly religious; and yet in this religious literature we find a work which, while it can hardly be called fiction, yet ranks high as a specimen of creative art — Bunyan's *Pilgrim's Progress* (1678). The plot is simple and direct; the characters, types clearly marked rather than individual; the descriptions, vivid and real — all these rank it as the greatest allegory in literature, in a way the predecessor of the novel with a purpose.

With the Restoration, prose devoted itself to the service of science and politics. In connection with the latter there came into existence a book written as a political satire, but read and enjoyed to-day as a masterpiece in the art of making the impossible seem real — Dean Swift's *Gulliver's Travels* (1726). The only other fiction of this age is De Foe's *Robinson Crusoe*, of whose art it is said, "The little art he is truly master of is of forging a story and imposing it on the world for truth." His tale is told as was Swift's with a minuteness of detail which makes you feel that you are talking with an eyewitness. Neither of these, however, have any real plot, in the working out of which the characters have a part; their interest lies wholly in incident. They are of importance as forming, with the De Coverley Sketches, the transition between the romantic tale of the Elizabethan era, and the novels of Richardson and Fielding.

In the *De Coverley Papers*, the joint work of Addison and Steele begun in the *Spectator* in 1711, we see the beginnings of character study and local color. Defoe and Swift had shown the charm of the unnatural and strange, Addison and Steele show the charm of the natural and familiar — the pioneers in that line of work in which George Eliot excelled, the study of character. Each character, whether lightly sketched or fully drawn, is individual, real; they talk and act just as men talked and acted in the world around. Nor is this the only contribution made by the Spectator to English prose. Before this the language of prose has been stiff, formal, precise; even *Robinson Crusoe* is not entirely free from this; but the Spectator writes in the simple easy manner of the nineteenth century; we owe it to him that writing became easy and natural, and assumed attractive form.

With the middle of the eighteenth century, the real novel begins. Samuel Richardson and Henry Fielding are the makers of the modern novel — a story which centers about some great passion and works it out to a sad or a happy conclusion. With far more opportunity for character study and action than the drama, it is no wonder that the novel has replaced the drama as the medium through which creative genius speaks.

Pamela, the first of Richardson's novels, appeared in 1740. Like the second, *Clarissa Harlowe* (1748), it is written in the form of letters, thus affording opportunity for a minute study of character, and a close examination of the motives of action. The book took the reading world by storm, and with the appearance of *Sir Charles Grandison*, Richardson's fame was secured. To the modern reader they seem at first long drawn out and sentimental in the extreme, yet if we have the patience to read, we find ourselves rewarded by insight into pure, noble womanhood, and by a simplicity and pathos that belong only to a noble nature revealing itself before our very eyes.

Henry Fielding, mocking the sentimentality of *Pamela*, began *Joseph Andrews* (1742) purposely to burlesque it, but forgot his purpose in the fascination of creation. Later, in *Tom Jones* (1749), he gave us what Thackeray considered the finest English novel. Fielding surpasses Richardson in his power of developing a plot steadily and clearly and in his ability to make each character work out a definite part in the action of the story. He is often coarse, but thoroughly realistic.

A host of imitators followed — chief among them Tobias Smollett with *Roderick Random* and *Humphrey Clinker*, and Laurence Sterne with *Tristram Shandy*, hardly worthy the name of novel save for the admirable development of the characters. To this period, too, belong three new types — Dr. Johnson's novel with a moral, *Rasselas* (1759), Goldsmith's novel of country life, *The Vicar of Wakefield* (1766), and Miss Burney's society novels, *Evelina* (1778) and *Cecelia*.

The last of the eighteenth century saw the novel practically the chief literary type. Thomas Holcroft and William Godwin made use of it as a medium for the preaching of political or socialistic doctrines — the latter a use so popular to-day. Mrs. Radcliffe with *The Mysteries of Udolpho* introduced the romantic novel at almost the same time that Charles Brockden Brown, here in America, was writing of the vague, mysterious horrors of *Wieland*. Mrs. Inchbald began the novel of passion with her *Simple Story*, while Mrs. Opie, Miss Edgeworth, and, above all, Miss Austen showed us the possibilities in stories of domestic life, in the novel of national character, and in tales of every day society. Samuel Lever created for us *Handy Andy* and a host of other characters; but the work of all these is overshadowed by the creations of one man whose genius shared all these powers and more — Walter Scott.

Not until the time of Scott, however, did the novel become one of the great shaping influences in human thought. In his hands the characters are no longer mere lay figures, but living, breathing human beings; the art of fiction is perfected. Not only do his tales abound in the strange and the romantic — he has also opened to us the possibilities of the historical romance and brought the past vividly before the eyes of the present. He is at his best in his presentation of Scottish national life. We feel that Jeanie Deans, Old Mortality, Ellen Douglas are human beings whom we know and whose life we share. His novels and metrical romances touch almost every department of fiction — the historical romance, the story of every-day life, the romance of the sea, the tale colored by the supernatural — and all breathe the spirit and character of the age and land they present so clearly as to seem almost a picture gallery painted by an artist's brush.

Before his death the nineteenth century had fairly begun with its three great names which lead the honor roll of novelists — Dickens, Thackeray, George Eliot. In the hands of Dickens the novel became a powerful weapon for the correction of existing abuses, as well as a mere source of pleasure — *Nicholas Nickleby* forever killed the schools of the class represented by Dotheboy's Hall, *Oliver Twist* brought about a reform in the poor laws, *Bleak House* put the Court of Chancery to the blush, because of the evils wrought by its methods. Hardly one of his tales has not some great aim, some specific abuse to remedy. With Thackeray, too, the novel becomes a weapon against evil, but here more against the shams and hypocrisy of society. To Thackeray we owe the creation of the autobiographical novel — *Henry Esmond*, ranked by many as the finest novel in the English language, by others as second only to Dickens' *Tale of Two Cities*, or George Eliot's *Silas Marner*. Thackeray it is more than Dickens, who makes use of close analysis and minute study of character development — a method which George Eliot brought to perfection.

George Eliot began her literary work as a translator, essayist, and editor — novel writing was at first a side issue. When she did take it up, her habits of thought were already formed; the translator's exactness, the scholar's careful and minute analysis, the critic's care for perfection of form are all found in her work. Brought up as she was among the middle class and with plenty of opportunity to know the working class from her father's position, she is at her best in presenting to us the thoughts and lives of the workers. No other writer has quite her gift of entering into the personality of the character and interesting the reader in the seemingly trivial details, the sordid tragedies and comedies of peasant life. Nor is this all. Her works deserve to rank as classics to be placed among the truly great examples of modern art, because they never lose sight of the fact that literature, fiction though it may be, has a higher aim than merely to entertain — its true purpose should be to teach and guide, to put before us the working out of the great truths which shape life, that, by seeing this, we may guide our own lives aright.

THE STRUCTURE OF THE NOVEL

Fiction may be divided broadly into two classes, the romance and the novel. The romance, or romantic novel, deals with the unreal — that is, with scenes foreign to those of our everyday life, in time or nature. The novel presents phases of everyday life, the working out of causes into their results, such as appear in our own experience and influence our own lives.

With both classes the essentials are character, action, plot. The story must be about somebody who does something against certain definite obstacles. This struggle of the individual against an obstacle constitutes plot. According to the type of novel, it may be man against nature, as in tales of exploration and discovery; man against man, as in stories of adventure, daring, and the greater number of romances; and finally man against himself, the working out of his higher or lower self, as in the so-called problem novels of to-day. The characters must be consistent throughout. We should never feel that a man in a book has done a thing which that man's own nature would prevent him from doing in real life. For every act we must be able to trace a cause in the man himself, and his character must unfold consistently with the analysis of it indicated by the author.

There is always one main plot centering around the chief actor; there may be other plots interwoven with this, but centering around minor characters. Often the two are kept distinct until at some crisis the actions touch. In *Silas Marner* the plot centering around Silas is entirely distinct from that centering around Godfrey Cass, except at the two critical points, the finding of Eppie and Godfrey's final losing of her. The two are brought in touch at first by the theft of the miser's gold by Dunstan Cass, and later by Silas' adoption of Godfrey Cass's unclaimed daughter; but the action of each is distinct. In the first part of the story certain forces are at work complicating or entangling the characters; after the climax other forces, or possibly another phase of these, disentangle the snarl caused in the first part. For example, Silas' dependence on something to love leads him to rely blindly on William Dane and his church. This taken away, he clings to gold as an idol which cannot harm him; when this, too, is removed his heart is ready to receive the child, and later this love for her leads to his regeneration.

These forces work out the action of the plot, in obedience to certain laws called by the German critic, Freytag, the laws of the drama. These laws apply equally to all plots — not alone to those of the drama.

In every action or plot are three decisive steps — the incentive moment, the climax, the catastrophe or outcome. The incentive may be defined as the moment when the hero decides upon that course of action which brings about the rest of the plot. From here the action ascends steadily to the climax, the highest point of interest, at which the action turns, and the actor who has been before successful now begins to lose in power; from here the action descends until the outcome or catastrophe, which shows the final consequence of the action begun by the hero at the incentive.

Other dramatic moments than these three may be found in very intricate plots. Tragic moments may occur before or after the climax — minor crises, to be distinguished from the climax by the fact that the action does not turn at these, as it does at the climax. Shortly before the catastrophe is often found the moment of last suspense, a point when, for a short time, it seems possible that the catastrophe which the climax made inevitable should be averted. These points, however, are not essential to the action as are the incentive, the climax, the catastrophe.

In the action of a comic or happy-ending plot the villain is in power up to the climax, then the hero governs the descending action. In the tragic plot the efforts of the hero are foiled at the climax by his adversary, who brings about the hero's undoing at the catastrophe.

Formerly it was the custom to give a more or less formal introduction, showing setting, time, and place, as in *Ivanhoe*. Nowadays the story usually begins in the midst of the action, and whatever introductory matter is necessary for a clear understanding of the plot is told incidentally, usually in the conversation of the characters as the story unfolds. So, too, with the conclusion, since the climax practically decides the catastrophe, the descending action must be shorter than the ascending or interest will be lost. The sixteen years during which Godfrey Cass's punishment is working out are passed over in a few words, and we are brought at once from the climax to the outcome. The outcome concludes the action — it brings to a logical conclusion the action begun at the incentive and shows the final step in the development of the chief characters.

So, from a simple narrative of a single event as told by the minstrels of old, has evolved the complex novel of the present day with its careful study of character, its complicated plot, and its interwoven action, presenting to us a picture of human life and, by showing the working out of the laws of life, making us wiser to shape our own destinies.

CRITICAL OPINIONS

In her personal bearing George Eliot was seldom moved by the hurry which mars all dignity in action. Her commanding brows and deep, penetrating eyes were seconded by the sweet, restrained, impressive speech, which claimed something like an awed attention from strangers. But to those very near to her there was another side of her nature, scarcely suspected by outside friends and acquaintances. No one could be more capable of enjoying and of communicating genuine, loving, hearty, uncontrollable laughter. It was a deep-seated wish, expressed in the poem of *Agatha* — "I would have young things merry." And I remember many years ago, at the time of our first acquaintance, how deeply it pained her when, in reply to a direct question, I was obliged to admit that, with all my admiration for her books, I found them, on the whole, profoundly sad. But sadness was certainly not the note of her intimate converse, for she had the distinctively feminine qualities which lend a rhythm to the movement of life. The quick sympathy that understands without words; the capacity for creating a complete atmosphere of loving interest; the detachment from outside influences; the delight of everything worthy — even the smallest thing — for its own sake; the readiness to receive as well as to give impressions; the disciplined mental habit which can hold in check and conquer the natural egoism of a massive, powerful personality; the versatility of mind; the varied accomplishments — these are characteristics to be found more highly developed among gifted women than among gifted men. Add to these the crowning gift of genius, and, in such companionship, we may possess the world without belonging to it.— *Life of George Eliot*, by her husband, J. W. Cross.

The plot of *Silas Marner* is good, and the delineation of character is excellent. But other writers who have the power of story-telling compose plots as interesting, and perhaps sketch charcters as well. It is in the portraiture of the poor, and of what it is now fashionable to call " the lower middle class," that this writer is without a rival, and no phase of life could be harder to draw. The gift is so special, the difficulty is so great, the success is so complete, that the works of George Eliot come on us as a new revelation of what society in quiet English parishes really is and has been. . . . Within its limits *Silas Marner* is quite equal to either of its predecessors, and in combining the display of the author's characteristic excellences with freedom from blemishes and defects is perhaps superior.— *Saturday Review*, xi, 369.

George Eliot is one of the few thinkers who can see the weakness of humanity, and the comparatively disappointing and mean nature of most objects of pursuit, without being driven by the violence of a common reaction into transcendental artifices. Nobody in her books is made to talk of rapture as a mood of happiness, or as the remedy for failure and the littleness of things. Practical resignation to the harshness and inflexibility of many of those conditions which are the material that a man has to make his life out of, and a sober, not ecstatic, resolution to seize such elements as remain, and force them into the pattern which we have chosen for ourselves,— this is a state of feeling and will which seems to count for a great deal more with her than any solace which can come of beatific visions and discourse of eternal, unspeakable aspirations. . . . Like Mr. Carlyle, too, in this, as in a great many other points, George Eliot perceives that the only course for honest and worthy folk in the tangle which fools contrive to make of the world is to stick to the work that the hand findeth to do.— John Morley: *Macmillan's Magazine*, xiv, 272.

Certain that she belongs to the foremost intellectual forces of our time, and seeing that she is a novelist (for neither poems nor essays express her genius truly) some are apt to decide that she stands in the very front rank of the artists of the modern world. That is surely to claim a great deal too much. Cervantes, Fielding, Scott, of course stand immeasurably apart and above, by virtue of their wealth of imagination, their range of insight into manners, and sympathies with characters of every type. . . . The place of George Eliot will ultimately be found in the group where are set George Sand, Balzac, Jane Austen, Dickens, Thackeray, the Brontés. Judging her purely as an artist, we can hardly hope that her ultimate popularity will quite equal theirs. That she is immeasurably superior to them all as a thinker, teacher, inspirer of thought and purifier of soul, will perhaps be little disputed. As facile creator of types, painter of varied character, veracious chronicler of manners, she has not their range, vivacity, irrepressible energy. . . . The inexhaustible charm of George Sand, the microscopic vivacity of Jane Austen, the pathetic oddities of Charles Dickens, the terrible Hogarthian pencil of Balzac and Thackeray, were all deliberately foregone by a novelist who read so deeply, who looked on life so profoundly, and who meditated so conscientiously as George Eliot.— Frederick Harrison: *Fortnightly Review*, xliii, 716.

Complete in all its parts, and strong in all, the nature of George Eliot is yet not one of those rare natures, which without effort are harmonious. There is no impression made more decisively upon the readers of her books than this. No books bear more unmistakably the pain of moral conflict, and the pain of moral victory, only less bitter than that of defeat. Great forces warring with one another, a sorrowful and pathetic victory,— that is what we discern.— E. Dowden: *Studies in Literature*, 258.

There is no danger of arousing any controversy in saying that the works of her first period, the *Scenes of Clerical Life, Adam Bede, Silas Marner,* and *The Mill on the*

Floss, have the unmistakable mark of high genius. They are something for which it is simply out of the question to find any substitute. Strike them out of English literature, and we feel that there would be a gap not to be filled up; a distinct vein of thought and feeling unrepresented; a characteristic and delightful type of social development left without any adequate interpreter. A second-rate writer can be more or less displaced. When you have read Shakespeare you can do very well without Beaumont and Fletcher, and a study of the satires of Pope makes it unnecessary to plod through the many volumes filled by his imitators. But we feel that, however much we may admire the other great English novelists, there is none who would make the study of George Eliot superfluous. The sphere which she has made specially her own is that quiet English country life which she knew in early youth. It has been described with more or less vivacity and sympathy by many observers. Nobody has approached George Eliot in the power of seizing its essential characteristics and exhibiting its real charm. She has done for it what Scott did for the Scotch peasantry, or Fielding for the eighteenth-century Englishman, or Thackeray for the higher social stratum of his time. Its last traces are vanishing so rapidly amidst the changes of modern revolution that its picture could hardly be drawn again, even if there were an artist of equal skill and penetration. And thus when the name of George Eliot is mentioned, it calls up to me at least, and, I suspect, to most readers, not so much her later and more ambitious works, as the exquisite series of scenes so lovingly and vividly presented in the earlier stage.— Leslie Stephen: *Cornhill Magazine for February,* 1881.

REFERENCES FOR LIFE AND WORKS

Life of George Eliot. J. W. Cross.

Life of George Eliot. M. Blind in *Famous Women*.

The Childhood of Maggie Tulliver, in *The Mill on the Floss*.

The English Novel. Sidney Lanier.

Life of George Eliot. Henry James, Jr., *Atlantic Monthly*, May, 1885.

George Eliot. *Dictionary of National Biography*, Vol. xiii, pp. 216–222.

Scenes from the George Eliot Country. S. Parkinson.

Life of George Eliot. Oscar Browning.

Pancoast. Introduction to English Literature, pp. 446–458.

Saintsbury. Nineteenth Century Literature, pp. 321–324.

Dowden. Studies in Literature, pp. 240–272.

SILAS MARNER

SILAS MARNER

THE WEAVER OF RAVELOE

PART I

CHAPTER I

In the days when the spinning-wheels hummed bus-
ily in the farmhouses—and even great ladies, clothed
in silk and thread-lace, had their toy spinning-wheels
of polished oak—there might be seen in districts far
away among the lanes, or deep in the bosom of the
hills, certain pallid undersized men, who, by the side
of the brawny country-folk, looked like the remnants
of a disinherited race. The shepherd's dog barked
fiercely when one of these alien-looking men appeared on the upland, dark against the early winter
sunset; for what dog likes a figure bent under a
heavy bag?—and these pale men rarely stirred abroad
without that mysterious burden. The shepherd himself, though he had good reason to believe that the
bag held nothing but flaxen thread, or else the long
rolls of strong linen spun from that thread, was not
quite sure that this trade of weaving, indispensable

though it was, could be carried on entirely without the help of the Evil One. In that far-off time superstition clung easily round every person or thing that was at all unwonted, or even intermittent and occasional merely, like the visits of the pedler or the knifegrinder. No one knew where wandering men had their homes or their origin; and how was a man to be explained unless you at least knew somebody who knew his father and mother? To the peasants of old times, the world outside their own direct experience was a region of vagueness and mystery: to their untraveled thought a state of wandering was a conception as dim as the winter life of the swallows that came back with the spring; and even a settler, if he came from distant parts, hardly ever ceased to be viewed with a remnant of distrust, which would have prevented any surprise if a long course of inoffensive conduct on his part had ended in the commission of a crime; especially if he had any reputation for knowledge, or showed any skill in handicraft. All cleverness, whether in the rapid use of that difficult instrument the tongue, or in some other art unfamiliar to villagers, was in itself suspicious: honest folk, born and bred in a visible manner, were mostly not over wise or clever—at least, not beyond such a matter as knowing the signs of the weather; and the process by which rapidity and dexterity of any kind were acquired was so wholly hidden, that they partook of the nature of conjuring. In this way it came to pass that those scattered linen-weavers

—emigrants from the town into the country—were to the last regarded as aliens by their rustic neighbors, and usually contracted the eccentric habits which belong to a state of loneliness.

In the early years of this century, such a linen-weaver, named Silas Marner, worked at his vocation in a stone cottage that stood among the nutty hedge-rows near the village of Raveloe, and not far from the edge of a deserted stone-pit. The questionable sound of Silas's loom, so unlike the natural cheerful trotting of the winnowing-machine, or the simpler rhythm of the flail,[1] had a half-fearful fascination for the Raveloe boys, who would often leave off their nutting or birds'-nesting to peep in at the window of the stone cottage, counterbalancing a certain awe at the mysterious action of the loom, by a pleasant sense of scornful superiority, drawn from the mockery of its alternating noises, along with the bent, tread-mill attitude of the weaver. But sometimes it happened that Marner, pausing to adjust an irregularity in his thread, became aware of the small scoundrels, and, though chary of his time, he liked their intrusion so ill that he would descend from his loom, and, opening the door, would fix on them a gaze that was always enough to make them take to their legs in terror. For how was it possible to believe that those large, brown, protuberant eyes in Silas Marner's pale face really saw nothing very distinctly that was not close to them, and not rather that their dreadful stare could dart cramp, or rickets, or a wry mouth at any

boy who happened to be in the rear? They had, perhaps, heard their fathers and mothers hint that Silas
Marner could cure folk's rheumatism if he had a
mind, and add, still more darkly, that if you could
only speak the devil fair [1] enough, he might save
you the cost of the doctor. Such strange lingering
echoes of the old demon-worship might perhaps even
now be caught by the diligent listener among the
gray-haired peasantry; for the rude mind with difficulty associates the ideas of power and benignity. A
shadowy conception of power that by much persua-
sion can be induced to refrain from inflicting harm,
is the shape most easily taken by the sense of the
Invisible in the minds of men who have always been
pressed close by primitive wants,[2] and to whom a
life of hard toil has never been illuminated by any
enthusiastic religious faith.[3] To them pain and mis-
hap present a far wider range of possibilities than
gladness and enjoyment: their imagination is almost
barren of the images that feed desire and hope, but
is all overgrown by recollections that are a perpetual
pasture to fear. "Is there anything you can fancy
that you would like to eat?" I once said to an old
laboring man, who was in his last illness, and who
had refused all the food his wife had offered him.
"No," he answered, "I've never been used to nothing
but common victual, and I can't eat that." Experience had bred no fancies in him that could raise the
phantasm of appetite.

And Raveloe was a village where many of the old

echoes lingered, undrowned by new voices. Not
that it was one of those barren parishes lying on the
outskirts of civilization—inhabited by meager sheep
and thinly-scattered shepherds: on the contrary, it
lay in the rich central plain of what we are pleased
to call Merry England, and held farms which, speaking from a spiritual point of view, paid highly desirable tithes. But it was nestled in a snug well-
wooded hollow, quite an hour's journey on horseback
from any turnpike, where it was never reached by the
vibrations of the coach-horn, or of public opinion.
It was an important-looking village, with a fine old
church and large churchyard in the heart of it, and
two or three large brick-and-stone homesteads, with
well-walled orchards and ornamental weathercocks,
standing close upon the road, and lifting more imposing fronts than the rectory, which peeped from
among the trees on the other side of the churchyard:
—a village which showed at once the summits of its
social life, and told the practiced eye that there was
no great park and manor-house [1] in the vicinity, but
that there were several chiefs in Raveloe who could
farm badly quite at their ease,[2] drawing enough
money from their bad farming, in those war times,
to live in a rollicking fashion, and keep a jolly Christmas, Whitsun, and Easter tide.

It was fifteen years since Silas Marner had first
come to Raveloe; he was then simply a pallid young
man, with prominent, short-sighted, brown eyes,
whose appearance would have had nothing strange for

people of average culture and experience, but for the
villagers near whom he had come to settle it had mysterious peculiarities which corresponded with the exceptional nature of his occupation, and his advent
from an unknown region called "North'ard." So
had his way of life:—he invited no comer to step
across his door-sill, and he never strolled into the
village to drink a pint at the Rainbow,[1] or to gossip
at the wheelwright's: he sought no man or woman,
save for the purposes of his calling, or in order to
supply himself with necessaries; and it was soon clear
to the Raveloe lasses that he would never urge one of
them to accept him against her will—quite as if he
had heard them declare that they would never marry
a dead man come to life again. This view of Marner's personality was not without another ground
than his pale face and unexampled eyes;[2] for Jem
Rodney, the mole-catcher, averred that one evening
as he was returning homeward he saw Silas Marner
leaning against a stile with a heavy bag on his back,
instead of resting the bag on the stile as a man in his
senses would have done; and that, on coming up to
him, he saw that Marner's eyes were set like a dead
man's, and he spoke to him, and shook him, and his
limbs were stiff, and his hands clutched the bag as if
they'd been made of iron; but just as he had made
up his mind that the weaver was dead, he came all
right again, like, as you might say, in the winking of
an eye, and said "Good-night," and walked off. All
this Jem swore he had seen, more by token that it was

the very day he had been mole-catching on Squire Cass's land, down by the old saw-pit. Some said Marner must have been in a "fit," a word which seemed to explain things otherwise incredible; but the argumentative Mr. Macey, clerk of the parish, shook his head, and asked if anybody was ever known to go off in a fit and not fall down. A fit was a stroke wasn't it? and it was in the nature of a stroke to partly take away the use of a man's limbs and throw him on the parish, if he'd got no children to look to. No, no; it was no stroke that would let a man stand on his legs; like a horse between the shafts, and then walk off as soon as you can say "Gee!" But there might be such a thing as a man's soul being loose from his body, and going out and in, like a bird out of its nest and back; and that was how folks got over-wise, for they went to school in this shell-less state to those who could teach them more than their neighbors could learn with their five senses and the parson. And where did Master Marner get his knowledge of herbs from—and charms too, if he liked to give them away? Jem Rodney's story was no more than what might have been expected by anybody who had seen how Marner had cured Sally Oates, and made her sleep like a baby, when her heart had been beating enough to burst her body, for two months and more, while she had been under the doctor's care. He might cure more folks if he would; but he was worth speaking fair, if it was only to keep him from doing you a mischief.

It was partly to this vague fear that Marner was indebted for protecting him from the persecution that his singularities might have drawn upon him, but still more to the fact that, the old linen-weaver in the neighboring parish of Tarley being dead, his handicraft made him a highly welcome settler to the richer housewives of the district, and even to the more provident cottagers, who had their little stock of yarn at the year's end. Their sense of his usefulness would have counteracted any repugnance or suspicion which was not confirmed by a deficiency in the quality or the tale of the cloth he wove for them. And the years had rolled on without producing any change in the impressions of the neighbors concerning Marner, except the change from novelty to habit. At the end of fifteen years the Raveloe men said just the same things about Silas Marner as at the beginning : they did not say them quite so often, but they believed them much more strongly when they did say them. There was only one important addition which the years had brought : it was, that Master Marner had laid by a fine sight of money somewhere, and that he could buy up "bigger men" than himself.

But while opinion concerning him had remained nearly stationary, and his daily habits had presented scarcely any visible change, Marner's inward life had been a history and a metamorphosis, as that of every fervid nature must be when it has fled, or been condemned to solitude. His life, before he came to Raveloe, had been filled with the movement, the mental

activity, and the close fellowship, which, in that day
as in this, marked the life of an artisan early incorporated in a narrow religious sect,[1] where the poorest
layman has the chance of distinguishing himself by
gifts of speech, and has, at the very least, the weight
of a silent voter in the government of his community.
Marner was highly thought of in that little hidden
world, known to itself as the church assembling in
Lantern Yard; he was believed to be a young man of
exemplary life and ardent faith; and a peculiar interest had been centered in him ever since he had fallen,
at a prayer-meeting, into a mysterious rigidity and
suspension of consciousness, which, lasting for an
hour or more, had been mistaken for death. To have
sought a medical explanation for this phenomenon
would have been held by Silas himself, as well as by
his minister and fellow-members, a willful self-exclu-
sion from the spiritual significance that might lie
therein. Silas was evidently a brother selected for a
peculiar discipline; and though the effort to interpret
this discipline was discouraged by the absence, on his
part, of any spiritual vision during his outward
trance, yet it was believed by himself and others that
its effect was seen in an accession of light and fervor.
A less truthful man than he might have been tempted
into the subsequent creation of a vision in the form of
resurgent memory; a less sane man might have believed in such a creation; but Silas was both sane and
honest, though, as with many honest and fervent men,
culture had not defined any channels for his sense of

mystery, and so it spread itself over the proper pathway of inquiry and knowledge. He had inherited
from his mother some acquaintance with medicinal
herbs and their preparation—a little store of wisdom
which she had imparted to him as a solemn bequest—
but of late years he had had doubts about the lawful-
ness of applying this knowledge, believing that herbs
could have no efficacy without prayer, and that prayer
might suffice without herbs; so that his inherited delight to wander through the fields in search of foxglove and dandelion and coltsfoot began to wear to
him the character of a temptation.

Among the members of his church there was one
young man, a little older than himself, with whom he
had long lived in such close friendship that it was the
custom of their Lantern Yard brethren to call them
David and Jonathan.[1] The real name of the friend
was William Dane, and he, too, was regarded as a
shining instance of youthful piety, though somewhat
given to over-severity towards weaker brethren, and
to be so dazzled by his own light as to hold himself
wiser than his teachers. But whatever blemishes
others might discern in William, to his friend's mind
he was faultless; for Marner had one of those impress-
ible self-doubting natures which, at an inexperienced
age, admire imperativeness and lean on contradiction.
The expression of trusting simplicity in Marner's
face, heightened by that absence of special observation, that defenseless, deer-like gaze which belongs to
large prominent eyes, was strongly contrasted by the

self-complacent suppression of inward triumph that
lurked in the narrow slanting eyes and compressed
lips of William Dane. One of the most frequent topics of conversation between the two friends was Assurance of Salvation: Silas confessed that he could
never arrive at anything higher than hope mingled
with fear, and listened with longing wonder when
William declared that he had possessed unshaken
assurance ever since, in the period of his conversion,
he had dreamed that he saw the words "calling and
election sure" standing by themselves on a white page
in the open Bible. Such colloquies have occupied
many a pair of pale-faced weavers, whose unnur-
tured souls have been like young winged things, flut-
tering forsaken in the twilight.

It had seemed to the unsuspecting Silas that the
friendship had suffered no chill even from his forma-
tion of another attachment of a closer kind. For
some months he had been engaged to a young servant-
woman, waiting only for a little increase to their
mutual savings in order to their marriage; and it
was a great delight to him that Sarah did not object
to William's occasional presence in their Sunday interviews. It was at this point in their history that
Silas's cataleptic fit occurred during the prayer-meeting; and amidst the various queries and expressions
of interst addressed to him by his fellow-members,
William's suggestion alone jarred with the general
sympathy towards a brother thus singled out for special dealings. He observed that, to him, this trance

looked more like a visitation of Satan than a proof
of divine favor, and exhorted his friend to see that
he hid no accursed thing within his soul. Silas, feeling bound to accept rebuke and admonition as a brotherly office, felt no resentment, but only pain, at his
friend's doubts concerning him; and to this was soon
added some anxiety at the perception that Sarah's
manner towards him began to exhibit a strange fluc-
tuation between an effort at an increased manifesta-
tion of regard and involuntary signs of shrinking and
dislike. He asked her if she wished to break off their
engagement; but she denied this: their engagement
was known to the church, and had been recognized in
the prayer-meetings; it could not be broken off without strict investigation, and Sarah could render no
reason that would be sanctioned by the feeling of the
community. At this time the senior deacon was
taken dangerously ill, and, being a childless widower,
he was tended night and day by some of the younger
brethren or sisters. Silas frequently took his turn in
the night-watching with William, the one relieving
the other at two in the morning. The old man, contrary to expectation, seemed to be on the way to re-
covery, when one night Silas, sitting up by his bedside,
observed that his usual audible breathing had ceased.
The candle was burning low, and he had to lift it to
see the patient's face distinctly. Examination convinced him that the deacon was dead—had been dead
some time, for the limbs were rigid. Silas asked himself if he had been asleep, and looked at the clock: it

was already four in the morning. How was it that
William had not come? In much anxiety he went to
seek for help, and soon there were several friends
assembled in the house, the minister among them,
while Silas went away to his work, wishing he could
have met William to know the reason of his non-
appearance. But at six o'clock, as he was thinking
of going to seek his friend, William came, and with
him the minister. They came to summon him to Lantern Yard, to meet the church members there; and to
his inquiry concerning the cause of the summons the
only reply was, "You will hear." Nothing further
was said until Silas was seated in the vestry, in front
of the minister, with the eyes of those who to him
represented God's people fixed solemnly upon him.
Then the minister, taking out a pocket-knife, showed
it to Silas, and asked him if he knew where he had
left that knife? Silas said, he did not know that he
had left it anywhere out of his own pocket—but he
was trembling at this strange interrogation. He was
then exhorted not to hide his sin, but to confess and
repent. The knife had been found in the bureau by
the departed deacon's bedside—found in the place
where the little bag of church money had lain, which
the minister himself had seen the day before. Some
hand had removed that bag; and whose hand could
it be, if not that of the man to whom the knife belonged? For some time Silas was mute with astonishment: then he said, "God will clear me: I know
nothing about the knife being there, or the money

being gone. Search me and my dwelling; you will find nothing but three pound five of my own savings, which William Dane knows that I have had these six months." At this William groaned, but the minister said, "The proof is heavy against you, brother Marner. The money was taken in the night last past, and no man was with our departed brother but you, for William Dane declares to us that he was hindered by sudden sickness from going to take his place as usual, and you yourself said that he had not come; and, moreover, you neglected the dead body."

"I must have slept," said Silas. Then, after a pause, he added, "Or I must have had another visitation like that which you have all seen me under, so that the thief must have come and gone while I was not in the body, but out of the body. But, I say again, search me and my dwelling, for I have been nowhere else."

The search was made, and it ended—in William Dane's finding the well-known bag empty, tucked behind the chest of drawers in Silas's chamber! On this William exhorted his friend to confess, and not to hide his sin any longer. Silas turned a look of keen reproach on him, and said, "William, for nine years that we have gone in and out together, have you ever known me to tell a lie? But God will clear me."

" Brother," said William, "how do I know what you may have done in the secret chambers of your heart, to give Satan an advantage over you?"

Silas was still looking at his friend. Suddenly a

deep flush came over his face, and he was about to
speak impetuously, when he seemed checked again by
some inward shock, that sent the flush back and made
him tremble. But at last he spoke feebly, looking at
William.

"I remember now—the knife wasn't in my pocket."

William said, "I know nothing of what you mean."
The other persons present, however, began to inquire
where Silas meant to say that the knife was, but he
would give no further explanation: he only said, "I
am sore stricken; I can say nothing. God will clear
me."

On their return to the vestry there was further de-
liberation. Any resort to legal measures for ascertain-
ing the culprit was contrary to the principles of the
church in Lantern Yard, according to which prosecu-
tion was forbidden to Christians even had the case
held less scandal to the community. But the members
were bound to take other measures for finding out the
truth, and they resolved on praying and drawing lots.
This resolution can be a ground of surprise only to
those who are unacquainted with that obscure religious life which has gone on in the alleys of our
towns. Silas knelt with his brethren, relying on his
own innocence being certified by immediate divine
interference, but feeling that there was sorrow and
mourning behind for him even then—that his trust in
man had been cruelly bruised. *The lots* [1] *declared
that Silas Marner was guilty.* He was solemnly suspended from church-membership, and called upon to

render up the stolen money: only on confession, as the sign of repentance, could he be received once more within the folds of the church. Marner listened in silence. At last, when every one rose to depart, he went towards William Dane and said, in a voice shaken by agitation—

"The last time I remember using my knife, was when I took it out to cut a strap for you. I don't remember putting it in my pocket again. *You* stole the money, and you have woven a plot to lay the sin at my door. But you may prosper, for all that: there is no just God that governs the earth righteously, but a God of lies, that bears witness against the innocent."

There was a general shudder at this blasphemy.

William said meekly, "I leave our brethren to judge whether this is the voice of Satan or not. I can do nothing but pray for you, Silas."

Poor Marner went out with that despair in his soul —that shaken trust in God and man, which is little short of madness to a loving nature. In the bitterness of his wounded spirit, he said to himself, "*She* will cast me off too." And he reflected that, if she did not believe the testimony against him, her whole faith must be upset as his was. To people accustomed to reason about the forms in which their religious feeling has incorporated itself, it is difficult to enter into that simple, untaught state of mind in which the form and the feeling have never been severed by an act of reflection. We are apt to think it inevitable that a man in Marner's position should have begun to question the validity of an appeal to the divine judgment by drawing lots: but to him this would have been an effort of independent thought such as he had never known; and he must have made the effort at a moment when all his energies were turned into the anguish of disappointed faith. If there is an angel who records the sorrows of men as well as their sins, he knows how many and deep are the sorrows that spring from false ideas for which no man is culpable.

Marner went home, and for a whole day sat alone, stunned by despair, without any impulse to go to Sarah and attempt to win her belief in his innocence. The second day he took refuge from benumbing unbelief, by getting into his loom and working away as usual; and before many hours were past, the minister and one of the deacons came to him with the message from Sarah, that she held her engagement to him at an end. Silas received the message mutely, and then turned away from the messengers to work at his loom again. In little more than a month from that time, Sarah was married to William Dane; and not long afterwards it was known to the brethren in Lantern Yard that Silas Marner had departed from the town.

CHAPTER II

EVEN people whose lives have been made various by learning,[1] sometimes find it hard to keep a fast hold on their habitual views of life, on their faith in the Invisible, nay, on the sense that their past joys and sorrows are a real experience, when they are suddenly transported to a new land, where the beings around them know nothing of their history, and share none of their ideas—where their mother earth shows another lap, and human life has other forms than those on which their souls have been nourished. Minds that have been unhinged from their old faith and love have perhaps sought this Lethean influence of exile, in which the past becomes dreamy because its symbols have all vanished, and the present too is dreamy because it is linked with no memories. But even *their* experience may hardly enable them thoroughly to imagine what was the effect on a simple weaver like Silas Marner, when he left his own country and people and came to settle in Raveloe. Nothing could be more unlike his native town, set within sight of the widespread hillsides, than this low, wooded region, where he felt hidden even from the heavens by the screening trees and hedgerows. There was nothing here, when he rose in the deep morning quiet and looked out on the dewy brambles and rank tufted grass, that seemed to have any relation with that life centering in Lantern Yard, which had once been to him the altar-place of high dispensations. The whitewashed walls; the little pews where well-known figures entered with a subdued rustling, and where first one well-known voice and then another, pitched in a peculiar key of petition, uttered phrases at once occult and familiar, like the amulet [1] worn on the heart; the pulpit where the minister delivered unquestioned doctrine, and swayed to and fro, and handled the book in a long-accustomed manner; the very pauses between the couplets of the hymn, as it was given out, and the recurrent swell of voices in song: these things had been the channel of divine influences to Marner—they were the fostering home of his religious emotions—they were Christianity and God's kingdom upon earth. A weaver who finds hard words in his hymn-book knows nothing of abstractions; as the little child knows nothing of parental love, but only knows one face and one lap towards which it stretches its arms for refuge and nurture.

And what could be more unlike that Lantern Yard world than the world in Raveloe?—orchards looking lazy with neglected plenty; the large church in the wide church-yard, which men gazed at lounging at their own doors in service-time; the purple-faced farmers jogging along the lanes or turning in at the Rainbow; homesteads, where men supped heavily and

slept in the light of the evening hearth, and where
women seemed to be laying up a stock of linen for the
life to come. There were no lips in Raveloe from
which a word could fall that would stir Silas Marner's benumbed faith to a sense of pain. In the early
ages of the world, we know, it was believed that each
territory was inhabited and ruled by its own divini-
ties, so that a man could cross the bordering heights
and be out of the reach of his native gods, whose
presence was confined to the streams and the groves
and the hills among which he had lived from his
birth. And poor Silas was vaguely conscious of
something not unlike the feeling of primitive men,
when they fled thus, in fear or in sullenness, from the
face of an unpropitious deity. It seemed to him that
the Power he had vainly trusted in among the streets
and at the prayer-meetings, was very far away [1] from
this land in which he had taken refuge, where men
lived in careless abundance, knowing and needing
nothing of that trust, which, for him, had been turned
to bitterness. The little light he possessed spread its
beams so narrowly, that frustrated belief [2] was a cur-
tain broad enough to create for him the blackness of
night.

His first movement after the shock had been to
work in his loom; and he went on with this unremit-
tingly, never asking himself why, now he was come to
Raveloe, he worked far on into the night to finish the
tale of Mrs. Osgood's table-linen [3] sooner than she
expected—without contemplating beforehand the

money she would put into his hand for the work. He
seemed to weave, like the spider, from pure impulse,
without reflection. Every man's work, pursued
steadily, tends in this way to become an end in itself,
and so to bridge over the loveless chasms of his life.
Silas's hand satisfied itself with throwing the shuttle,[1]
and his eye with seeing the little squares in the cloth
complete themselves under his effort. Then there
were the calls of hunger; and Silas, in his solitude,
had to provide his own breakfast, dinner, and supper,
to fetch his own water from the well, and put his own
kettle on the fire; and all these immediate promptings helped, along with the weaving, to reduce his life
to the unquestioning activity of a spinning insect.
He hated the thought of the past; there was nothing
that called out his love and fellowship towards the
strangers he had come among; and the future was all
dark, for there was no Unseen Love that cared for
him. Thought was arrested by utter bewilderment,
now its old narrow pathway was closed, and affection
seemed to have died under the bruise that had fallen
on its keenest nerves.

But at last Mrs. Osgood's table-linen was finished,
and Silas was paid in gold. His earnings in his native town, where he worked for a wholesale dealer,
had been after a lower rate; he had been paid
weekly, and of his weekly earnings a large proportion had gone to objects of piety and charity.
Now, for the first time in his life, he had five bright
guineas put into his hand; no man expected a share

of them, and he loved no man that he should offer
him a share. But what were the guineas to him
who saw no vista beyond countless days of weaving?
It was needless for him to ask that, for it was pleasant to him to feel them in his palm, and look at their
bright faces, which were all his own: it was another
element of life, like the weaving and the satisfaction
of hunger, subsisting quite aloof from the life of belief and love from which he had been cut off. The
weaver's hand had known the touch of hard-won
money even before the palm had grown to its full
breadth; for twenty years, mysterious money had
stood to him as the symbol of earthly good, and the
immediate object of toil. He had seemed to love it
little in the years when every penny had its purpose
for him; for he loved the *purpose* then. But now,
when all purpose was gone, that habit of looking towards the money and grasping it with a sense of ful-
filled effort made a loam that was deep enough for
the seeds of desire; and as Silas walked homeward
across the fields in the twilight, he drew out the money
and thought it was brighter in the gathering gloom.

About this time an incident happened which
seemed to open a possibility of some fellowship with
his neighbors. One day, taking a pair of shoes to be
mended, he saw the cobbler's wife seated by the fire,
suffering from the terrible symptoms of heart-disease
and dropsy, which he had witnessed as the precur-
sors of his mother's death. He felt a rush of pity at
the mingled sight and remembrance, and, recalling

the relief his mother had found from a simple preparation of foxglove, he promised Sally Oates to bring
her something that would ease her, since the doctor
did her no good. In this office of charity, Silas
felt, for the first time since he had come to Raveloe,
a sense of unity between his past and present life,
which might have been the beginning of his rescue
from the insect-like existence into which his nature
had shrunk. But Sally Oates's disease had raised
her into a personage of much interest and importance
among the neighbors, and the fact of her having
found relief from drinking Silas Marner's "stuff"
became a matter of general discourse. When Doctor
Kimble gave physic, it was natural that it should have
an effect; but when a weaver, who came from nobody
knew where, worked wonders with a bottle of brown
waters, the occult character of the process was evident.
Such a sort of thing had not been known since the
Wise Woman at Tarley died; and she had charms
as well as "stuff": everybody went to her when their
children had fits. Silas Marner must be a person of
the same sort, for how did he know what would bring
back Sally Oates's breath, if he didn't know a fine
sight more than that? The Wise Woman had words
that she muttered to herself, so that you couldn't hear
what they were, and if she tied a bit of red thread
round the child's toe the while, it would keep off the
water in the head. There were women in Raveloe,
at that present time, who had worn one of the Wise
Woman's little bags round their necks, and, in con-

sequence, had never had an idiot child, as Ann Coulter had. Silas Marner could very likely do as much, and more; and now it was all clear how he should have come from unknown parts, and be so "comical-looking." But Sally Oates must mind and not tell the doctor, for he would be sure to set his face against Marner: he was always angry about the Wise Woman, and used to threaten those who went to her that they should have none of his help any more.

Silas now found himself and his cottage suddenly beset by mothers who wanted him to charm away the whooping-cough, or bring back the milk, and by men who wanted stuff against the rheumatics or the knots in the hands; and, to secure themselves against a refusal, the applicants brought silver in their palms. Silas might have driven a profitable trade in charms as well as in his small list of drugs; but money on this condition was no temptation to him: he had never known an impulse towards falsity, and he drove one after another away with growing irritation, for the news of him as a wise man had spread even to Tarley, and it was long before people ceased to take long walks for the sake of asking his aid. But the hope in his wisdom was at length changed into dread, for no one believed him when he said he knew no charms and could work no cures, and every man or woman who had an accident or a new attack after applying to him, set the misfortune down to Master Marner's ill-will and irritated glances. Thus it came to pass that his movement of pity towards Sally Oates, which had given him a transient sense of brotherhood, heightened the repulsion between him and his neighbors, and made his isolation more complete.

Gradually the guineas, the crowns, and the half-crowns grew to a heap, and Marner drew less and less for his own wants, trying to solve the problem of keeping himself strong enough to work sixteen hours a day on as small an outlay as possible. Have not men, shut up in solitary imprisonment, found an interest in marking the moments by straight strokes of a certain length on the wall, until the growth of the sum of straight strokes, arranged in triangles, has become a mastering purpose? Do we not wile away moments of inanity or fatigued waiting by repeating some trivial movement or sound, until the repetition has bred a want, which is incipient habit? That will help us to understand how the love of accumulating money grows an absorbing passion in men whose imaginations, even in the very beginning of their hoard, showed them no purpose beyond it. Marner wanted the heaps of ten to grow into a square, and then into a larger square; and every added guinea, while it was itself a satisfaction, bred a new desire. In this strange world, made a hopeless riddle to him, he might, if he had had a less intense nature, have sat weaving, weaving—looking towards the end of his pattern, or towards the end of his web, till he forgot the riddle, and everything else but his immediate sensations; but the money had come to mark off his weaving into periods, and the money not only grew, but it remained with him. He began to think it was conscious of him, as his loom was, and he would on no account have exchanged those coins, which had become his familiars, for other coins with unknown faces. He handled them, he counted them, till their form and color were like the satisfaction of a thirst to him; but it was only in the night, when his work was done, that he drew them out to enjoy their companionship. He had taken up some bricks in his floor underneath his loom, and here he had made a hole in which he set the iron pot that contained his guineas and silver coins, covering the bricks with sand whenever he replaced them. Not that the idea of being robbed presented itself often or strongly to his mind; hoarding was common in country districts in those days; there were old laborers in the parish of Raveloe who were known to have their savings by them, probably inside their flock-beds; but their rustic neighbors, though not all of them as honest as their ancestors in the days of King Alfred,[1] had not imaginations bold enough to lay a plan of burglary. How could they have spent the money in their own village without betraying themselves? They would be obliged to "run away"—a course as dark and dubious as a balloon journey.

So, year after year, Silas Marner had lived in this solitude, his guineas rising in the iron pot, and his life narrowing and hardening itself more and more into a mere pulsation of desire and satisfaction that had no relation to any other being. His life had reduced itself to the functions of weaving and hoarding, without any contemplation of an end towards which the functions tended. The same sort of process has perhaps been undergone by wiser men, when they have been cut off from faith and love—only, instead of a loom and a heap of guineas, they have had some erudite research, some ingenious project, or some well-knit theory. Strangely Marner's face and figure shrank and bent themselves into a constant mechanical relation to the objects of his life, so that he produced the same sort of impression as a handle or a crooked tube, which has no meaning standing apart. The prominent eyes that used to look trusting and dreamy, now looked as if they had been made to see only one kind of thing that was very small, like tiny grain, for which they hunted everywhere: and he was so withered and yellow, that, though he was not yet forty, the children always called him "Old Master Marner."

Yet even in this stage of withering a little incident happened, which showed that the sap of affection was not all gone. It was one of his daily tasks to fetch his water from a well a couple of fields off, and for this purpose, ever since he came to Raveloe, he had had a brown earthenware pot, which he held as his most precious utensil among the very few conveniences he had granted himself. It had been his companion for twelve years, always standing on the same spot, always lending its handle to him in the early morning, so that its form had an expression for him of willing helpfulness, and the impress of its handle

on his palm gave a satisfaction mingled with that of
having the fresh clear water. One day as he was
returning from the well, he stumbled against the step
of the stile, and his brown pot, falling with force
against the stones that overarched the ditch below
him, was broken in three pieces. Silas picked up
the pieces and carried them home with grief in his
heart. The brown pot could never be of use to him
any more, but he stuck the bits together and propped
the ruin in its old place for a memorial.

This is the history of Silas Marner, until the fifteenth year after he came to Raveloe. The livelong
day he sat in his loom, his ear filled with its monotony, his eyes bent close down on the slow growth of
sameness in the brownish web,[1] his muscles moving
with such even repetition that their pause seemed almost as much a constraint as the holding of his breath.
But at night came his revelry: at night he closed his
shutters, and made fast his doors, and drew forth his
gold. Long ago the heap of coins had become too
large for the iron pot to hold them, and he had made
for them two thick leather bags, which wasted no
room in their resting-place, but lent themselves flexi-
bly to every corner. How the guineas shone as they
came pouring out of the dark leather mouths! The
silver bore no large proportion in amount to the gold,
because the long pieces of linen which formed his chief
work were always partly paid for in gold, and out of
the silver he supplied his own bodily wants, choosing
always the shillings and sixpences to spend in this

way. He loved the guineas best, but he would not change the silver—the crowns and half-crowns that were his own earnings, begotten by his labor; he loved them all. He spread them out in heaps and bathed his hands in them; then he counted them and set them up in regular piles, and felt their rounded outline between his thumb and fingers, and thought fondly of the guineas that were only half earned by the work in his loom, as if they had been unborn children—thought of the guineas that were coming slowly through the coming years, through all his life, which spread far away before him, the end quite hidden by countless days of weaving. No wonder his thoughts were still with his loom and his money when he made his journeys through the fields and the lanes to fetch and carry home his work, so that his steps never wandered to the hedge-banks and the lane-side in search of the once familiar herbs: these too belonged to the past, from which his life had shrunk away, like a rivulet that has sunk far down from the grassy fringe of its old breadth into a little shivering thread, that cuts a groove for itself in the barren sand.

But about the Christmas of that fifteenth year, a second great change came over Marner's life, and his history became blent in a singular manner with the life of his neighbors.

CHAPTER III

THE greatest man in Raveloe was Squire Cass, who
lived in the large red house with the handsome flight
of stone steps in front and the high stables behind it,
nearly opposite the church. He was only one among
several landed parishioners, but he alone was honored
with the title of Squire; for though Mr. Osgood's
family was also understood to be of timeless origin—
the Raveloe imagination having never ventured back
to that fearful blank when there were no Osgoods—
still, he merely owned the farm he occupied; whereas
Squire Cass had a tenant or two, who complained of
the game to him quite as if he had been a lord.

It was still that glorious war-time which was felt
to be a peculiar favor of Providence towards the
landed interest, and the fall of prices [1] had not yet
come to carry the race of small squires and yeomen
down that road to ruin for which extravagant habits
and bad husbandry were plentifully anointing their
wheels. I am speaking now in relation to Raveloe
and the parishes that resembled it; for our old-fashioned country life had many different aspects, as all
life must have when it is spread over a various surface, and breathed on variously by multitudinous currents, from the winds of heaven to the thoughts of

men, which are forever moving and crossing each
other with incalculable results. Raveloe lay low
among the bushy trees and the rutted lanes, aloof from
the currents of industrial energy and Puritan earnest-
ness: the rich ate and drank freely, accepting gout
and apoplexy as things that ran mysteriously in respectable families, and the poor thought that the rich
were entirely in the right of it to lead a jolly life;
besides, their feasting caused a multiplication of orts,[1]
which were the heirlooms of the poor. Betty Jay
scented the boiling of Squire Cass's hams, but her
longing was arrested by the unctuous liquor in which
they were boiled; and when the seasons brought round
the great merry-makings, they were regarded on all
hands as a fine thing for the poor. For the Raveloe
feasts were like the rounds of beef and the barrels
of ale—they were on a large scale, and lasted a good
while, especially in the winter-time. After ladies
had packed up their best gowns and top-knots in
bandboxes, and had incurred the risk of fording
streams on pillions with the precious burden in rainy
or snowy weather, when there was no knowing how
high the water would rise, it was not to be supposed
that they looked forward to a brief pleasure. On
this ground it was always contrived in the dark
seasons, when there was little work to be done, and
the hours were long, that several neighbors should
keep open house in succession. So soon as Squire
Cass's standing dishes diminished in plenty and freshness, his guests had nothing to do but to walk a little

higher up the village to Mr. Osgood's, at the Orchards, and they found hams and chines[1] uncut, pork-pies with the scent of the fire in them; spun butter in all its freshness—everything, in fact, that appetites at leisure could desire, in perhaps greater perfection, though not in greater abundance, than at Squire Cass's.

For the Squire's wife had died long ago, and the Red House was without that presence of the wife and mother which is the fountain of wholesome love and fear in parlor and kitchen; and this helped to account not only for there being more profusion than finished excellence in the holiday provisions, but also for the frequency with which the proud Squire condescended to preside in the parlor of the Rainbow rather than under the shadow of his own dark wainscot; perhaps, also, for the fact that his sons had turned out rather ill. Raveloe was not a place where moral censure was severe, but it was thought a weakness in the Squire that he had kept all his sons at home in idleness; and though some license was to be allowed to young men whose fathers could afford it, people shook their heads at the courses of the second son, Dunstan, commonly called Dunsey Cass, whose taste for swopping and betting might turn out to be a sowing of something worse than wild oats. To be sure, the neighbors said, it was no matter what became of Dunsey—a spiteful jeering fellow, who seemed to enjoy his drink the more when other people went dry—always provided that his doings did not bring trouble on a family like Squire Cass's, with a monument in the church, and tankards older than King George. But it would be a thousand pities if Mr. Godfrey, the eldest, a fine open-faced good-natured young man who was to come into the land some day, should take to going along the same road with his brother, as he had seemed to do of late. If he went on in that way, he would lose Miss Nancy Lammeter; for it was well known that she had looked very shyly on him ever since last Whitsuntide twelvemonth, when there was so much talk about his being away from home days and days together. There was something wrong more than common—that was quite clear; for Mr. Godfrey didn't look half so fresh-colored and open as he used to do. At one time everybody was saying, What a handsome couple he and Miss Nancy Lammeter would make! and if she could come to be mistress at the Red House, there would be a fine change, for the Lammeters had been brought up in that way, that they never suffered a pinch of salt to be wasted, and yet everybody in their household had of the best, according to his place. Such a daughter-in-law would be a saving to the old Squire, if she never brought a penny to her fortune; for it was to be feared that, notwithstanding his incomings, there were more holes in his pocket than the one where he put his own hand in. But if Mr. Godfrey didn't turn over a new leaf, he might say "Good-by" to Miss Nancy Lammeter.

It was the once hopeful Godfrey who was standing, with his hands in his side-pockets and his back to the fire, in the dark wainscoted parlor, one late November afternoon in that fifteenth year of Silas Marner's life at Raveloe. The fading gray light fell dimly on the walls decorated with guns, whips, and foxes' brushes, on coats and hats flung on the chairs, on tankards sending forth a scent of flat ale, and on a half-choked fire, with pipes propped up in the chimney-corners: signs of a domestic life destitute of any hallowing charm, with which the look of gloomy vexation on Godfrey's blond face was in sad accordance. He seemed to be waiting and listening for some one's approach, and presently the sound of a heavy step, with an accompanying whistle, was heard across the large empty entrance-hall.

The door opened, and a thick-set, heavy-looking young man entered, with the flushed face and the gratuitously elated bearing which mark the first stage of intoxication. It was Dunsey, and at the sight of him Godfrey's face parted with some of its gloom to take on the more active expression of hatred. The handsome brown spaniel that lay on the hearth retreated under the chair in the chimney-corner.

"Well, Master Godfrey, what do you want with me?" said Dunsey, in a mocking tone. "You're my elders and betters, you know; I was obliged to come when you sent for me."

"Why, this is what I want—and just shake yourself sober and listen, will you?" said Godfrey, savagely. He had himself been drinking more than was good for him, trying to turn his gloom into uncalculating anger. "I want to tell you, I must hand over that rent of Fowler's to the Squire, or else tell him I gave it you; for he's threatening to distrain [1] for it, and it'll all be out soon, whether I tell him or not. He said, just now, before he went out, he should send word to Cox to distrain, if Fowler didn't come and pay up his arrears this week. The Squire's short o' cash, and in no humor to stand any nonsense; and you know what he threatened, if ever he found you making away with his money again. So, see and get the money, and pretty quickly, will you?"

"Oh!" said Dunsey, sneeringly, coming nearer to his brother and looking in his face. "Suppose, now, you get the money yourself, and save me the trouble, eh? Since you was so kind as to hand it over to me, you'll not refuse me the kindness to pay it back for me: it was your brotherly love made you do it, you know."

Godfrey bit his lips and clenched his fist. "Don't come near me with that look, else I'll knock you down."

"Oh, no, you won't," said Dunsey, turning away on his heel, however. "Because I'm such a good-natured brother, you know, I might get you turned out of house and home, and cut off with a shilling any day. I might tell the Squire how his handsome son was married to that nice young woman, Molly Farren, and was very unhappy because he couldn't live with his drunken wife, and I should slip into your place as comfortable as could be. But you see,

I don't do it—I'm so easy and good-natured. You'll take any trouble for me. You'll get the hundred pounds for me—I know you will.''

"How can I get the money?" said Godfrey, quivering. "I haven't a shilling to bless myself with. And it's a lie that you'd slip into my place: you'd get yourself turned out too, that's all. For if you begin telling tales, I'll follow. Bob's my father's favorite—you know that very well. He'd only think himself well rid of you.''

"Never mind," said Dunsey, nodding his head sideways as he looked out of the window. "It 'ud be very pleasant to me to go in your company— you're such a handsome brother, and we've always been so fond of quarreling with one another, I shouldn't know what to do without you. But you'd like better for us both to stay at home together; I know you would. So you'll manage to get that little sum o' money, and I'll bid you good-by, though I'm sorry to part.''

Dunstan was moving off, but Godfrey rushed after him and seized him by the arm, saying, with an oath—

"I tell you, I have no money: I can get no money.''

"Borrow of old Kimble.''

"I tell you, he won't lend me any more, and I shan't ask him.''

"Well, then, sell Wildfire.''

"Yes, that's easy talking. I must have the money directly.''

"Well, you've only got to ride him to the hunt to-morrow. There'll be Bryce and Keating there, for sure. You'll get more bids than one."

"I daresay, and get back home at eight o'clock, splashed up to the chin. I'm going to Mrs. Osgood's birthday dance."

"Oho!" said Dunsey, turning his head on one side, and trying to speak in a small mincing treble. "And there's sweet Miss Nancy coming; and we shall dance with her, and promise never to be naughty again, and be taken into favor, and—"

"Hold your tongue about Miss Nancy, you fool," said Godfrey, turning red, "else I'll throttle you."

"What for?" said Dunsey, still in an artificial tone, but taking a whip from the table and beating the butt-end of it on his palm. "You've a very good chance. I'd advise you to creep up her sleeve [1] again: it 'ud be saving time, if Molly should happen to take a drop too much laudanum some day, and make a widower of you. Miss Nancy wouldn't mind being a second, if she didn't know it. And you've got a good-natured brother, who'll keep your secret well, because you'll be so very obliging to him."

"I'll tell you what it is," said Godfrey, quivering, and pale again, "my patience is pretty near at an end. If you'd a little more sharpness in you, you might know that you may urge a man a bit too far, and make one leap as easy as another. I don't know but what it is so now: I may as well tell the Squire everything myself—I should get you off my

back, if I got nothing else.   And, after all, he'll know
some time.   She's been threatening to come herself
and tell him.   So, don't flatter yourself that your
secrecy's worth any price you choose to ask.   You
drain me of money till I have got nothing to pacify
her with, and she'll do as she threatens some day.
It's all one.   I'll tell my father everything myself,
and you may go to the devil.''

Dunsey perceived that he had overshot his mark,
and that there was a point at which even the hesitating Godfrey might be driven into decision.   But
he said, with an air of unconcern—

"As you please; but I'll have a draught of ale
first.''   And ringing the bell, he threw himself across
two chairs, and began to rap the window-seat with
the handle of his whip.

Godfrey stood, still with his back to the fire uneasily moving his fingers among the contents of his
side-pockets, and looking at the floor.   That big
muscular frame of his held plenty of animal courage,
but helped him to no decision when the dangers to
be braved were such as could neither be knocked down
nor throttled.   His natural irresolution and moral
cowardice were exaggerated by a position in which
dreaded consequences seemed to press equally on all
sides, and his irritation had no sooner provoked him
to defy Dunstan and anticipate all possible betrayals,
than the miseries he must bring on himself by such a
step seemed more unendurable to him than the present
evil.   The results of confession were not contingent,

they were certain; whereas betrayal was not certain.
From the near vision of that certainty he fell back on
suspense and vacillation with a sense of repose. The
disinherited son of a small squire, equally disinclined
to dig and to beg,[1] was almost as helpless as an up-
rooted tree, which, by the favor of earth and sky, has
grown to a handsome bulk on the spot where it first
shot upward. Perhaps it would have been possible
to think of digging with some cheerfulness if Nancy
Lammeter were to be won on those terms; but, since
he must irrevocably lose *her* as well as the inheritance,
and must break every tie but the one that degraded
him and left him without motive for trying to recover his better self, he could imagine no future for
himself on the other side of confession but that of
"'listing for a soldier"—the most desperate step,
short of suicide, in the eyes of respectable families.
No! he would rather trust to casualties than to his
own resolve—rather go on sitting at the feast, and
sipping the wine he loved, though with the sword
hanging over him,[2] and terror in his heart, than rush
away into the cold darkness where there was no pleasure left. The utmost concession to Dunstan about
the horse began to seem easy, compared with the ful-
fillment of his own threat. But his pride would not
let him recommence the conversation otherwise than
by continuing the quarrel. Dunstan was waiting for
this, and took his ale in shorter draughts than usual.

"It's just like you," Godfrey burst out, in a bitter
tone, "to talk about my selling Wildfire in that cool

way—the last thing I've got to call my own, and the best bit of horse-flesh I ever had in my life. And if you'd got a spark of pride in you, you'd be ashamed to see the stables emptied, and everybody sneering about it. But it's my belief you'd sell yourself, if it was only for the pleasure of making somebody feel he'd got a bad bargain.''

"Ay, ay," said Dunstan, very placably, "you do me justice, I see. You know I'm a jewel for 'ticing people into bargains. For which reason I advise you to let *me* sell Wildfire. I'd ride him to the hunt to-morrow for you, with pleasure. I shouldn't look so handsome as you in the saddle, but it's the horse they'll bid for, and not the rider."

"Yes, I daresay—trust my horse to you!"

"As you please," said Dunstan, rapping the window-seat again with an air of great unconcern. "It's *you* have got to pay Fowler's money; it's none of my business. You received the money from him when you went to Bramcote, and *you* told the Squire it wasn't paid. I'd nothing to do with that; you chose to be so obliging as to give it me, that was all. If you don't want to pay the money, let it alone; it's all one to me. But I was willing to accommodate you by undertaking to sell the horse, seeing it's not convenient to you to go so far to-morrow."

Godfrey was silent for some moments. He would have liked to spring on Dunstan, wrench the whip from his hand, and flog him to within an inch of his life; and no bodily fear could have deterred him;

but he was mastered by another sort of fear, which was fed by feelings stronger even than his resentment. When he spoke again it was in a half-conciliatory tone.

"Well, you mean no nonsense about the horse, eh? You'll sell him all fair, and hand over the money? If you don't, you know, everything 'ull go to smash, for I've got nothing else to trust to. And you'll have less pleasure in pulling the house over my head, when your own skull's to be broken too."

"Ay, ay," said Dunstan, rising; "all right. I thought you'd come round. I'm the fellow to bring old Bryce up to the scratch. I'll get you a hundred and twenty for him, if I get you a penny."

"But it'll perhaps rain cats and dogs [1] to-morrow, as it did yesterday, and then you can't go," said Godfrey, hardly knowing whether he wished for that obstacle or not.

"Not *it*," said Dunstan. "I'm always lucky in my weather. It might rain if you wanted to go yourself. You never hold trumps, you know—I always do. You've got the beauty, you see, and I've got the luck, so you must keep me by you for your crooked sixpence; [2] you'll *ne*-ver get along without me."

"Confound you, hold your tongue!" said Godfrey, impetuously. "And take care to keep sober to-morrow, else you'll get pitched on your head coming home, and Wildfire might be the worse for it."

"Make your tender heart easy," said Dunstan, opening the door. "You never knew me see double

when I'd got a bargain to make; it 'ud spoil the fun.
Besides, whenever I fall, I'm warranted to fall on
my legs.''

With that, Dunstan slammed the door behind him,
and left Godfrey to that bitter rumination on his
personal circumstances which was now unbroken from
day to day save by the excitement of sporting, drinking, card-playing, or the rare and less oblivious pleasure of seeing Miss Nancy Lammeter. The subtle
and varied pains springing from the higher sensibility that accompanies higher culture are perhaps less
pitiable than that dreary absence of impersonal enjoyment and consolation which leaves ruder minds to
the perpetual urgent companionship of their own
griefs and discontents. The lives of those rural forefathers, whom we are apt to think very prosaic figures
—men whose only work was to ride round their land,
getting heavier and heavier in their saddles, and who
passed the rest of their days in the half-listless gratification of senses dulled by monotony—had a certain
pathos in them nevertheless. Calamities came to
them too, and their early errors carried hard consequences: perhaps the love of some sweet maiden, the
image of purity, order, and calm, had opened their
eyes to the vision of a life in which the days would
not seem too long, even without rioting; but the
maiden was lost, and the vision passed away, and
then what was left to them, especially when they had
become too heavy for the hunt, or for carrying a gun
over the furrows, but to drink and get merry, or to

drink and get angry, so that they might be independent of variety, and say over again with eager emphasis the things they had said already any time that twelvemonth? Assuredly, among these flushed and dull-eyed men there were some whom—thanks to their native human-kindness—even riot could never drive into brutality; men who, when their cheeks were fresh, had felt the keen point of sorrow or remorse, had been pierced by the reeds they leaned on, or had lightly put their limbs in fetters from which no struggle could loose them; and under these sad circumstances, common to us all, their thoughts could find no resting-place outside the ever-trodden round of their own petty history.

That, at least, was the condition of Godfrey Cass in this six-and-twentieth year of his life. A movement of compunction, helped by those small indefinable influences which every personal relation exerts on a pliant nature, had urged him into a secret marriage, which was a blight on his life. It was an ugly story of low passion, delusion, and waking from delusion, which needs not to be dragged from the privacy of Godfrey's bitter memory. He had long known that the delusion was partly due to a trap laid for him by Dunstan, who saw in his brother's degrading marriage the means of gratifying at once his jealous hate and his cupidity. And if Godfrey could have felt himself simply a victim, the iron bit that destiny had put into his mouth would have chafed him less intolerably. If the curses he muttered half aloud when he was alone had had no other object than Dunstan's diabolical cunning, he might have shrunk less from the consequences of avowal. But he had something else to curse—his own vicious folly, which now seemed as mad and unaccountable to him as almost all our follies and vices do when their promptings have long passed away. For four years he had thought of Nancy Lammeter, and wooed her with tacit patient worship, as the woman who made him think of the future with joy; she would be his wife, and would make home lovely to him, as his father's home had never been; and it would be easy, when she was always near, to shake off those foolish habits that were no pleasures, but only a feverish way of annulling vacancy. Godfrey's was an essentially domestic nature, bred up in a home where the hearth had no smiles, and where the daily habits were not chastised by the presence of household order. His easy disposition made him fall in unresistingly with the family courses, but the need of some tender permanent affection, the longing for some influence that would make the good he preferred easy to pursue, caused the neatness, purity, and liberal orderliness of the Lammeter household, sunned by the smile of Nancy, to seem like those fresh bright hours of the morning when temptations go to sleep and leave the ear open to the voice of the good angel, inviting to industry, sobriety, and peace. And yet the hope of this paradise had not been enough to save him from a course which shut him out of it forever. Instead of keeping fast hold of the strong silken rope by which Nancy would have drawn him safe to the green banks where it was easy to step firmly, he had let himself be dragged back into mud and slime, in which it was useless to struggle. He had made ties for himself which robbed him of all wholesome motive and were a constant exasperation.

Still, there was one position worse than the present: it was the position he would be in when the ugly secret was disclosed; and the desire that continually triumphed over every other was that of warding off the evil day, when he would have to bear the consequences of his father's violent resentment for the wound inflicted on his family pride—would have, perhaps, to turn his back on that hereditary ease and dignity which, after all, was a sort of reason for living, and would carry with him the certainty that he was banished forever from the sight and esteem of Nancy Lammeter. The longer the interval, the more chance there was of deliverance from some, at least, of the hateful consequences to which he had sold himself; the more opportunities remained for him to snatch the strange gratification of seeing Nancy, and gathering some faint indications of her lingering regard. Towards this gratification he was impelled, fitfully, every now and then, after having passed weeks in which he had avoided her as the far-off bright-winged prize that only made him spring forward and find his chain all the more galling. One of those fits of yearning was on him now, and it would have been strong enough to have persuaded him to trust Wildfire to Dunstan rather than disappoint the yearning, even if he had not had another reason for his disinclination towards the morrow's hunt. That other reason was the fact that the morning's meet was near Batherley, the market-town where the unhappy woman lived, whose image became more odious to him every day; and to his thought the whole vicinage was haunted by her. The yoke a man creates for himself by wrong-doing will breed hate in the kindliest nature; and the good-humored, affectionate-hearted Godfrey Cass was fast becoming a bitter man, visited by cruel wishes, that seemed to enter, and depart, and enter again, like demons who had found in him a ready-garnished home.

What was he to do this evening to pass the time? He might as well go to the Rainbow, and hear the talk about the cock-fighting: everybody was there, and what else was there to be done? Though, for his own part, he did not care a button for cock-fighting. Snuff, the brown spaniel, who had placed herself in front of him, and had been watching him for some time, now jumped up in impatience for the expected caress. But Godfrey thrust her away without looking at her, and left the room, followed humbly by the unresenting Snuff—perhaps because she saw no other career open to her.

CHAPTER IV

DUNSTAN CASS, setting off in the raw morning, at the judiciously quiet pace of a man who is obliged to ride to cover on his hunter, had to take his way along the lane which, at its farther extremity, passed by the piece of unenclosed ground called the Stone-pit, where stood the cottage, once a stone-cutter's shed, now for fifteen years inhabited by Silas Marner. The spot looked very dreary at this season, with the moist trodden clay about it, and the red, muddy water high up in the deserted quarry. That was Dunstan's first thought as he approached it; the second was, that the old fool of a weaver, whose loom he heard rattling already, had a great deal of money hidden somewhere. How was it that he, Dunstan Cass, who had often heard talk of Marner's miserliness, had never thought of suggesting to Godfrey that he should frighten or persuade the old fellow into lending the money on the excellent security of the young Squire's prospects? The resource occurred to him now as so easy and agreeable, especially as Marner's hoard was likely to be large enough to leave Godfrey a handsome surplus beyond his immediate needs, and enable him to accommodate his faithful brother, that he had almost turned the horse's head towards home again. Godfrey would be ready enough to accept the suggestion: he would snatch eagerly at a plan that might save him from parting with Wildfire. But when Dunstan's meditation reached this point, the inclination to go on grew strong and prevailed. He didn't want to give Godfrey that pleasure: he preferred that Master Godfrey should be vexed. Moreover, Dunstan enjoyed the self-important consciousness of having a horse to sell, and the opportunity of driving a bargain, swaggering, and possibly taking somebody in. He might have all the satisfaction attendant on selling his brother's horse, and not the less have the further satisfaction of setting Godfrey to borrow Marner's money. So he rode on to cover.

Bryce and Keating were there, as Dunstan was quite sure they would be—he was such a lucky fellow.

"Heyday!" said Bryce, who had long had his eye on Wildfire, "you're on your brother's horse to-day: how's that?"

"Oh, I've swopped with him," said Dunstan, whose delight in lying, grandly independent of utility, was not to be diminished by the likelihood that his hearer would not believe him—"Wildfire's mine now."

"What! has he swopped with you for that big-boned hack of yours?" said Bryce, quite aware that he should get another lie in answer.

"Oh, there was a little account between us," said Dunsey carelessly, "and Wildfire made it even. I accommodated him by taking the horse, though it was against my will, for I'd got an itch for a mare o'

Jortin's—as rare a bit o' blood as ever you threw your leg across. But I shall keep Wildfire, now I've got him, though I'd a bid of a hundred and fifty for him the other day, from a man over at Flitton—he's buying for Lord Cromleck—a fellow with a cast in his eye, and a green waistcoat. But I mean to stick to Wildfire: I shan't get a better at a fence in a hurry. The mare's got more blood, but she's a bit too weak in the hind-quarters.''

Bryce of course divined that Dunstan wanted to sell the horse, and Dunstan knew that he divined it (horse-dealing is only one of many human transactions carried on in this ingenious manner); and they both considered that the bargain was in its first stage, when Bryce replied, ironically—

''I wonder at that now; I wonder you mean to keep him; for I never heard of a man who didn't want to sell his horse getting a bid of half as much again as the horse was worth. You'll be lucky if you get a hundred.''

Keating rode up now, and the transaction became more complicated. It ended in the purchase of the horse by Bryce for a hundred and twenty, to be paid on the delivery of Wildfire, safe and sound, at the Batherley stables. It did occur to Dunsey that it might be wise for him to give up the day's hunting, proceed at once to Batherley, and, having waited for Bryce's return, hire a horse to carry him home with the money in his pocket. But the inclination for a run, encouraged by confidence in his luck and by a

draught of brandy from his pocket-pistol at the conclusion of the bargain, was not easy to overcome, especially with a horse under him that would take the
fences to the admiration of the field. Dunstan, however, took one fence too many, and got his horse
pierced with a hedge-stake. His own ill-favored person, which was quite unmarketable, escaped without
injury; but poor Wildfire, unconscious of his price,
turned on his flank and painfully panted his last.
It happened that Dunstan, a short time before, having had to get down to arrange his stirrup, had muttered a good many curses at this interruption, which
had thrown him in the rear of the hunt near the
moment of glory, and under this exasperation had
taken the fences more blindly. He would soon have
been up with the hounds again, when the fatal accident happened; and hence he was between eager riders
in advance, not troubling themselves about what happened behind them, and far-off stragglers, who were
as likely as not to pass quite aloof from the line of
road in which Wildfire had fallen. Dunstan, whose
nature it was to care more for immediate annoyances
than for remote consequences, no sooner recovered
his legs, and saw that it was all over with Wildfire,
than he felt a satisfaction at the absence of witnesses
to a position which no swaggering could make envia-
ble. Reinforcing himself, after his shake, with a little
brandy and much swearing, he walked as fast as he
could to a coppice on his right hand, through which it
occurred to him that he could make his way to Bath-

erley without danger of encountering any member of
the hunt. His first intention was to hire a horse
there and ride home forthwith, for to walk many
miles without a gun in his hand and along an ordinary
road, was as much out of the question to him as to
other spirited young men of his kind. He did not
much mind about taking the bad news to Godfrey,
for he had to offer him at the same time the resource
of Marner's money; and if Godfrey kicked, as he always did, at the notion of making a fresh debt from
which he himself got the smallest share of advantage,
why, he wouldn't kick long: Dunstan felt sure that he
could worry Godfrey into anything. The idea of
Marner's money kept growing in vividness, now the
want of it had become immediate; the prospect of
having to make his appearance with the muddy boots
of a pedestrian at Batherley, and to encounter the
grinning queries of stablemen, stood unpleasantly in
the way of his impatience to be back at Raveloe and
carry out his felicitous plan; and a casual visitation
of his waistcoat-pocket, as he was ruminating,
awakened his memory to the fact that the two or
three small coins his fore-finger encountered there,
were of too pale a color to cover that small debt, without payment of which the stable-keeper had declared
he would never do any more business with Dunsey
Cass. After all, according to the direction in which
the run had brought him, he was not so very much
farther from home than he was from Batherley; but
Dunsey, not being remarkable for clearness of head,

was only led to this conclusion by the gradual perception that there were other reasons for choosing the unprecedented course of walking home. It was now nearly four o'clock, and a mist was gathering: the sooner he got into the road the better. He remembered having crossed the road and seen the finger-post only a little while before Wildfire broke down; so, buttoning his coat, twisting the lash of his hunting-whip compactly round the handle, and rapping the tops of his boots with a self-possessed air, as if to assure himself that he was not at all taken by surprise, he set off with the sense that he was undertaking a remarkable feat of bodily exertion, which somehow and at some time he should be able to dress up and magnify to the admiration of a select circle at the Rainbow. When a young gentleman like Dunsey is reduced to so exceptional a mode of locomotion as walking, a whip in his hand is a desirable corrective to a too bewildering dreamy sense of unwontedness in his position; and Dunstan, as he went along through the gathering mist, was always rapping his whip somewhere. It was Godfrey's whip, which he had chosen to take without leave because it had a gold handle; [1] of course no one could see, when Dunstan held it, that the name *Godfrey Cass* was cut in deep letters on that gold handle—they could only see that it was a very handsome whip. Dunsey was not without fear that he might meet some acquaintance in whose eyes he would cut a pitiable figure for mist is no screen when people get close to each other; but

when he at last found himself in the well-known
Raveloe lanes without having met a soul, he silently
remarked that that was part of his usual good-luck.
But now the mist, helped by the evening darkness,
was more of a screen than he desired, for it hid the
ruts into which his feet were liable to slip—hid everything, so that he had to guide his steps by dragging
his whip along the low bushes in advance of the
hedgerow. He must soon, he thought, be getting near
the opening at the Stone-pits: he should find it out
by the break in the hedgerow. He found it out, however, by another circumstance which he had not expected—namely, by certain gleams of light, which he
presently guessed to proceed from Silas Marner's
cottage. That cottage and the money hidden within
it had been in his mind continually during his walk,
and he had been imagining ways of cajoling and
tempting the weaver to part with the immediate possession of his money for the sake of receiving interest. Dunstan felt as if there must be a little fright-
ening added to the cajolery, for his own arithmetical
convictions were not clear enough to afford him any
forcible demonstration as to the advantages of interest; and as for security, he regarded it vaguely as
a means of cheating a man by making him believe
that he would be paid. Altogether, the operation on
the miser's mind was a task that Godfrey would be
sure to hand over to his more daring and cunning
brother: Dunstan had made up his mind to that; and
by the time he saw the light gleaming through the

chinks of Marner's shutters, the idea of a dialogue
with the weaver had become so familiar to him, that
it occurred to him as quite a natural thing to make
the acquaintance forthwith. There might be several
conveniences attending this course: the weaver had
possibly got a lantern, and Dunstan was tired of feeling his way. He was still nearly three-quarters of a
mile from home, and the lane was becoming unpleasantly slippery, for the mist was passing into rain.
He turned up the bank, not without some fear lest
he might miss the right way, since he was not certain
whether the light were in front or on the side of the
cottage. But he felt the ground before him cau-
tiously with his whip-handle, and at last arrived
safely at the door. He knocked loudly, rather enjoying the idea that the old fellow would be frightened
at the sudden noise. He heard no movement in reply: all was silence in the cottage. Was the weaver
gone to bed, then? If so, why had he left a light?
That was a strange forgetfulness in a miser. Dunstan knocked still more loudly, and, without pausing
for a reply, pushed his fingers through the latch-hole,
intending to shake the door and pull the latch-string [1]
up and down not doubting that the door was fastened.
But, to his surprise, at this double motion the door
opened, and he found himself in front of a bright
fire which lit up every corner of the cottage—the bed,
the loom, the three chairs, and the table—and showed
him that Marner was not there.

Nothing at that moment could be much more invit-

ing to Dunsey that the bright fire on the brick hearth:
he walked in and seated himself by it at once. There
was something in front of the fire, too, that would
have been inviting to a hungry man, if it had been
in a different stage of cooking. It was a small bit of
pork suspended from the kettle-hanger by a string
passed through a large door-key, in a way known to
primitive house-keepers unpossessed of jacks.[1] But
the pork had been hung at the farthest extremity of
the hanger, apparently to prevent the roasting from
proceeding too rapidly during the owner's absence.
The old staring simpleton had hot meat for his supper, then? thought Dunstan. People had always said
he lived on moldy bread, on purpose to check his
appetite. But where could he be at this time, and
on such an evening, leaving his supper in this stage
of preparation, and his door unfastened? Dunstan's
own recent difficulty in making his way suggested to
him that the weaver had perhaps gone outside his
cottage to fetch in fuel, or for some such brief purpose, and had slipped into the Stone-pit. That was
an interesting idea to Dunstan, carrying consequences
of entire novelty. If the weaver was dead, who had
a right to his money? Who would know where his
money was hidden? *Who would know that anybody
had come to take it away?* He went no farther into
the subtleties of evidence: the pressing question,
"Where *is* the money?" now took such entire possession of him as to make him quite forget that the
weaver's death was not a certainty. A dull mind,

once arriving at an inference that flatters a desire,[1]
is rarely able to retain the impression that the notion
from which the inference started was purely prob-
lematic. And Dunstan's mind was as dull as the
mind of a possible felon usually is. There were only
three hiding-places where he had ever heard of cottagers' hoards being found: the thatch, the bed, and
a hole in the floor. Marner's cottage had no thatch;
and Dunstan's first act, after a train of thought made
rapid by the stimulus of cupidity, was to go up to the
bed; but while he did so, his eyes traveled eagerly
over the floor, where the bricks, distinct in the fire-
light, were discernible under the sprinkling of sand.
But not everywhere; for there was one spot, and one
only, which was quite covered with sand, and sand
showing the marks of fingers, which had apparently
been careful to spread it over a given space. It was
near the treadles of the loom. In an instant Dunstan
darted to that spot, swept away the sand with his
whip, and, inserting the thin end of the hook between
the bricks, found that they were loose. In haste he
lifted up two bricks, and saw what he had no doubt
was the object of his search; for what could there be
but money in those two leathern bags? And, from
their weight, they must be filled with guineas. Dunstan felt round the hole, to be certain that it held no
more; then he hastily replaced the bricks, and spread
the sand over them. Hardly more than five minutes
had passed since he had entered the cottage, but it
seemed to Dunstan like a long while; and though he

was without any distinct recognition of the possibility that Marner might be alive, and might re-enter the cottage at any moment, he felt an undefinable dread laying hold on him, as he rose to his feet with the bags in his hand. He would hasten out into the darkness, and then consider what he should do with the bags. He closed the door behind him immediately, that he might shut in the stream of light: a few steps would be enough to carry him beyond betrayal by the gleams from the shutter-chinks and the latch-hole. The rain and darkness had got thicker, and he was glad of it; though it was awkward walking with both hands filled, so that it was as much as he could do to grasp his whip along with one of the bags. But when he had gone a yard or two, he might take his time. So he stepped forward into the darkness.

CHAPTER V

WHEN Dunstan Cass turned his back on the cottage, Silas Marner was not more than a hundred yards away from it, plodding along from the village with a sack thrown round his shoulders as an overcoat, and with a horn lantern in his hand. His legs were weary, but his mind was at ease, free from the presentiment of change. The sense of security more frequently springs from habit than from conviction, and for this reason it often subsists after such a change in the conditions as might have been expected to suggest alarm. The lapse of time during which a given event has not happened, is, in this logic of habit, constantly alleged as a reason why the event should never happen, even when the lapse of time is precisely the added condition which makes the event imminent. A man will tell you that he has worked in a mine for forty years unhurt by an accident as a reason why he should apprehend no danger, though the roof is beginning to sink; and it is often observable, that the older a man gets, the more difficult it is to him to retain a believing conception of his own death. This influence of habit was necessarily strong in a man whose life was so monotonous as Marner's— who saw no new people and heard of no new events to keep alive in him the idea of the unexpected and the changeful; and it explains simply enough, why his mind could be at ease, though he had left his house and his treasure more defenseless than usual. Silas was thinking with double complacency of his supper: first, because it would be hot and savory; and secondly, because it would cost him nothing. For the little bit of pork was a present from the excellent housewife, Miss Priscilla Lammeter, to whom he had this day carried home a handsome piece of linen; and it was only on occasion of a present like this, that Silas indulged himself with roast meat. Supper was his favorite meal, because it came at his time of revelry, when his heart warmed over his gold; whenever he had roast meat, he always chose to have it for supper. But this evening, he had no sooner ingeniously knotted his string fast round his bit of pork, twisted the string according to rule over his door-key, passed it through the handle, and made it fast on the hanger, than he remembered that a piece of very fine twine was indispensable to his ''setting up'' a new piece of work in his loom early in the morning. It had slipped his memory, because, in coming from Mr. Lammeter's, he had not had to pass through the village; but to lose time by going on errands in the morning was out of the question. It was a nasty fog to turn out into, but there were things Silas loved better than his own comfort; so, drawing his pork to the extremity of the hanger, and arming himself with his lantern and his old sack, he set out on what, in

ordinary weather, would have been a twenty minutes'
errand. He could not have locked his door without
undoing his well-knotted string and retarding his
supper; it was not worth his while to make that sacrifice. What thief would find his way to the Stone-
pits on such a night as this? and why should he come
on this particular night, when he had never come
through all the fifteen years before? These questions were not distinctly present in Silas's mind; they
merely serve to represent the vaguely-felt foundation
of his freedom from anxiety.

He reached his door in much satisfaction that his
errand was done: he opened it, and to his short-
sighted eyes everything remained as he had left it,
except that the fire sent out a welcome increase of
heat. He trod about the floor while putting by his
lantern and throwing aside his hat and sack, so as to
merge the marks of Dunstan's feet on the sand in the
marks of his own nailed boots. Then he moved his
pork nearer to the fire, and sat down to the agreeable
business of tending the meat and warming himself at
the same time.

Any one who had looked at him as the red light
shone upon his pale face, strange straining eyes, and
meager form, would perhaps have understood the
mixture of contemptuous pity, dread, and suspicion
with which he was regarded by his neighbors in Raveloe. Yet few men could be more harmless than poor
Marner. In his truthful simple soul, not even the
growing greed and worship of gold could beget any

vice directly injurious to others. The light of his faith quite put out, and his affections made desolate, he had clung with all the force of his nature to his work and his money; and like all objects to which a man devotes himself, they had fashioned him into correspondence with themselves. His loom, as he wrought in it without ceasing, had in its turn wrought on him, and confirmed more and more the monotonous craving for its monotonous response. His gold, as he hung over it and saw it grow, gathered his power of loving together into a hard isolation like its own.

As soon as it was warm he began to think it would be a long while to wait till after supper before he drew out his guineas, and it would be pleasant to see them on the table before him as he ate his unwonted feast. For joy is the best of wine, and Silas's guineas were a golden wine of that sort.

He rose and placed his candle unsuspectingly on the floor near his loom, swept away the sand without noticing any change, and removed the bricks. The sight of the empty hole made his heart leap violently, but the belief that his gold was gone could not come at once—only terror, and the eager effort to put an end to the terror. He passed his trembling hand all about the hole, trying to think it possible that his eyes had deceived him; then he held the candle in the hole and examined it curiously, trembling more and more. At last he shook so violently that he let fall the candle, and lifted his hands to his head, trying

to steady himself, that he might think. Had he put
his gold somewhere else, by a sudden resolution last
night, and then forgotten it? A man falling into
dark waters seeks a momentary footing even on slid-
ing stones; and Silas, by acting as if he believed in
false hopes, warded off the moment of despair. He
searched in every corner, he turned his bed over, and
shook it, and kneaded it; he looked in his brick oven
where he laid his sticks. When there was no other
place to be searched, he kneeled down again and felt
once more all round the hole. There was no untried
refuge left for a moment's shelter from the terrible
truth.

Yes, there was a sort of refuge which always comes
with the prostration of thought under an overpower-
ing passion: it was that expectation of impossibilities,
that belief in contradictory images, which is still distinct from madness, because it is capable of being dissipated by the external fact. Silas got up from his
knees trembling, and looked round at the table:
didn't the gold lie there after all? The table was
bare. Then he turned and looked behind him—
looked all round his dwelling, seeming to strain his
brown eyes after some possible appearance of the
bags where he had already sought them in vain. He
could see every object in his cottage—and his gold
was not there.

Again he put his trembling hands to his head, and
gave a wild ringing scream, the cry of desolation.
For a few moments after, he stood motionless; but

the cry had relieved him from the first maddening
pressure of the truth. He turned, and tottered towards his loom, and got into the seat where he
worked, instinctively seeking this as the strongest
assurance of reality.

And now that all the false hopes had vanished, and
the first shock of certainty was past, the idea of a
thief began to present itself, and he entertained it
eagerly, because a thief might be caught and made to
restore the gold. The thought brought some new
strength with it, and he started from his loom to the
door. As he opened it the rain beat in upon him, for
it was falling more and more heavily. There were no
footsteps to be tracked on such a night—footsteps?
When had the thief come? During Silas's absence
in the daytime the door had been locked, and there
had been no marks of any inroad on his return
by daylight. And in the evening, too, he said to himself, everything was the same as when he had left it.
The sand and bricks looked as if they had not been
moved. *Was* it a thief who had taken the bags? or
was it a cruel power that no hands could reach which
had delighted in making him a second time desolate?
He shrank from this vaguer dread, and fixed his mind
with struggling effort on the robber with hands, who
could be reached by hands. His thoughts glanced at
all the neighbors who had made any remarks, or asked
any questions which he might now regard as a ground
of suspicion. There was Jem Rodney, a known
poacher, and otherwise disreputable; he had often

met Marner in his journeys across the fields, and had
said something jestingly about the weaver's money;
nay, he had once irritated Marner, by lingering at
the fire when he called to light his pipe, instead of going about his business. Jem Rodney was the man—
there was ease in the thought. Jem could be found
and made to restore the money: Marner did not want
to punish him, but only to get back his gold which
had gone from him, and left his soul like a forlorn
traveler on an unknown desert. The robber must be
laid hold of. Marner's ideas of legal authority were
confused, but he felt that he must go and proclaim
his loss; and the great people in the village—the clergyman, the constable, and Squire Cass—would make
Jem Rodney, or somebody else, deliver up the stolen
money. He rushed out in the rain, under the stimulus of this hope, forgetting to cover his head, not
caring to fasten his door; for he felt as if he had
nothing left to lose. He ran swiftly, till want of
breath compelled him to slacken his pace as he was
entering the village at the turning close to the Rainbow.

The Rainbow, in Marner's view, was a place of
luxurious resort for rich and stout husbands, whose
wives had superfluous stores of linen; it was the
place where he was likely to find the powers and dig-
nities of Raveloe, and where he could most speedily
make his loss public. He lifted the latch, and turned
into the bright bar or kitchen on the right hand,
where the less lofty customers of the house were in

the habit of assembling, the parlor on the left being
reserved for the more select society in which Squire
Cass frequently enjoyed the double pleasure of con-
viviality and condescension. But the parlor was
dark to-night, the chief personages who ornamented
its circle being all at Mrs. Osgood's birthday dance,
as Godfrey Cass was. And in consequence of this,
the party on the high-screened seats in the kitchen
was more numerous than usual; several personages,
who would otherwise have been admitted into the parlor and enlarged the opportunity of hectoring and
condescension for their betters, being content this
evening to vary their enjoyment by taking their spirits-and-water where they could themselves hector and
condescend in company that called for beer.

CHAPTER VI

THE conversation, which was at a high pitch of animation when Silas approached the door of the Rainbow, had, as usual, been slow and intermittent when the company first assembled. The pipes began to be puffed in a silence which had an air of severity; the more important customers, who drank spirits and sat nearest the fire, staring at each other as if a bet were depending on the first man who winked; while the beer-drinkers, chiefly men in fustian jackets and smock-frocks, kept their eyelids down and rubbed their hands across their mouths, as if their draughts of beer were a funeral duty attended with an embarrassing sadness. At last, Mr. Snell, the landlord, a man of a neutral disposition, accustomed to stand aloof from human differences as those of beings who were all alike in need of liquor, broke silence, by saying in a doubtful tone to his cousin the butcher—

"Some folks 'ud say that was a fine beast you druv in yesterday, Bob?"

The butcher, a jolly, smiling, red-haired man, was not disposed to answer rashly. He gave a few puffs before he spat and replied, "And they wouldn't be fur wrong, John."

After this feeble delusive thaw, the silence set in as severely as before.

"Was it a red Durham?" said the farrier,[1] taking up the thread of discourse after the lapse of a few minutes.

The farrier looked at the landlord, and the landlord looked at the butcher, as the person who must take the responsibility of answering.

"Red it was," said the butcher, in his good-humored husky treble—"and a Durham it was."

"Then you needn't tell *me* who you bought it of," said the farrier, looking round with some triumph; "I know who it is has got the red Durhams o' this country-side. And she'd a white star on her brow, I'll bet a penny?" The farrier leaned forward with his hands on his knees as he put this question, and his eyes twinkled knowingly.

"Well; yes—she might," said the butcher, slowly, considering that he was giving a decided affirmative. "I don't say contrairy."

"I knew that very well," said the farrier, throwing himself backward again, and speaking defiantly; "if *I* don't know Mr. Lammeter's cows, I should like to know who does—that's all. And as for the cow you've bought, bargain or no bargain, I've been at the drenching of her—contradick me who will."

The farrier looked fierce, and the mild butcher's conversational spirit was roused a little.

"I'm not contradicking no man," he said; "I'm for peace and quietness. Some are for cutting long

ribs—I'm for cutting 'em short myself; but *I* don't
quarrel with 'em. All I say is, it's a lovely carkiss—
and anybody as was reasonable, it 'ud bring tears
into their eyes to look at it.''

''Well, it's the cow as I drenched, whatever it is,''
pursued the farrier, angrily; ''and it was Mr. Lammeter's cow, else you told a lie when you said it was
a red Durham.''

''I tell no lies,'' said the butcher, with the same
mild huskiness as before, ''and I contradick none—
not if a man was to swear himself black: he's no meat
o' mine, nor none o' my bargains. All I say is, it's
a lovely carkiss. And what I say I'll stick to; but
I'll quarrel wi' no man.''

''No,'' said the farrier, with bitter sarcasm, looking at the company generally; ''and p'rhaps you
aren't pig-headed; and p'rhaps you didn't say the
cow was a red Durham; and p'rhaps you didn't say
she'd got a star on her brow—stick to that, now
you're at it.''

''Come, come,'' said the landlord; ''let the cow
alone. The truth lies atween you: you're both right
and both wrong, as I allays say. And as for the
cow's being Mr. Lammeter's, I say nothing to that;
but this I say, as the Rainbow's the Rainbow. And
for the matter o' that, if the talk is to be o' the Lammeters, *you* know the most upo' that head, eh, Mr.
Macey? You remember when first Mr. Lammeter's
father come into these parts, and took the Warrens?''

Mr. Macey, tailor and parish-clerk,[1] the latter of

which functions rheumatism had of late obliged him to share with a small-featured young man who sat opposite him, held his white head on one side, and twirled his thumbs with an air of complacency, slightly seasoned with criticism. He smiled pityingly, in answer to the landlord's appeal, and said—

"Ay, ay; I know, I know; but let other folks talk. I've laid by now, and gev up to the young uns. Ask them as have been to school at Tarley: they've learnt pernouncing; that's come up since my day."

"If you're pointing at me, Mr. Macey," said the deputy-clerk, with an air of anxious propriety, "I'm nowise a man to speak out of my place. As the psalm says—

> ' I know what's right, nor only so,
>   But also practise what I know.' "

"Well, then, I wish you'd keep hold o' the tune, when it's set for you; if you're for prac*tis*ing, I wish you'd prac*tise* that," said a large jocose-looking man, an excellent wheelwright in his week-day capacity, but on Sundays leader of the choir. He winked, as he spoke, at two of the company, who were known officially as the "bassoon" and the "key-bugle," in the confidence that he was expressing the sense of the musical profession in Raveloe.

Mr. Tookey, the deputy-clerk, who shared the unpopularity common to deputies, turned very red, but replied, with careful moderation—"Mr. Winthrop, if you'll bring me any proof as I'm in the wrong, I'm not the man to say I won't alter. But there's people set up their own ears for a standard, and expect the whole choir to follow 'em. There may be two opinions, I hope.''

"Ay, ay,'' said Mr. Macey, who felt very well satisfied with this attack on youthful presumption; "you're right there, Tookey; there's allays two 'pinions; there's the 'pinion a man has of himsen, and there's the 'pinion other folks have on him. There'd be two 'pinions about a cracked bell, if the bell could hear itself.''

"Well, Mr. Macey,'' said poor Tookey, serious amidst the general laughter, "I undertook to partially fill up the office of parish-clerk by Mr. Crackenthorp's desire, whenever your infirmities should make you unfitting; and it's one of the rights thereof to sing in the choir—else why have you done the same yourself?''

"Ah! but the old gentleman and you are two folks,'' said Ben Winthrop. "The old gentleman's got a gift. Why, the Squire used to invite him to take a glass, only to hear him sing the 'Red Rovier'; didn't he, Mr. Macey? It's a nat'ral gift. There's my little lad, Aaron, he's got a gift—he can sing a tune off straight, like a throstle. But as for you, Master Tookey, you'd better stick to your 'Amens': your voice is well enough when you keep it up in your nose. It's your inside as isn't right made for music: it's no better nor a hollow stalk.''

This kind of unflinching frankness was the most piquant form of joke to the company at the Rainbow, and Ben Winthrop's insult was felt by everybody to have capped Mr. Macey's epigram.

"I see what it is plain enough," said Mr. Tookey, unable to keep cool any longer. "There's a consperacy to turn me out o' the choir, as I shouldn't share the Christmas money—that's where it is. But I shall speak to Mr. Crackenthorp; I'll not be put upon by no man."

"Nay, nay, Tookey," said Ben Winthrop. "We'll pay you your share to keep out of it—that's what we'll do. There's things folks 'ud pay to be rid on, besides varmin."

"Come, come," said the landlord who felt that paying people for their absence was a principle dangerous to society; "a joke's a joke. We're all good friends here, I hope. We must give and take. You're both right and you're both wrong, as I say. I agree wi' Mr. Macey here, as there's two opinions; and if mine was asked, I should say they're both right. Tookey's right and Winthrop's right, and they've only got to split the difference and make themselves even."

The farrier was puffing his pipe rather fiercely, in some contempt at this trivial discussion. He had no ear for music himself, and never went to church, as being of the medical profession, and likely to be in requisition for delicate cows. But the butcher, having music in his soul, had listened with a divided desire for Tookey's defeat and for the preservation of the peace.

"To be sure," he said, following up the landlord's conciliatory view, "we're fond of our old clerk; it's nat'ral and him used to be such a singer, and got a brother as is known for the first fiddler in this country-side. Eh, it's a pity but what Solomon lived in our village, and could give us a tune when we liked; eh, Mr. Macey? I'd keep him in liver and lights for nothing—that I would."

"Ay, ay," said Mr. Macey, in the height of complacency; "our family's been known for musicianers as far back as anybody can tell. But them things are dying out, as I tell Solomon every time he comes round; there's no voices like what there used to be, and there's nobody remembers what we remember, if it isn't the old crows."

"Ay, you remember when first Mr. Lammeter's father come into these parts, don't you, Mr. Macey?" said the landlord.

"I should think I did," said the old man, who had now gone through that complimentary process necessary to bring him up to the point of narration; "and a fine old gentleman he was—as fine, and finer nor the Mr. Lammeter as now is. He came from a bit north'ard, so far as I could ever make out. But there's nobody rightly knows about those parts: only it couldn't be far north'ard, nor much different from this country, for he brought a fine breed o' sheep with him, so there must be pastures there, and everything reasonable. We heared tell as he'd sold his own land to come and take the Warrens, and that seemed odd for a man as had land of his own, to come and rent a farm in a strange place. But they said it was along of his wife's dying; though there's reasons in things as nobody knows on—that's pretty much what I've made out; yet some folks are so wise, they'll find you fifty reasons straight off, and all the while the real reason's winking at 'em in the corner, and they niver see't. Howsomever, it was soon seen as we'd got a new parish'ner as know'd the rights and customs o' things, and kep a good house, and was well looked on by everybody. And the young man—that's the Mr. Lammeter as now is, for he'd niver a sister—soon begun to court Miss Osgood, that's the sister o' the Mr. Osgood as now is, and a fine handsome lass she was—eh, you can't think—they pretend this young lass is like her, but that's the way wi' people as don't know what come before 'em. *I* should know, for I helped the old rector, Mr. Drumlow as was, I helped him marry 'em.''

Here Mr. Macey paused; he always gave his narrative in installments, expecting to be questioned according to precedent.

"Ay, and a partic'lar thing happened, didn't it, Mr. Macey, so as you were likely to remember that marriage?'' said the landlord, in a congratulatory tone.

"I should think there did—a *very* partic'lar thing,'' said Mr. Macey, nodding sideways. "For Mr. Drumlow—poor old gentleman. I was fond on him, though he'd got a bit confused in his head, what

wi' age and wi' taking a drop o' summat warm when
the service come of a cold morning. And young Mr.
Lammeter he'd have no way but he must be married
in Janiwary, which, to be sure, 's a unreasonable
time to be married in, for it isn't like a christening
or a burying, as you can't help; and so Mr. Drumlow—poor old gentleman, I was fond on him—but
when he come to put the questions, he put 'em by the
rule o' contrairy, like, and he says, 'Wilt thou have
this man to thy wedded wife?' says he, and then he
says 'Wilt thou have this woman to thy wedded husband?' says he. But the partic'larest thing of all is,
as nobody took any notice on it but me, and they answered straight off 'yes,' like as if it had been me
saying 'Amen' i' the right place, without listening to
what went before.''

"But *you* knew what was going on well enough,
didn't you, Mr. Macey? You were live enough, eh?''
said the butcher.

"Lor bless you!'' said Mr. Macey, pausing, and
smiling in pity at the impotence of his hearer's imagination—"why, I was all of a tremble: it was as if
I'd been a coat pulled by the two tails like; for I
couldn't stop the parson, I couldn't take upon me to
do that; and yet I said to myself, I says, 'Suppose
they shouldn't be fast married, 'cause the words are
contrairy?' and my head went working like a mill,
for I was allays uncommon for turning things over
and seeing all round 'em; and I says to myself, 'Is't
the meanin' or the words as makes folks fast i' wed-

lock?' For the parson meant right, and the bride and bridegroom meant right. But then, when I come to think on it, meanin' goes but a little way i' most things, for you may mean to stick things together and your glue may be bad, and then where are you? And so I says to mysen, 'It isn't the meanin', it's the glue.' And I was worreted as if I'd got three bells to pull at once, when we went into the vestry, and they begun to sign their names. But where's the use o' talking?—you can't think what goes on in a 'cute man's inside.''

"But you held in for all that, didn't you, Mr. Macey?" said the landlord.

"Ay, I held in tight till I was by mysen wi' Mr. Drumlow, and then I out wi' everything, but respectful, as I allays did. And he made light on it, and he says, 'Pooh, pooh, Macey, make yourself easy,' he says; 'it's neither the meaning nor the words—it's the *regis*ter does it—that's the glue.' So you see he settled it easy; for parsons and doctors know everything by heart, like, so as they aren't worreted wi' thinking what's the rights and wrongs o' things, as I'n been many and many's the time. And sure enough the wedding turned out all right, on'y poor Mrs. Lammeter—that's Miss Osgood as was—died afore the lasses was growed up; but for prosperity and everything respectable, there's no family more looked on."

Every one of Mr. Macey's audience had heard this story many times, but it was listened to as if it had been a favorite tune, and at certain points the puffing of the pipes was momentarily suspended, that the listeners might give their whole minds to the expected words. But there was more to come; and Mr. Snell, the landlord, duly put the leading question.

"Why, old Mr. Lammeter had a pretty fortin, didn't they say, when he come into these parts?"

"Well, yes," said Mr. Macey; "but I dare say it's as much as this Mr. Lammeter's done to keep it whole. For there was allays a talk as nobody could get rich on the Warrens: though he holds it cheap, for it's what they call Charity Land."

"Ay, and there's few folks know so well as you how it come to be Charity Land, eh, Mr. Macey?" said the butcher.

"How should they?" said the old clerk, with some contempt. "Why, my grandfather made the grooms' livery for that Mr. Cliff as came and built the big stables at the Warrens. Why, they're stables four times as big as Squire Cass's, for he thought o' nothing but hosses and hunting, Cliff didn't—a Lunnon tailor, some folks said, as had gone mad wi' cheating. For he couldn't ride; lor bless you! they said he'd got no more grip o' the hoss than if his legs had been cross-sticks: my grandfather heared old Squire Cass say so many and many a time. But ride he would as if Old Harry had been a-driving him; and he'd a son, a lad o' sixteen; and nothing would his father have him do, but he must ride and ride—though the lad was frighted, they said. And it was a common saying as the father wanted to ride the tailor out o' the

lad, and make a gentleman on him—not but what I'm
a tailor myself, but in respect as God made me such,
I'm proud on it, for 'Macey, tailor,' 's been wrote up
over our door since afore the Queen's heads went out
on the shillings.[1] But Cliff, he was ashamed o' being called a tailor, and he was sore vexed as his riding
was laughed at, and nobody o' the gentlefolks here-
about could abide him. Howsomever, the poor lad
got sickly and died, and the father didn't live long
after him, for he got queerer nor ever, and they said
he used to go out i' the dead o' the night, wi' a lantern in his hand, to the stables, and set a lot o' lights
burning, for he got as he couldn't sleep; and there
he'd stand, cracking his whip and looking at his
hosses; and they said it was a mercy as the stables
didn't get burned down wi' the poor dumb creaturs
in 'em. But at last he died raving, and they found
as he'd left all his property, Warrens and all, to a
Lunnon Charity, and that's how the Warrens come to
be Charity Land; though, as for the stables, Mr. Lammeter never uses 'em—they're out o' all charicter—
lor bless you! if you was to set the doors a-banging
in 'em, it 'ud sound like thunder half o'er the parish.''

''Ay, but there's more going on in the stables than
what folks see by daylight, eh, Mr. Macey?'' said the
landlord.

''Ay, ay; go that way of a dark night, that's all,''
said Mr. Macey, winking mysteriously, ''and then
make believe, if you like, as you didn't see lights i'

the stables, nor hear the stamping o' the hosses, nor
the cracking o' the whips, and howling, too, if it's
tow'rt daybreak. 'Cliff's Holiday' has been the
name of it ever sin' I were a boy; that's to say, some
said as it was the holiday Old Harry gev him from
roasting, like. That's what my father told me, and
he was a reasonable man, though there's folks nowadays know what happened afore they were born better nor they know their own business.''

''What do you say to that, eh, Dowlas?'' said the
landlord, turning to the farrier, who was swelling
with impatience for his cue. ''There's a nut for *you*
to crack.''

Mr. Dowlas was the negative spirit in the company,
and was proud of his position.

''Say? I say what a man *should* say as doesn't
shut his eyes to look at a finger-post. I say, as I'm
ready to wager any man ten pound, if he'll stand out
wi' me any dry night in the pasture before the War-
ren stables, as we shall neither see lights nor hear
noises, if it isn't the blowing of our own noses. That's
what I say, and I've said it many a time; but there's
nobody 'ull ventur a ten-pun' note on their ghos'es
as they make so sure of.''

''Why, Dowlas, that's easy betting, that is,'' said
Ben Winthrop. ''You might as well bet a man as
he wouldn't catch the rheumatize if he stood up to 's
neck in the pool of a frosty night. It 'ud be fine fun
for a man to win his bet, as he'd catch the rheumatize. Folks as believe in Cliff's Holiday aren't

a-going to ventur near it for a matter o' ten pound.''

"If Master Dowlas wants to know the truth on it,'' said Mr. Macey, with a sarcastic smile, tapping his thumbs together, "he's no call to lay any bet—let him go and stan' by himself—there's nobody 'ull hinder him; and then he can let the parish'ners know if they're wrong.''

"Thank you! I'm obliged to you,'' said the farrier, with a snort of scorn. "If folks are fools, it's no business o' mine. *I* don't want to make out the truth about ghos'es: I know it a'ready. But I'm not against a bet—everything fair and open. Let any man bet me ten pound as I shall see Cliff's Holiday, and I'll go and stand by myself. I want no company. I'd as lief do it as I'd fill this pipe.''

"Ah, but who's to watch you, Dowlas, and see you do it? That's no fair bet,'' said the butcher.

"No fair bet?'' replied Mr. Dowlas, angrily. "I should like to hear any man stand up and say I want to bet unfair. Come now, Master Lundy, I should like to hear you say it.''

"Very like you would,'' said the butcher. "But it's no business o' mine. You're none o' my bargains, and I aren't a-going to try and 'bate your price. If anybody 'll bid for you at your own vallying, let him. I'm for peace and quietness, I am.''

"Yes, that's what every yapping cur is, when you hold a stick up at him,'' said the farrier. "But I'm afraid o' neither man nor ghost, and I'm ready to lay a fair bet. *I* aren't a turn-tail cur.''

"Ay, but there's this in it, Dowlas," said the landlord, speaking in a tone of much candor and tolerance. "There's folks, i' my opinion, they can't see ghos'es, not if they stood as plain as a pike-staff before 'em. And there's reason i' that. For there's my wife, now, can't smell, not if she'd the strongest o' cheese under her nose. I never see'd a ghost myself; but then I says to myself, 'Very like I haven't got the smell for 'em.' I mean, putting a ghost for a smell, or else contrairiways. And so, I'm for holding with both sides; for, as I say, the truth lies between 'em. And if Dowlas was to go and stand, and say he'd never seen a wink o' Cliff's Holiday all the night through, I'd back him; and if anybody said as Cliff's Holiday was certain sure for all that, I'd back *him* too. For the smell's what I go by."

The landlord's analogical argument was not well received by the farrier—a man intensely opposed to compromise.

"Tut, tut," he said, setting down his glass with refreshed irritation; "what's the smell got to do with it? Did ever a ghost give a man a black eye? That's what I should like to know. If ghos'es want me to believe in 'em, let 'em leave off skulking i' the dark and i' lone places—let 'em come where there's company and candles."

"As if ghos'es 'ud want to be believed in by anybody so ignirant!" said Mr. Macey, in deep disgust at the farrier's crass incompetence to apprehend the conditions of ghostly phenomena.

CHAPTER VII

YET the next moment there seemed to be some evidence that ghosts had a more condescending disposition than Mr. Macey attributed to them; for the pale thin figure of Silas Marner was suddenly seen standing in the warm light, uttering no word, but looking round at the company with his strange unearthly eyes. The long pipes gave a simultaneous movement, like the antennæ of startled insects, and every man present, not excepting even the skeptical farrier, had an impression that he saw, not Silas Marner in the flesh, but an apparition; for the door by which Silas had entered was hidden by the high-screened seats, and no one had noticed his approach. Mr. Macey, sitting a long way off the ghost, might be supposed to have felt an argumentative triumph, which would tend to neutralize his share of the general alarm. Had he not always said that when Silas Marner was in that strange trance of his, his soul went loose from his body? Here was the demonstration: nevertheless, on the whole, he would have been as well contented without it. For a few moments there was a dead silence, Marner's want of breath and agitation not allowing him to speak. The landlord, under the habitual sense that he was bound to keep his house

111

open to all company, and confident in the protection of his unbroken neutrality, at last took on himself the task of adjuring the ghost.

"Master Marner," he said, in a conciliatory tone, "what's lacking to you? What's your business here?"

"Robbed!" said Silas, gaspingly. "I've been robbed! I want the constable—and the Justice—and Squire Cass—and Mr. Crackenthorp."

"Lay hold on him, Jem Rodney," said the landlord, the idea of a ghost subsiding; "he's off his head, I doubt. He's wet through."

Jem Rodney was the outermost man, and sat conveniently near Marner's standing-place; but he declined to give his services.

"Come and lay hold on him yourself, Mr. Snell, if you've a mind," said Jem, rather sullenly. "He's been robbed, and murdered too, for what I know," he added, in a muttering tone.

"Jem Rodney!" said Silas, turning and fixing his strange eyes on the suspected man.

"Ay, Master Marner, what do ye want wi' me?" said Jem, trembling a little, and seizing the drinking-can as a defensive weapon.

"If it was you stole my money," said Silas, clasping his hands entreatingly, and raising his voice to a cry, "give it me back,—and I won't meddle with you. I won't set the constable on you. Give it me back, and I'll let you—I'll let you have a guinea."

"Me stole your money!" said Jem, angrily. "I'll

pitch this can at your eye if you talk o' *my* stealing your money.''

"Come, come, Master Marner,'' said the landlord, now rising resolutely, and seizing Marner by the shoulder, "if you've got any information to lay, speak it out sensible, and show as you're in your right mind, if you expect anybody to listen to you. You're as wet as a drownded rat. Sit down and dry yourself, and speak straight forrard.''

"Ah, to be sure, man,'' said the farrier, who began to feel that he had not been quite on a par with himself and the occasion. "Let's have no more staring and screaming, else we'll have you strapped for a madman.[1] That was why I didn't speak at the first—thinks I, the man's run mad.''

"Ay, ay, make him sit down,'' said several voices at once, well pleased that the reality of ghosts remained still an open question.

The landlord forced Marner to take off his coat, and then to sit down on a chair aloof from every one else, in the center of the circle and in the direct rays of the fire. The weaver, too feeble to have any distinct purpose beyond that of getting help to recover his money, submitted unresistingly. The transient fears of the company were now forgotten in their strong curiosity, and all faces were turned towards Silas, when the landlord, having seated himself again, said—

"Now then, Master Marner, what's this you've got to say—as you've been robbed? Speak out.''

"He'd better not say again as it was me robbed him," cried Jem Rodney, hastily. "What could I ha' done with his money? I could as easily steal the parson's surplice, and wear it."

"Hold your tongue, Jem, and let's hear what he's got to say," said the landlord. "Now then, Master Marner."

Silas now told his story, under frequent questioning as the mysterious character of the robbery became evident.

This strangely novel situation of opening his trouble to his Raveloe neighbors, of sitting in the warmth of a hearth not his own, and feeling the presence of faces and voices which were his nearest promise of help, had doubtless its influence on Marner, in spite of his passionate preoccupation with his loss. Our consciousness rarely registers the beginning of a growth within us any more than without us: there have been many circulations of the sap before we detect the smallest sign of the bud.

The slight suspicion with which his hearers at first listened to him, gradually melted away before the convincing simplicity of his distress: it was impossible for the neighbors to doubt that Marner was telling the truth, not because they were capable of arguing at once from the nature of his statements to the absence of any motive for making them falsely, but because, as Mr. Macey observed, "Folks as had the devil to back 'em were not likely to be so mushed" as poor Silas was. Rather, from the strange fact that

the robber had left no traces, and had happened to
know the nick of time, utterly incalculable by mortal
agents, when Silas would go away from home without locking his door, the more probable conclusion
seemed to be, that his disreputable intimacy in that
quarter, if it ever existed, had been broken up, and
that, in consequence, this ill turn had been done to
Marner by somebody it was quite in vain to set the
constable after. Why this preternatural felon should
be obliged to wait till the door was left unlocked, was
a question which did not present itself.

"It isn't Jem Rodney as has done this work, Master Marner," said the landlord. "You mustn't be
a-casting your eye at poor Jem. There may be a bit
of a reckoning against Jem for the matter of a hare or
so, if anybody was bound to keep their eyes staring
open and niver to wink; but Jem's been a-sitting
here drinking his can, like the decentest man i' the
parish, since before you left your house, Master Marner, by your own account."

"Ay, ay," said Mr. Macey: "let's have no accus-
ing o' the innicent. That isn't the law. There must
be folks to swear again' a man before he can be ta'en
up. Let's have no accusin' o' the innicent, Master
Marner."

Memory was not so utterly torpid in Silas that it
could not be awakened by these words. With a movement of compunction as new and strange to him as
everything else within the last hour, he started from
his chair and went close up to Jem, looking at him as

if he wanted to assure himself of the expression in his face.

"I was wrong," he said—"yes, yes—I ought to have thought. There's nothing to witness against you, Jem. Only you'd been into my house oftener than anybody else, and so you came into my head. I don't accuse you—I won't accuse anybody—only," he added, lifting up his hands to his head, and turning away with bewildered misery, "I try—I try to think where my guineas can be."

"Ay, ay, they're gone where it's hot enough to melt 'em, I doubt," said Mr. Macey.

"Tchuh!" said the farrier. And then he asked, with a cross-examining air, "How much money might there be in the bags, Master Marner?"

"Two hundred and seventy-two pounds, twelve and sixpence, last night when I counted it," said Silas, seating himself again, with a groan.

"Pooh! why, they'd be none so heavy to carry. Some tramp's been in, that's all; and as for the no footmarks, and the bricks and the sand being all right—why, your eyes are pretty much like a insect's, Master Marner; they're obliged to look so close, you can't see much at a time. It's my opinion as, if I'd been you, or you'd been me—for it comes to the same thing—you wouldn't have thought you'd found everything as you left it. But what I vote is, as two of the sensiblest o' the company should go with you to Master Kench, the constable's—he's ill i' bed, I know that much—and get him to appoint one of us his deppity; for that's the law, and I don't think anybody 'ull take upon him to contradick me there. It isn't much of a walk to Kench's; and then, if it's me as is deppity, I'll go back with you, Master Marner, and examine your premises; and if anybody's got any fault to find with that, I'll thank him to stand up and say it out like a man."

By this pregnant speech the farrier had re-established his self-complacency, and waited with confidence to hear himself named as one of the superlatively sensible men.

"Let us see how the night is, though," said the landlord, who also considered himself personally concerned in this proposition. "Why, it rains heavy still," he said, returning from the door.

"Well, I'm not the man to be afraid o' the rain," said the farrier. "For it'll look bad when Justice Malam hears as respectable men like us had a information laid before 'em and took no steps."

The landlord agreed with this view, and after taking the sense of the company, and duly rehearsing a small ceremony known in high ecclesiastical life as the *nolo episcopari*,[1] he consented to take on himself the chill dignity of going to Kench's. But to the farrier's strong disgust, Mr. Macey now started an objection to his proposing himself as a deputy-constable; for that oracular old gentleman, claiming to know the law, stated, as a fact delivered to him by his father, that no doctor could be a constable.

"And you're a doctor, I reckon, though you're

only a cow-doctor—for a fly's a fly, though it may be a hoss-fly,'' concluded Mr. Macey, wondering a little at his own '' 'cuteness.''

There was a hot debate upon this, the farrier being of course indisposed to renounce the quality of doctor, but contending that a doctor could be a constable if he liked—the law meant, he needn't be one if he didn't like. Mr. Macey thought this was nonsense, since the law was not likely to be fonder of doctors than of other folks. Moreover, if it was in the nature of doctors more than of other men not to like being constables, how came Mr. Dowlas to be so eager to act in that capacity?

''I don't want to act the constable,'' said the farrier, driven into a corner by this merciless reasoning; ''and there's no man can say it of me, if he'd tell the truth. But if there's to be any jealousy and en*vy*ing about going to Kench's in the rain, let them go as like it—you won't get me to go, I can tell you.''

By the landlord's intervention, however, the dispute was accomodated. Mr. Dowlas consented to go as a second person disinclined to act officially; and so poor Silas, furnished with some old coverings, turned out with his two companions into the rain again, thinking of the long night-hours before him, not as those do who long to rest, but as those who expect to ''watch for the morning.''

CHAPTER VIII

WHEN Godfrey Cass returned from Mrs. Osgood's party at midnight, he was not much surprised to learn that Dunsey had not come home. Perhaps he had not sold Wildfire, and was waiting for another chance —perhaps, on that foggy afternoon, he had preferred housing himself at the Red Lion at Batherley for the night, if the run had kept him in that neighborhood; for he was not likely to feel much concern about leaving his brother in suspense. Godfrey's mind was too full of Nancy Lammeter's looks and behavior, too full of the exasperation against himself and his lot, which the sight of her always produced in him, for him to give much thought to Wildfire, or to the probabilities of Dunstan's conduct.

The next morning the whole village was excited by the story of the robbery, and Godfrey, like every one else, was occupied in gathering and discussing news about it, and in visiting the Stone-pits. The rain had washed away all possibility of distinguishing foot-marks, but a close investigation of the spot had disclosed, in the direction opposite to the village, a tinder-box, with a flint and steel, half sunk in the mud. It was not Silas's tinder-box, for the only one

119

he had ever had was still standing on his shelf; and
the inference generally accepted was, that the tinder-
box in the ditch was somehow connected with the robbery. A small minority shook their heads, and in-
timated their opinion that it was not a robbery to
have much light thrown on it by tinder-boxes, that
Master Marner's tale had a queer look with it, and
that such things had been known as a man's doing
himself a mischief, and then setting the justice to
look for the doer. But when questioned closely as
to their grounds for this opinion, and what Master
Marner had to gain by such false pretenses, they only
shook their heads as before, and observed that there
was no knowing what some folks counted gain; moreover, that everybody had a right to their own opinions, grounds or no grounds, and that the weaver, as
everybody knew, was partly crazy. Mr. Macey,
though he joined in the defense of Marner against all
suspicions of deceit, also pooh-poohed the tinder-box;
indeed, repudiated it as a rather impious suggestion,
tending to imply that everything must be done by
human hands, and that there was no power which
could make away with the guineas without moving the
bricks. Nevertheless, he turned round rather sharply
on Mr. Tookey, when the zealous deputy, feeling that
this was a view of the case peculiarly suited to a
parish-clerk, carried it still further, and doubted
whether it was right to inquire into a robbery at all
when the circumstances were so mysterious.

"As if," concluded Mr. Tookey—"as if there was

nothing but what could be made out by justices and constables.''

''Now, don't you be for overshooting the mark, Tookey,'' said Mr. Macey, nodding his head aside admonishingly. ''That's what you're allays at; if I throw a stone and hit, you think there's summat better than hitting, and you try to throw a stone beyond. What I said was against the tinder-box: I said nothing against justices and constables, for they're o' King George's making, and it 'ud be ill-becoming a man in a parish office to fly out again' King George.''

While these discussions were going on among the group outside the Rainbow, a higher consultation was being carried on within, under the presidency of Mr. Crackenthorp, the Rector, assisted by Squire Cass and other substantial parishioners. It had just occurred to Mr. Snell, the landlord—he being, as he observed, a man accustomed to put two and two together—to connect with the tinder-box, which as deputy-constable, he himself had had the honorable distinction of finding, certain recollections of a peddler who had called to drink at the house about a month before, and had actually stated that he carried a tinder-box about with him to light his pipe. Here, surely, was a clew to be followed out. And as memory, when duly impregnated with ascertained facts, is sometimes surprisingly fertile, Mr. Snell gradually recovered a vivid impression of the effect produced on him by the peddler's countenance and conversation. He had a ''look with his eye'' which fell unpleasantly on Mr. Snell's sensitive organism. To be sure, he didn't say anything particular—no, except that about the tinder-box—but it isn't what a man says, it's the way he says it. Moreover, he had a swarthy foreignness of complexion which boded little honesty.

"Did he wear ear-rings?" Mr. Crackenthorp wished to know, having some acquaintance with foreign customs.

"Well—stay—let me see," said Mr. Snell, like a docile clairvoyant, who would really not make a mistake if she could help it. After stretching the corners of his mouth and contracting his eyes, as if he were trying to see the ear-rings, he appeared to give up the effort, and said, "Well, he'd got ear-rings in his box to sell, so it's nat'ral to suppose he might wear 'em. But he called at every house, a'most, in the village; there's somebody else, mayhap, saw 'em in his ears, though I can't take upon me rightly to say."

Mr. Snell was correct in his surmise, that somebody else would remember the peddler's ear-rings. For on the spread of inquiry among the villagers it was stated with gathering emphasis, that the parson had wanted to know whether the peddler wore ear-rings in his ears, and an impression was created that a great deal depended on the eliciting of this fact. Of course, every one who heard the question, not having any distinct image of the peddler as *without* ear-rings, immediately had an image of him *with* ear-rings, larger or smaller, as the case might be;

and the image was presently taken for a vivid recollection, so that the glazier's wife, a well-intentioned
woman, not given to lying, and whose house was
among the cleanest in the village, was ready to declare, as sure as ever she meant to take the sacrament
the very next Christmas that was ever coming, that
she had seen big ear-rings, in the shape of the young
moon, in the peddler's two ears; while Jinny Oates,
the cobbler's daughter, being a more imaginative person, stated not only that she had seen them too, but
that they had made her blood creep, as it did at that
very moment while there she stood.

Also, by way of throwing further light on this
clew of the tinder-box, a collection was made of all
the articles purchased from the peddler at various
houses, and carried to the Rainbow to be exhibited
there. In fact, there was a general feeling in the
village, that for the clearing-up of this robbery there
must be a great deal done at the Rainbow, and that
no man need offer his wife an excuse for going there
while it was the scene of severe public duties.

Some disappointment was felt, and perhaps a little
indignation also, when it became known that Silas
Marner, on being questioned by the Squire and the
parson, had retained no other recollection of the peddler than that he had called at his door, but had not
entered his house, having turned away at once when
Silas, holding the door ajar, had said that he wanted
nothing. This had been Silas's testimony, though
he clutched strongly at the idea of the peddler's being

the culprit, if only because it gave him a definite
image of a whereabout for his gold after it had been
taken away from its hiding-place: he could see it
now in the peddler's box. But it was observed with
some irritation in the village, that anybody but a
"blind creatur" like Marner would have seen the
man prowling about, for how came he to leave his
tinder-box in the ditch close by, if he hadn't been
lingering there? Doubtless, he had made his ob-
servations when he saw Marner at the door. Anybody might know—and only look at him—that the
weaver was a half-crazy miser. It was a wonder the
peddler hadn't murdered him: men of that sort with
rings in their ears, had been known for murderers
often and often; there had been one tried at the
'sizes, not so long ago but what there were people
living who remembered it.

Godfrey Cass, indeed, entering the Rainbow during
one of Mr. Snell's frequently repeated recitals of his
testimony, had treated it lightly, stating that he himself had bought a pen-knife of the peddler, and thought
him a merry grinning fellow enough; it was all nonsense, he said, about the man's evil looks. But this
was spoken of in the village as the random talk of
youth, "as if it was only Mr. Snell who had seen
something odd about the peddler!" On the contrary,
there were at least half-a-dozen who were ready to
go before Justice Malam, and give in much more
striking testimony than any the landlord could fur-
nish. It was to be hoped Mr. Godfrey would not go

to Tarley and throw cold water on what Mr. Snell
said there, and so prevent the justice from drawing
up a warrant. He was suspected of intending this,
when, after mid-day, he was seen setting off on horseback in the direction of Tarley.

But by this time Godfrey's interest in the robbery
had faded before his growing anxiety about Dunstan
and Wildfire, and he was going, not to Tarley, but
to Batherly, unable to rest in uncertainty about them
any longer. The possibility that Dunstan had played
him the ugly trick of riding away with Wildfire, to
return at the end of a month, when he had gambled
away or otherwise squandered the price of the horse,
was a fear that urged itself upon him more, even than
the thought of an accidental injury; and now that
the dance at Mrs. Osgood's was past, he was irritated
with himself that he had trusted his horse to Dunstan. Instead of trying to still his fears he encouraged them, with that superstitious impression
which clings to us all, that if we expect evil very
strongly it is the less likely to come; and when he
heard a horse approaching at a trot, and saw a hat
rising above a hedge beyond an angle of the lane,
he felt as if his conjuration had succeeded. But no
sooner did the horse come within sight, than his heart
sank again. It was not Wildfire; and in a few moments more he discerned that the rider was not Dunstan, but Bryce, who pulled up to speak, with a face
that implied something disagreeable.

"Well, Mr. Godfrey, that's a lucky brother of yours, that Master Dunsey, isn't he?"

"What do you mean?" said Godfrey, hastily.

"Why, hasn't he been home yet?" said Bryce.

"Home? no. What has happened? Be quick. What has he done with my horse?"

"Ah, I thought it was yours, though he pretended you had parted with it to him."

"Has he thrown him down and broken his knees?" said Godfrey, flushed with exasperation.

"Worse than that," said Bryce. "You see, I'd made a bargain with him to buy the horse for a hundred and twenty—a swinging price, but I always liked the horse. And what does he do but go and stake him—fly at a hedge with stakes in it, atop of a bank with a ditch before it. The horse had been dead a pretty good while when he was found. So he hasn't been home since, has he?"

"Home? no," said Godfrey, "and he'd better keep away. Confound me for a fool! I might have known this would be the end of it."

"Well, to tell you the truth," said Bryce, "after I'd bargained for the horse, it did come into my head that he might be riding and selling the horse without your knowledge, for I didn't believe it was his own. I knew Master Dunsey was up to his tricks sometimes. But where can he be gone? He's never been seen at Batherly. He couldn't have been hurt, for he must have walked off."

"Hurt?" said Godfrey, bitterly. "He'll never be hurt—he's made to hurt other people."

"And so you *did* give him leave to sell the horse, eh?" said Bryce.

"Yes; I wanted to part with the horse—he was always a little too hard in the mouth for me," said Godfrey; his pride making him wince under the idea that Bryce guessed the sale to be a matter of necessity. "I was going to see after him—I thought some mischief had happened. I'll go back now," he added, turning the horse's head, and wishing he could get rid of Bryce; for he felt that the long-dreaded crisis in his life was close upon him. "You're coming on to Raveloe, aren't you?"

"Well, no, not now," said Bryce. "I *was* coming round there, for I had to go to Flitton, and I thought I might as well take you in my way, and just let you know all I knew myself about the horse. I suppose Master Dunsey didn't like to show himself till the ill news had blown over a bit. He's perhaps gone to pay a visit at the Three Crowns, by Whitbridge— I know he's fond of the house."

"Perhaps he is," said Godfrey, rather absently. Then rousing himself, he said, with an effort at carelessness, "We shall hear of him soon enough, I'll be bound."

"Well, here's my turning," said Bryce, not surprised to perceive that Godfrey was rather "down"; "so I'll bid you good-day, and wish I may bring you better news another time."

Godfrey rode along slowly, representing to himself the scene of confession to his father from which he felt that there was now no longer any escape. The revelation about the money must be made the very next morning; and if he withheld the rest, Dunstan would be sure to come back shortly, and, finding that he must bear the brunt of his father's anger, would tell the whole story out of spite, even though he had nothing to gain by it. There was one step, perhaps, by which he might still win Dunstan's silence and put off the evil day: he might tell his father that he had himself spent the money paid to him by Fowler; and as he had never been guilty of such an offense before, the affair would blow over after a little storming. But Godfrey could not bend himself to this. He felt that in letting Dunstan have the money, he had already been guilty of a breach of trust hardly less culpable than that of spending the money directly for his own behoof; and yet there was a distinction between the two acts which made him feel that the one was so much more blackening than the other as to be intolerable to him.

"I don't pretend to be a good fellow," he said to himself; "but I'm not a scoundrel—at least, I'll stop short somewhere. I'll bear the consequences of what I *have* done sooner than make believe I've done what I never would have done. I'd never have spent the money for my own pleasure—I was tortured into it."

Through the remainder of this day Godfrey, with only occasional fluctuations, kept his will bent in the

direction of a complete avowal to his father, and he
withheld the story of Wildfire's loss till the next
morning, that it might serve him as an introduction
to heavier matter. The old Squire was accustomed
to his son's frequent absence from home, and thought
neither Dunstan's nor Wildfire's non-appearance a
matter calling for remark. Godfrey said to himself
again and again, that if he let slip this one opportunity of confession, he might never have another;
the revelation might be made even in a more odious
way than by Dunstan's malignity: *she* might come [1]
as she had threatened to do. And then he tried to
make the scene easier to himself by rehearsal: he
made up his mind how he would pass from the ad-
mission of his weakness in letting Dunstan have the
money to the fact that Dunstan had a hold on him
which he had been unable to shake off, and how he
would work up his father to expect something very
bad before he told him the fact. The old Squire was
an implacable man: he made resolutions in violent
anger, and he was not to be moved from them after his
anger had subsided—as fiery volcanic matters cool
and harden into rock. Like many violent and implacable men, he allowed evils to grow under favor
of his own heedlessness, till they pressed upon him
with exasperating force, and then he turned round
with fierce severity and became unrelentingly hard.
This was his system with his tenants: he allowed them
to get into arrears, neglect their fences, reduce their
stock, sell their straw, and otherwise go the wrong

way,—and then, when he became short of money in
consequence of this indulgence, he took the hardest
measures and would listen to no appeal. Godfrey
knew all this and felt it with the greater force because he had constantly suffered annoyance from wit-
nessing his father's sudden fits of unrelentingness,
for which his own habitual irresolution deprived him
of all sympathy. (He was not critical on the faulty
indulgence which preceded these fits; *that* seemed to
him natural enough.) Still there was just the
chance, Godfrey thought, that his father's pride
might see this marriage in a light that would induce
him to hush it up, rather than turn his son out and
make the family the talk of the country for ten miles
round.

This was the view of the case that Godfrey man-
aged to keep before him pretty closely till midnight,
and he went to sleep thinking that he had done with
inward debating. But when he awoke in the still morning darkness he found it impossible to reawaken his
evening thoughts; it was as if they had been tired out
and were not to be roused to further work. Instead
of arguments for confession, he could now feel the
presence of nothing but its evil consequences: the old
dread of disgrace came back—the old shrinking from
the thought of raising a hopeless barrier between himself and Nancy—the old disposition to rely on chances
which might be favorable to him, and save him from
betrayal. Why, after all, should he cut off the hope
of them by his own act? He had seen the matter in

a wrong light yesterday. He had been in a rage with Dunstan, and had thought of nothing but a thorough break-up of their mutual understanding; but what it would be really wisest for him to do, was to try and soften his father's anger against Dunsey, and keep things as nearly as possible in their old condition. If Dunsey did not come back for a few days (and Godfrey did not know but that the rascal had enough money in his pocket to enable him to keep away still longer), everything might blow over.

CHAPTER IX

GODFREY rose and took his own breakfast earlier
than usual, but lingered in the wainscoted parlor till
his younger brothers had finished their meal and
gone out; awaiting his father, who always took a
walk with his managing-man before breakfast. Every
one breakfasted at a different hour in the Red House,
and the Squire was always the latest, giving a long
chance to a rather feeble morning appetite before he
tried it. The table had been spread with substantial
eatables nearly two hours before he presented himself
—a tall, stout man of sixty, with a face in which the
knit brow and rather hard glance seemed contra-
dicted by the slack and feeble mouth. His person
showed marks of habitual neglect, his dress was
slovenly; and yet there was something in the presence of the old Squire distinguishable from that of
the ordinary farmers in the parish, who were perhaps every whit as refined as he, but, having slouched
their way through life with a consciousness of being
in the vicinity of their "betters," wanted that self-
possession and authoritativeness of voice and carriage
which belonged to a man who thought of superiors
as remote existences with whom he had personally
little more to do than with America or the stars.

The Squire had been used to parish homage all his life, used to the presupposition that his family, his tankards, and everything that was his, were the oldest and best; and as he never associated with any gentry higher than himself, his opinion was not disturbed by comparison.

He glanced at his son as he entered the room, and said, "What, sir! haven't *you* had your breakfast yet?" but there was no pleasant morning greeting between them; not because of any unfriendliness, but because the sweet flower of courtesy is not a growth of such homes as the Red House.

"Yes, sir," said Godfrey, "I've had my breakfast, but I was waiting to speak to you."

"Ah! well," said the Squire, throwing himself indifferently into his chair, and speaking in a ponderous coughing fashion, which was felt in Raveloe to be a sort of privilege of his rank, while he cut a piece of beef, and held it up before the deer-hound that had come in with him. "Ring the bell for my ale, will you? You youngsters' business is your own pleasure, mostly. There's no hurry about it for anybody but yourselves."

The Squire's life was quite as idle as his sons', but it was a fiction kept up by himself and his contemporaries in Raveloe that youth was exclusively the period of folly, and that their aged wisdom was constantly in a state of endurance mitigated by sarcasm. Godfrey waited, before he spoke again, until the ale had been brought and the door closed—an interval during which Fleet, the deer-hound, had consumed enough bits of beef to make a poor man's holiday dinner.

"There's been a cursed piece of ill-luck with Wildfire," he began; "happened the day before yesterday."

"What! broke his knees?" said the Squire, after taking a draught of ale. "I thought you knew how to ride better than that, sir. I never threw a horse down in my life. If I had, I might ha' whistled for another, for *my* father wasn't quite so ready to unstring as some other fathers I know of. But they must turn over a new leaf—*they* must. What with mortgages and arrears, I'm as short o' cash as a roadside pauper. And that fool Kimble says the newspaper's talking about peace. Why, the country wouldn't have a leg to stand on. Prices 'ud run down like a jack,[1] and I should never get my arrears, not if I sold all the fellows up. And there's that damned Fowler, I won't put up with him any longer; I've told Winthrop to go to Cox this very day. The lying scoundrel told me he'd be sure to pay me a hundred last month. He takes advantage because he's on that outlying farm, and thinks I shall forget him."

The Squire had delivered this speech in a coughing and interrupted manner, but with no pause long enough for Godfrey to make it a pretext for taking up the word again. He felt that his father meant to ward off any request for money on the ground of the misfortune with Wildfire, and that the emphasis he had thus been led to lay on the shortness of cash and his arrears was likely to produce an attitude of mind the utmost unfavorable for his own disclosure. But he must go on, now he had begun.

"It's worse than breaking the horse's knees—he's been staked and killed," he said, as soon as his father was silent, and had begun to cut his meat. "But I wasn't thinking of asking you to buy me another horse; I was only thinking I'd lost the means of paying you with the price of Wildfire, as I'd meant to do. Dunsey took him to the hunt to sell him for me the other day, and after he'd made a bargain for a hundred and twenty with Bryce, he went after the hounds, and took some fool's leap or other that did for the horse at once. If it hadn't been for that, I should have paid you a hundred pounds this morning."

The Squire had laid down his knife and fork, and was staring at his son in amazement, not being sufficiently quick of brain to form a probable guess as to what could have caused so strange an inversion of the paternal and filial relations as this proposition of his son, to pay him a hundred pounds.

"The truth is, sir—I'm very sorry—I was quite to blame," said Godfrey. "Fowler did pay that hundred pounds. He paid it to me, when I was over there one day last month. And Dunsey bothered me for the money, and I let him have it, because I hoped I should be able to pay it you before this."

The Squire was purple with anger before his son had done speaking, and found utterance difficult. "You let Dunsey have it, sir? And how long have you been so thick with Dunsey that you must *collogue* with him to embezzle my money? Are you turning out a scamp? I tell you I won't have it. I'll turn the whole pack of you out of the house together, and marry again. I'd have you to remember, sir, my property's got no entail[1] on it;—since my grandfather's time the Casses can do as they like with their land. Remember that, sir. Let Dunsey have the money! Why should you let Dunsey have the money? There's some lie at the bottom of it."

"There's no lie, sir," said Godfrey. "I wouldn't have spent the money myself, but Dunsey bothered me, and I was a fool, and let him have it. But I meant to pay it, whether he did or not. That's the whole story. I never meant to embezzle money, and I'm not the man to do it. You never knew me to do a dishonest trick, sir."

"Where's Dunsey, then? What do you stand talking there for? Go and fetch Dunsey, as I tell you, and let him give account of what he wanted the money for, and what he's done with it. He shall repent it. I'll turn him out. I said I would, and I'll do it. He shan't brave me. Go and fetch him."

"Dunsey isn't come back, sir."

"What! did he break his own neck, then?" said the Squire, with some disgust at the idea that, in that case, he could not fulfill his threat.

"No, he wasn't hurt, I believe, for the horse was found dead, and Dunsey must have walked off. I dare say we shall see him again by-and-by. I don't know where he is."

"And what must you be letting him have my money for? Answer me that," said the Squire, attacking Godfrey again, since Dunsey was not within reach.

"Well, sir, I don't know," said Godfrey, hesitatingly. That was a feeble evasion, but Godfrey was not fond of lying, and, not being sufficiently aware that no sort of duplicity can long flourish without the help of vocal falsehoods, he was quite unprepared with invented motives.

"You don't know? I tell you what it is, sir. You've been up to some trick, and you've been bribing him not to tell," said the Squire, with a sudden acuteness which startled Godfrey who felt his heart beat violently at the nearness of his father's guess. The sudden alarm pushed him on to take the next step—a very slight impulse suffices for that on a downward road.

"Why, sir," he said, trying to speak with careless ease, "it was a little affair between me and Dunsey; it's no matter to anybody else. It's hardly worth while to pry into young men's fooleries: it wouldn't have made any difference to you, sir, if I'd not had the bad luck to lose Wildfire. I should have paid you the money."

"Fooleries! Pshaw! it's time you'd done with

fooleries. And I'd have you know, sir, you *must*
ha' done with 'em," said the Squire, frowning and
casting an angry glance at his son. "Your goings-
on are not what I shall find money for any longer.
There's my grandfather had his stables full o' horses,
and kept a good house, too, and in worse times, by
what I can make out; and so might I, if I hadn't
four good-for-nothing fellows to hang on me like
horse-leeches. I've been too good a father to you all
—that's what it is. But I shall pull up, sir."

Godfrey was silent. He was not likely to be very
penetrating in his judgments, but he had always
had a sense that his father's indulgence had not
been kindness, and had had a vague longing for some
discipline that would have checked his own errant [1]
weakness and helped his better will. The Squire
ate his bread and meat hastily, took a deep draught
of ale, then turned his chair from the table, and began to speak again.

"It'll be all the worse for you, you know—you'd
need try and help me keep things together."

"Well, sir, I've often offered to take the management of things, but you know you've taken it ill
always, and seemed to think I wanted to push you
out of your place."

"I know nothing o' your offering or o' my taking
it ill," said the Squire, whose memory consisted in
certain strong impressions unmodified by detail; "but
I know one while you seemed to be thinking o' marrying, and I didn't offer to put any obstacles in your

way, as some fathers would. I'd as lieve you married Lammeter's daughter as anybody. I suppose, if I'd said you nay, you'd ha' kept on with it; but, for want o' contradiction, you've changed your mind. You're a shilly-shally fellow: you take after your poor mother. She never had a will of her own; a woman has no call for one, if she's got a proper man for her husband. But *your* wife had need have one, for you hardly know your own mind enough to make both your legs walk one way. The lass hasn't said downright she won't have you, has she?"

"No," said Godfrey, feeling very hot and uncomfortable; "but I don't think she will."

"Think! why haven't you the courage to ask her? Do you stick to it, you want to have *her*—that's the thing?"

"There's no other woman I want to marry," said Godfrey, evasively.

"Well, then, let me make the offer for you, that's all, if you haven't the pluck to do it yourself. Lammeter isn't likely to be loath for his daughter to marry into *my* family, I should think. And as for the pretty lass, she wouldn't have her cousin—and there's nobody else, as I see, could ha' stood in your way."

"I'd rather let it be, please sir, at present," said Godfrey in alarm. "I think she's a little offended with me just now, and I should like to speak for myself. A man must manage these things for himself."

"Well, speak, then, and manage it, and see if you can't turn over a new leaf. That's what a man must do when he thinks o' marrying."

"I don't see how I can think of it at present, sir. You wouldn't like to settle me on one of the farms, I suppose, and I don't think she'd come to live in this house with all my brothers. It's a different sort of life to what she's been used to."

"Not come to live in this house? Don't tell me. You ask her, that's all," said the Squire, with a short, scornful laugh.

"I'd rather let the thing be, at present, sir," said Godfrey. "I hope you won't try to hurry it on by saying anything."

"I shall do what I choose," said the Squire, "and I shall let you know I'm master; else you may turn out, and find an estate to drop into somewhere else. Go out and tell Winthrop not to go to Cox's, but wait for me. And tell 'em to get my horse saddled. And stop: look out and get that hack o' Dunsey's sold, and hand me the money, will you? He'll keep no more hacks at my expense. And if you know where he's sneaking—I dare say you do—you may tell him to spare himself the journey o' coming back home. Let him turn ostler, and keep himself. He shan't hang on me any more."

"I don't know where he is; and if I did, it isn't my place to tell him to keep away," said Godfrey, moving towards the door.

"Confound it, sir, don't stay arguing, but go and

order my horse," said the Squire, taking up a pipe.

Godfrey left the room, hardly knowing whether he were more relieved by the sense that the interview was ended without having made any change in his position, or more uneasy that he had entangled himself still further in prevarication and deceit. What had passed about his proposing to Nancy had raised a new alarm, lest by some after-dinner words of his father's to Mr. Lammeter he should be thrown into the embarrassment of being obliged absolutely to decline her when she seemed to be within his reach. He fled to his usual refuge, that of hoping for some unforeseen turn of fortune, some favorable chance which would save him from unpleasant consequences —perhaps even justify his insincerity by manifesting its prudence.

In this point of trusting to some throw of fortune's dice Godfrey can hardly be called old-fashioned. Favorable Chance is the god of all men who follow their own devices instead of obeying a law they believe in. Let even a polished man of these days get into a position he is ashamed to avow, and his mind will be bent on all the possible issues that may deliver him from the calculable results of that position. Let him live outside his income, or shirk the resolute honest work that brings wages, and he will presently find himself dreaming of a possible benefactor, a possible simpleton who may be cajoled into using his interest, a possible state of mind in some possible person not yet forthcoming. Let him neglect the responsibilities of his office, and he will inevitably anchor himself on the chance, that the thing left undone may turn out not to be of the supposed importance. Let him betray his friend's confidence, and he will adore that same cunning complexity called Chance, which gives him the hope that his friend will never know. Let him forsake a decent craft that he may pursue the gentilities of a profession to which nature never called him, and his religion will infallibly be the worship of blessed Chance, which he will believe in as the mighty creator of success. The evil principle deprecated in that religion is the orderly sequence by which the seed brings forth a crop after its kind.

CHAPTER X

JUSTICE MALAM was naturally regarded in Tarley and Raveloe as a man of capacious mind, seeing that he could draw much wider conclusions without evidence than could be expected of his neighbors who were not on the Commission of the Peace. Such a man was not likely to neglect the clew of the tinderbox, and an inquiry was set on foot concerning a peddler, name unknown, with curly black hair and a foreign complexion, carrying a box of cutlery and jewelry, and wearing large rings in his ears. But either because inquiry was too slow-footed to overtake him, or because the description applied to so many peddlers that inquiry did not know how to choose among them, weeks passed away, and there was no other result concerning the robbery than a gradual cessation of the excitement it had caused in Raveloe. Dunstan Cass's absence was hardly a subject of remark: he had once before had a quarrel with his father, and had gone off, nobody knew whither, to return at the end of six weeks, take up his old quarters unforbidden and swagger as usual. His own family, who equally expected this issue, with the sole difference that the Squire was determined this time to forbid him the old quarters, never mentioned his

absence; and when his uncle Kimble or Mr. Osgood
noticed it, the story of his having killed Wildfire and
committed some offense against his father was enough
to prevent surprise. To connect the fact of Dunsey's disappearance with that of the robbery occur-
ring on the same day, lay quite away from the track
of every one's thought—even Godfrey's, who had
better reason than any one else to know what his
brother was capable of. He remembered no mention
of the weaver between them since the time, twelve
years ago, when it was their boyish sport to deride
him; and, besides, his imagination constantly created
an *alibi* for Dunstan: he saw him continually in some
congenial haunt, to which he had walked off on leaving Wildfire—saw him sponging on chance acquaintances, and meditating a return home to the old
amusement of tormenting his elder brother. Even
if any brain in Raveloe had put the said two facts
together, I doubt whether a combination so injurious
to the prescriptive respectability of a family with a
mural monument and venerable tankards,[1] would not
have been suppressed as of unsound tendency. But
Christmas puddings, brawn, and abundance of spirit-
uous liquors, throwing the mental originality into the
channel of nightmare, are great preservatives against
a dangerous spontaneity of waking thought.

When the robbery was talked of at the Rainbow
and elsewhere, in good company, the balance continued to waver between the rational explanation
founded on the tinder-box, and the theory of an im-

penetrable mystery that mocked investigation. The
advocates of the tinder-box-and-peddler view considered the other side a muddle-headed and cred-
ulous set, who, because they themselves were wall-
eyed, supposed everybody else to have the same blank
outlook; and the adherents of the inexplicable more
than hinted that their antagonists were animals inclined to crow before they had found any corn—
mere skimming-dishes in point of depth—whose clear-
sightedness consisted in supposing there was nothing
behind a barn-door because they couldn't see through
it; so that, though their controversy did not serve to
elicit the fact concerning the robbery, it elicited
some true opinions of collateral importance.

But while poor Silas's loss served thus to brush the
slow current of Raveloe conversation, Silas himself
was feeling the withering desolation of that bereavement about which his neighbors were arguing at their
ease. To any one who had observed him before he
lost his gold, it might have seemed that so withered
and shrunken a life as his could hardly be susceptible of a bruise, could hardly endure any substrac-
tion but such as would put an end to it altogether.
But in reality it had been an eager life, filled with
immediate purpose which fenced him in from the
wide, cheerless unknown. It had been a clinging
life; and though the object round which its fibers
had clung was a dead disrupted thing, it satisfied
the need for clinging. But now the fence was broken
down—the support was snatched away. Marner's

thoughts could no longer move in their old round,
and were baffled by a blank like that which meets a
plodding ant when the earth has broken away on its
homeward path. The loom was there, and the weaving, and the growing pattern in the cloth; but the
bright treasure in the hole under his feet was gone;
the prospect of handling and counting it was gone:
the evening had no phantasm of delight [1] to still the
poor soul's craving. The thought of the money he
would get by his actual work could bring no joy,
for its meager image was only a fresh reminder of
his loss; and hope was too heavily crushed by the
sudden blow, for his imagination to dwell on the
growth of a new hoard from that small beginning.

He filled up the blank with grief. As he sat weaving, he every now and then moaned low, like one in
pain: it was the sign that his thoughts had come
round again to the sudden chasm—to the empty
evening time. And all the evening, as he sat in his
loneliness by his dull fire, he leaned his elbows on
his knees, and clasped his head with his hands, and
moaned very low—not as one who seeks to be heard.

And yet he was not utterly forsaken in his trouble.
The repulsion Marner had always created in his
neighbors was partly dissipated by the new light in
which this misfortune had shown him. Instead of a
man who had more cunning than honest folks could
come by, and, what was worse, had not the inclination to use that cunning in a neighborly way, it
was now apparent that Silas had not cunning enough

to keep his own. He was generally spoken of as a
"poor mushed creatur;" and that avoidance of his
neighbors, which had before been referred to his ill-
will and to a probable addiction to worse company,
was now considered mere craziness.

This change to a kindlier feeling was shown in
various ways. The odor of Christmas cooking being
on the wind, it was the season when superfluous
pork and black puddings are suggestive of charity in
well-to-do families; and Silas's misfortune had
brought him uppermost in the memory of house-
keepers like Mrs. Osgood. Mr. Crackenthorp, too,
while he admonished Silas that his money had probably been taken from him because he thought too
much of it and never came to church, enforced the
doctrine by a present of pigs' pettitoes,[1] well cal-
culated to dissipate unfounded prejudices against
the clerical character. Neighbors who had nothing
but verbal consolation to give showed a disposition
not only to greet Silas and discuss his misfortune at
some length when they encountered him in the village, but also to take the trouble of calling at his
cottage and getting him to repeat all the details on
the very spot; and then they would try to cheer him
by saying, "Well, Master Marner, you're no worse
off nor other poor folks, after all; and if you was to
be crippled, the parish 'ud give you a 'lowance."

I suppose one reason why we are seldom able to
comfort our neighbors with our words is that our
goodwill gets adulterated, in spite of ourselves, be-

fore it can pass our lips. We can send black puddings and pettitoes without giving them a flavor of
our own egoism; but language is a stream that is
almost sure to smack of a mingled soil. There was a
fair proportion of kindness in Raveloe; but it was
often of a beery and bungling sort, and took the
shape least allied to the complimentary and hypo-
critical.

Mr. Macey, for example, coming one evening ex-
pressly to let Silas know that recent events had given
him the advantage of standing more favorably in the
opinion of a man whose judgment was not formed
lightly, opened the conversation by saying, as soon
as he had seated himself and adjusted his thumbs—

"Come, Master Marner, why, you've no call to sit
a-moaning. You're a deal better off to ha' lost your
money, nor to ha' kep it by foul means. I used to
think, when you first come into these parts, as you
were no better nor you should be; you were younger
a deal than what you are now; but you were allays
a staring, white-faced creatur, partly like a bald-
faced calf, as I may say. But there's no knowing:
it isn't every queer-looksed thing as Old Harry's
had the making of—I mean, speaking o' toads and
such; for they're often harmless, and useful against
varmin. And it's pretty much the same wi' you,
as fur as I can see. Though as to the yarbs and stuff
to cure the breathing, if you brought that sort o'
knowledge from distant parts, you might ha' been a
bit freer of it. And if the knowledge wasn't well

come by, why, you might ha' made up for it by
coming to church reg'lar; for as for the children as
the Wise Woman charmed, I've been at the christening of 'em again and again, and they took the water
just as well. And that's reasonable; for if Old
Harry's a mind to do a bit o' kindness for a holiday,
like, who's got anything against it? That's my
thinking; and I've been clerk o' this parish forty
years, and I know, when the parson and me does the
cussing of a Ash Wednesday,[1] there's no cussing o'
folks as have a mind to be cured without a doctor,
let Kimble say what he will. And so, Master Marner, as I was saying—for there's windings i' things
as they may carry you to the fur end o' the prayer-
book afore you get back to 'em—my advice is, as
you keep up your sperrits; for as for thinking you're
a deep un, and ha' got more inside you nor 'ull bear
daylight, I'm not o' that opinion at all, and so I
tell the neighbors. For, says I, you talk o' Master
Marner making out a tale—why, it's nonsense, that
is: it 'ud take a 'cute man to make a tale like that;
and, says I, he looked as scared as a rabbit.''

During this discursive address Silas had continued
motionless in his previous attitude, leaning his elbows on his knees, and pressing his hands against his
head. Mr. Macey, not doubting that he had been
listened to, paused, in the expectation of some ap-
preciatory reply, but Marner remained silent. He
had a sense that the old man meant to be good-
natured and neighborly; but the kindness fell on him

as sunshine falls on the wretched—he had no heart to taste it, and felt that it was very far off him.

"Come, Master Marner, have you got nothing to say to that?" said Mr. Macey at last, with a slight accent of impatience.

"Oh," said Marner, slowly, shaking his head between his hands, "I thank you—thank you—kindly."

"Ay, ay, to be sure: I thought you would," said Mr. Macey; "and my advice is—have you got a Sunday suit?"

"No," said Marner.

"I doubted it was so," said Mr. Macey. "Now, let me advise you to get a Sunday suit: there's Tookey, he's a poor creatur, but he's got my tailoring business, and some o' my money in it, and he shall make a suit at a low price, and give you trust, and then you can come to church, and be a bit neighborly. Why, you've never heared me say 'Amen' since you come into these parts, and I recommend you to lose no time, for it'll be poor work when Tookey has it all to himself, for I mayn't be equil to stand i' the desk at all, come another winter." Here Mr. Macey paused, perhaps expecting some sign of emotion in his hearer; but not observing any, he went on. "And as for the money for the suit o' clothes, why, you get a matter of a pound a-week at your weaving, Master Marner, and you're a young man, eh, for all you look so mushed. Why, you couldn't ha' been five-and-twenty when you come into these parts, eh?"

Silas started a little at the change to a questioning

tone, and answered mildly, "I don't know; I can't rightly say—it's a long while since."

After receiving such an answer as this, it is not surprising that Mr. Macey observed, later on in the evening at the Rainbow, that Marner's head was "all of a muddle," and that it was to be doubted if he ever knew when Sunday came round, which showed him a worse heathen than many a dog.

Another of Silas's comforters, besides Mr. Macey, came to him with a mind highly charged on the same topic. This was Mrs. Winthrop,[1] the wheelwright's wife. The inhabitants of Raveloe were not severely regular in their church-going, and perhaps there was hardly a person in the parish who would not have held that to go to church every Sunday in the calendar would have shown a greedy desire to stand well with Heaven, and get an undue advantage over their neighbors—a wish to be better than the "common run," that would have implied a reflection on those who had had godfathers and godmothers as well as themselves, and had an equal right to the burying-service. At the same time, it was understood to be requisite for all who were not household servants, or young men, to take the sacrament at one of the great festivals: Squire Cass himself took it on Christmas-day; while those who were held to be "good livers" went to church with greater, though still with moderate, frequency.

Mrs. Winthrop was one of these: she was in all respects a woman of scrupulous conscience, so eager for

duties that life seemed to offer them too scantily unless she rose at half-past four, though this threw a
scarcity of work over the more advanced hours of
the morning, which it was a constant problem with
her to remove. Yet she had not the vixenish temper
which is sometimes supposed to be a necessary condition of such habits: she was a very mild, patient
woman, whose nature it was to seek out all the sadder
and more serious elements of life, and pasture her mind
upon them. She was the person always first thought
of in Raveloe when there was illness or death in a
family, when leeches were to be applied, or there was
a sudden disappointment in a monthly nurse. She
was a "comfortable woman"—good-looking, fresh-
complexioned, having her lips always slightly
screwed, as if she felt herself in a sick-room with the
doctor or the clergyman present. But she was never
whimpering; no one had seen her shed tears; she was
simply grave and inclined to shake her head and sigh,
almost imperceptibly, like a funeral mourner who is
not a relation. It seemed surprising that Ben Winthrop, who loved his quart-pot and his joke, got along
so well with Dolly; but she took her husband's jokes
and joviality as patiently as everything else, considering that "men *would* be so," and viewing the
stronger sex in the light of animals whom it had
pleased Heaven to make naturally troublesome, like
bulls and turkey-cocks.

This good, wholesome woman could hardly fail to
have her mind drawn strongly towards Silas Marner,

now that he appeared in the light of a sufferer; and one Sunday afternoon, she took her little boy Aaron with her, and went to call on Silas, carrying in her hand some small lard-cakes, flat paste-like articles much esteemed in Raveloe. Aaron, an apple-cheeked youngster of seven, with a clean starched frill which looked like a plate for the apples, needed all his adventurous curiosity to embolden him against the possibility that the big-eyed weaver might do him some bodily injury; and his dubiety was much increased when, on arriving at the Stone-pits, they heard the mysterious sound of the loom.

"Ah, it is as I thought," said Mrs. Winthrop, sadly.

They had to knock loudly before Silas heard them; but when he did come to the door he showed no impatience, as he would once have done, at a visit that had been unasked for and unexpected. Formerly, his heart had been as a locked casket with its treasure inside; but now the casket was empty, and the lock was broken. Left groping in darkness, with his prop utterly gone, Silas had inevitably a sense, though a dull and half-despairing one, that if any help came to him it must come from without; and there was a slight stirring of expectation at the sight of his fellow-men, a faint consciousness of dependence on their good-will. He opened the door wide to admit Dolly, but without otherwise returning her greeting than by moving the arm-chair a few inches as a sign that she was to sit down in it. Dolly, as soon as she was seated, removed the white cloth that covered her lard-cakes, and said in her gravest way—

"I'd a baking yisterday, Master Marner, and the lard-cakes turned out better nor common, and I'd ha' asked you to accept some, if you'd thought well. I don't eat such things myself, for a bit o' bread's what I like from one year's end to the other; but men's stomichs are made so comical, they want a change—they do, I know, God help 'em."

Dolly sighed gently as she held out the cakes to Silas, who thanked her kindly and looked very close at them, absently, being accustomed to look so at everything he took into his hand—eyed all the while by the wondering bright orbs of the small Aaron, who had made an outwork of his mother's chair, and was peeping round from behind it.

"There's letters pricked on 'em," said Dolly. "I can't read 'em myself, and there's nobody, not Mr. Macey himself, rightly knows what they mean; but they've a good meaning, for they're the same as is on the pulpit-cloth at church. What are they, Aaron, my dear?"

Aaron retreated completely behind his outwork.

"Oh go, that's naughty," said his mother, mildly. "Well, whativer the letters are, they've a good meaning; and it's a stamp as has been in our house, Ben says, ever since he was a little un, and his mother used to put it on the cakes, and I've allays put it on too; for if there's any good, we've need of it i' this world."

"It's I. H. S.," [1] said Silas, at which proof of learning Aaron peeped round the chair again.

"Well, to be sure, you can read 'em off," said Dolly. "Ben's read 'em to me many and many a time, but they slip out o' my mind again; the more's the pity, for they're good letters, else they wouldn't be in the church; and so I prick 'em on all the loaves and all the cakes, though sometimes they won't hold, because o' the rising—for, as I said, if there's any good to be got we've need of it i' this world—that we have; and I hope they'll bring good to you, Master Marner, for it's wi' that will I brought you the cakes; and you see the letters have held better nor common."

Silas was as unable to interpret the letters as Dolly, but there was no possibility of misunderstanding the desire to give comfort that made itself heard in her quiet tones. He said, with more feeling than before— "Thank you—thank you kindly." But he laid down the cakes and seated himself absently—drearily unconscious of any distant benefit towards which the cakes and the letters, or even Dolly's kindness could tend for him.

"Ah, if there's good anywhere, we've need of it," repeated Dolly, who did not lightly forsake a serviceable phrase. She looked at Silas pityingly as she went on. "But you didn't hear the church-bells this morning, Master Marner? I doubt you didn't know it was Sunday. Living so lone here, you lose your count, I dare say; and then, when your loom makes a noise, you can't hear the bells, more partic'lar now the frost kills the sound.''

"Yes, I did; I heard 'em," said Silas, to whom Sunday bells were a mere accident of the day, and not part of its sacredness. There had been no bells in Lantern Yard.

"Dear heart!" said Dolly, pausing before she spoke again. "But what a pity it is you should work of a Sunday, and not clean yourself—if you *didn't* go to church; for if you'd a roasting bit, it might be as you couldn't leave it, being a lone man. But there's the bakehus, if you could make up your mind to spend a twopence on the oven now and then,— not every week, in course—I shouldn't like to do that myself,—you might carry your bit o' dinner there. for it's nothing but right to have a bit o' summat hot of a Sunday, and not to make it as you can't know your dinner from Saturday. But now, upo' Christmas-day, this blessed Christmas as is ever coming, if you was to take your dinner to the bakehus, and go to church, and see the holly and the yew, and hear the anthim, and then take the sacramen', you'd be a deal the better, and you'd know which end you stood on, and you could put your trust i' Them as knows better nor we do, seein' you'd ha' done what it lies on us all to do.''

Dolly's exhortation, which was an unusually long effort of speech for her, was uttered in the soothing persuasive tone with which she would have tried to prevail on a sick man to take his medicine, or a basin of gruel for which he had no appetite. Silas had never before been closely urged on the point of his absence from church, which had only been thought of as a part of his general queerness; and he was too direct and simple to evade Dolly's appeal.

"Nay, nay," he said, "I know nothing o' church. I've never been to church."

"No!" said Dolly, in a low tone of wonderment. Then bethinking herself of Silas's advent from an unknown country, she said, "Could it ha' been as they'd no church where you was born?"

"Oh yes," said Silas, meditatively, sitting in his usual posture of leaning on his knees, and supporting his head. "There was churches—a many—it was a big town. But I knew nothing of 'em—I went to chapel."

Dolly was much puzzled at this new word, but she was rather afraid of inquiring further, lest "chapel" might mean some haunt of wickedness. After a little thought, she said—

"Well, Master Marner, it's niver too late to turn over a new leaf, and if you've niver had no church, there's no telling the good it'll do you. For I feel so set up and comfortable as niver was, when I've been and heard the prayers, and the singing to the praise and glory o' God, as Mr. Macey gives out— and Mr. Crackenthorp saying good words, and more partic'lar on sacramen' Day; and if a bit o' trouble comes, I feel as I can put up wi' it, for I've looked for help i' the right quarter, and gev myself up to

Them as we must all give ourselves up to at the
last; and if we'n done our part, it isn't to be believed as Them as are above [1] us 'ull be worse nor we
are, and come short o' Their'n.''

Poor Dolly's exposition of her simple Raveloe
theology fell rather unmeaningly on Silas's ears, for
there was no word in it that could rouse a memory
of what he had known as religion, and his compre-
hension was quite baffled by the plural pronoun,
which was no heresy of Dolly's, but only her way of
avoiding a presumptuous familiarity. He remained
silent, not feeling inclined to assent to the part of
Dolly's speech which he fully understood—her rec-
ommendation that he should go to church. Indeed,
Silas was so unaccustomed to talk beyond the brief
questions and answers necessary for the transaction of
his simple business, that words did not easily come to
him without the urgency of a distinct purpose.

But now, little Aaron, having become used to the
weaver's awful presence, had advanced to his mother's side, and Silas, seeming to notice him for the
first time, tried to return Dolly's signs of goodwill
by offering the lad a bit of lard-cake. Aaron shrank
back a little, and rubbed his head against his mother's
shoulder, but still thought the piece of cake worth
the risk of putting his hand out for it.

''Oh, for shame, Aaron,'' said his mother, taking
him on her lap, however; ''why, you don't want cake
again yet awhile. He's wonderful hearty,'' she went

on, with a little sigh—"that he is, God knows. He's
my youngest, and we spoil him sadly, for either me or
the father must allays hev him in our sight—that we
must."

She stroked Aaron's brown head, and thought it
must do Master Marner good to see such a "pictur
of a child." But Marner, on the other side of the
hearth, saw the neat-featured rosy face as a mere dim
round, with two dark spots in it.

"And he's got a voice like a bird—you wouldn't
think," Dolly went on; "he can sing a Christmas
carril as his father's taught him; and I take it for a
token as he'll come to good, as he can learn the good
tunes so quick. Come, Aaron, stan' up and sing the
carril to Master Marner, come."

Aaron replied by rubbing his forehead against his
mother's shoulder.

"Oh, that's naughty," said Dolly, gently. "Stan'
up, when mother tells you, and let me hold the cake
till you've done."

Aaron was not indisposed to display his talents,
even to an ogre, under protecting circumstances; and
after a few more signs of coyness, consisting chiefly
in rubbing the backs of his hands over his eyes, and
then peeping between them at Master Marner, to see
if he looked anxious for the "carril," he at length
allowed his head to be duly adjusted, and standing
behind the table, which let him appear above it only
as far as his broad frill, so that he looked like a

cherubic head untroubled with a body, he began with
a clear chirp, and in a melody that had the rhythm of
an industrious hammer—

> "God rest you, merry gentlemen,
> Let nothing you dismay,
> For Jesus Christ our Saviour
> Was born on Christmas-day."

Dolly listened with a devout look, glancing at
Marner in some confidence that this strain would
help to allure him to church.

"That's Christmas music," she said, when Aaron
had ended, and had secured his piece of cake again.
"There's no other music equil to the Christmas
music—'Hark the erol angils sing.' And you may
judge what it is at church, Master Marner, with the
bassoon and the voices, as you can't help thinking
you've got to a better place a'ready—for I wouldn't
speak ill o' this world, seeing as Them put us in it as
knows best—but what wi' the drink, and the quarreling, and the bad illnesses, and the hard dying, as
I've seen times and times, one's thankful to hear of
a better. The boy sings pretty don't he, Master
Marner?"

"Yes," said Silas, absently, "very pretty."

The Christmas carol, with its hammer-like rhythm,
had fallen on his ears as strange music, quite unlike
a hymn, and could have none of the effect Dolly con-
templated. But he wanted to show her that he was
grateful, and the only mode that occurred to him was
to offer Aaron a bit more cake.

"Oh, no, thank you, Master Marner," said Dolly, holding down Aaron's willing hands. "We must be going home now. And so I wish you good-by, Master Marner; and if you ever feel anyways bad in your inside, as you can't fend for yourself, I'll come and clean up for you, and get you a bit o' victual, and willing. But I beg and pray of you to leave off weaving of a Sunday, for it's bad for soul and body —and the money as comes i' that way 'ull be a bad bed to lie down on at the last, if it doesn't fly away, nobody knows where, like the white frost. And you'll excuse me being that free with you, Master Marner, for I wish you well—I do. Make your bow, Aaron."

Silas said "Good-by, and thank you kindly," as he opened the door for Dolly, but he couldn't help feeling relieved when she was gone—relieved that he might weave again and moan at his ease. Her simple view of life and its comforts, by which she had tried to cheer him, was only like a report of unknown objects, which his imagination could not fashion. The fountains of human love and of faith in a divine love had not yet been unlocked, and his soul was still the shunken rivulet, with only this difference, that its little groove of sand was blocked up, and it wandered confusedly against dark obstruction.

And so, notwithstanding the honest persuasions of Mr. Macey and Dolly Winthrop, Silas spent his Christmas-day in loneliness, eating his meat in sadness of heart, though the meat had come to him as a neighborly present. In the morning he looked out on the black frost that seemed to press cruelly on every blade of grass, while the half-icy red pool shivered under the bitter wind; but towards evening the snow began to fall, and curtained from him even that dreary outlook, shutting him close up with his narrow grief. And he sat in his robbed home through the livelong evening, not caring to close his shutters or lock his door, pressing his head between his hands and moaning, till the cold grasped him and told him that his fire was gray.

Nobody in this world but himself knew that he was the same Silas Marner who had once loved his fellow with tender love, and trusted in an unseen goodness. Even to himself that past experience had become dim.

But in Raveloe village the bells rang merrily, and the church was fuller than all through the rest of the year, with red faces among the abundant dark-green boughs—faces prepared for a longer service than usual by an odorous breakfast of toast and ale. Those green boughs, the hymn and anthem never heard but at Christmas—even the Athanasian Creed,[1] which was discriminated from the others only as being longer and of exceptional virtue, since it was only read on rare occasions—brought a vague exulting sense, for which the grown men could as little have found words as the children, that something great and mysterious had been done for them in heaven above and in earth below, which they were appropriating by their presence. And then the red faces

made their way through the black biting frost to
their own homes, feeling themselves free for the rest
of the day to eat, drink, and be merry, and using that
Christian freedom without diffidence.

At Squire Cass's family party that day nobody
mentioned Dunstan—nobody was sorry for his absence, or feared it would be too long. The doctor
and his wife, uncle and aunt Kimble, were there, and
the annual Christmas talk was carried through without any omissions, rising to the climax of Mr. Kimble's experience when he walked the London hospitals
thirty years back, together with striking professional
anecdotes then gathered. Whereupon cards followed,
with aunt Kimble's annual failure to follow suit,
and uncle Kimble's irascibility concerning the odd
trick which was rarely explicable to him when it
was not on his side, without a general visitation of
tricks to see that they were formed on sound principles: the whole being accompanied by a strong steam-
ing odor of spirits-and-water.

But the party on Christmas-day, being a strictly
family party, was not the pre-eminently brilliant cel-
ebration of the season at the Red House. It was the
great dance on New Year's Eve that made the glory
of Squire Cass's hospitality, as of his forefathers',
time out of mind. This was the occasion when all
the society of Raveloe and Tarley, whether old acquaintances separated by long rutty distances, or
cooled acquaintances separated by misunderstand-
ings concerning run-away calves, or acquaintances

founded on intermittent condescension, counted on
meeting and on comporting themselves with mutual
appropriateness. This was the occasion on which fair
dames who came on pillions [1] sent their bandboxes
before them, supplied with more than their evening
costume; for the feast was not to end with a single
evening, like a paltry town entertainment, where the
whole supply of eatables is put on the table at once,
and bedding is scanty. The Red House was pro-
visioned as if for a siege; and as for the spare feather-
beds ready to be laid on floors, they were as plentiful
as might naturally be expected in a family that had
killed its own geese for many generations.

Godfrey Cass was looking forward to this New
Year's Eve with a foolish reckless longing, that made
him half deaf to his importunate companion, Anxiety.

"Dunsey will be coming home soon: there will be
a great blow-up, and how will you bribe his spite to
silence?" said Anxiety.

"Oh, he won't come home before New Year's Eve,
perhaps," said Godfrey; "and I shall sit by Nancy
then, and dance with her, and get a kind look from
her in spite of herself."

"But money is wanted in another quarter," said
Anxiety, in a louder voice, "and how will you get it
without selling your mother's diamond pin? And
if you don't get it . . . ?"

"Well, but something may happen to make things

easier. At any rate, there's one pleasure for me close at hand: Nancy is coming."

"Yes, and suppose your father should bring matters to a pass that will oblige you to decline marrying her—and to give your reasons?"

"Hold your tongue, and don't worry me. I can see Nancy's eyes, just as they will look at me, and feel her hand in mine already."

But Anxiety went on, though in noisy Christmas company; refusing to be utterly quieted even by much drinking.

CHAPTER XI

SOME women, I grant, would not appear to advantage seated on a pillion, and attired in a drab joseph [1] and a drab beaver bonnet, with a crown resembling a small stew-pan; for a garment suggesting a coachman's greatcoat, cut out under an exiguity of cloth that would only allow of miniature capes, is not well adapted to conceal deficiencies of contour, nor is drab a color that will throw sallow cheeks into lively contrast. It was all the greater triumph to Miss Nancy Lammeter's beauty that she looked thoroughly bewitching in that costume, as, seated on the pillion behind her tall, erect father, she held one arm round him, and looked down, with open-eyed anxiety, at the treacherous snow-covered pools and puddles, which sent up formidable splashings of mud under the stamp of Dobbin's foot. A painter would, perhaps, have preferred her in those moments when she was free from self-consciousness; but certainly the bloom on her cheeks was at its highest point of contrast with the surrounding drab when she arrived at the door of the Red House, and saw Mr. Godfrey Cass ready to lift her from the pillion. She wished her sister Priscilla had come up at the same time behind the servant, for then she would have contrived that Mr.

Godfrey should have lifted off Priscilla first, and, in the meantime, she would have persuaded her father to go round to the horse-block instead of alighting at the door-steps. It was very painful, when you had made it quite clear to a young man that you were determined not to marry him, however much he might wish it, that he would still continue to pay you marked attentions; besides, why didn't he always show the same attentions, if he meant them sincerely, instead of being so strange as Mr. Godfrey Cass was, sometimes behaving as if he didn't want to speak to her, and taking no notice of her for weeks and weeks, and then, all on a sudden, almost making love again? Moreover, it was quite plain he had no real love for her, else he would not let people have *that* to say of him which they did say. Did he suppose that Miss Nancy Lammeter was to be won by any man, squire or no squire, who led a bad life? That was not what she had been used to see in her own father, who was the soberest and best man in that country-side, only a little hot and hasty now and then, if things were not done to the minute.

All these thoughts rushed through Miss Nancy's mind, in their habitual succession, in the moments between her first sight of Mr. Godfrey Cass standing at the door and her own arrival there. Happily, the Squire came out too and gave a loud greeting to her father, so that, somehow, under cover of this noise she seemed to find concealment for her confusion and neglect of any suitably formal behavior, while she

was being lifted from the pillion by strong arms
which seemed to find her ridiculously small and light.
And there was the best reason for hastening into the
house at once, since the snow was beginning to fall
again, threatening an unpleasant journey for such
guests as were still on the road. These were a small
minority; for already the afternoon was beginning
to decline, and there would not be too much time for
the ladies who came from a distance to attire themselves in readiness for the early tea which was to in-
spirit them for the dance.

There was a buzz of voices through the house, as
Miss Nancy entered, mingled with the scrape of a
fiddle preluding in the kitchen; but the Lammeters
were guests whose arrival had evidently been thought
of so much that it had been watched for from the win-
dows, for Mrs. Kimble, who did the honors at the Red
House on these great occasions, came forward to
meet Miss Nancy in the hall, and conduct her up-
stairs. Mrs. Kimble was the Squire's sister, as well
as the doctor's wife—a double dignity, with which
her diameter was in direct proportion; so that, a
journey up-stairs being rather fatiguing to her, she
did not oppose Miss Nancy's request to be allowed to
find her way alone to the Blue Room, where the Miss
Lammeters' bandboxes had been deposited on their
arrival in the morning.

There was hardly a bedroom in the house where
feminine compliments were not passing and feminine
toilettes going forward, in various stages, in space

made scanty by extra beds spread upon the floor; and Miss Nancy, as she entered the Blue Room, had to make her little formal curtsy to a group of six. On the one hand, there were ladies no less important than the two Miss Gunns, the wine merchant's daughters from Lytherly, dressed in the height of fashion, with the tightest skirts and the shortest waists, and gazed at by Miss Ladbrook (of the Old Pastures) with a shyness not unsustained by inward criticism. Partly, Miss Ladbrook felt that her own skirt must be regarded as unduly lax by the Miss Gunns, and partly, that it was a pity the Miss Gunns did not show that judgment which she herself would show if she were in their place, by stopping a little on this side of the fashion. On the other hand, Mrs. Ladbrook was standing in skull-cap and front, with her turban in her hand, curtsying and smiling blandly and saying, "After you, ma'am," to another lady in similar circumstances, who had politely offered the precedence at the looking-glass.

But Miss Nancy had no sooner made her curtsy than an elderly lady came forward, whose full white muslin kerchief, and mob-cap round her curls of smooth gray hair, were in daring contrast with the puffed yellow satins and top-knotted caps of her neighbors. She approached Miss Nancy with much primness, and said, with a slow, treble suavity—

"Niece, I hope I see you well in health." Miss Nancy kissed her aunt's cheek dutifully, and answered, with the same sort of amiable primness, "quite well, I thank you, aunt; and I hope I see you the same."

"Thank you, niece; I keep my health for the present. And how is my brother-in-law?"

These dutiful questions and answers were continued until it was ascertained in detail that the Lammeters were all as well as usual, and the Osgoods likewise, also that niece Priscilla must certainly arrive shortly, and that traveling on pillions in snowy weather was unpleasant, though a joseph was a great protection. Then Nancy was formally introduced to her aunt's visitors, the Miss Gunns, as being the daughters of a mother known to *their* mother, though now for the first time induced to make a journey into these parts; and these ladies were so taken by surprise at finding such a lovely face and figure in an out-of-the-way country place, that they began to feel some curiosity about the dress she would put on when she took off her joseph. Miss Nancy, whose thoughts were always conducted with the propriety and moderation conspicuous in her manners, remarked to herself that the Miss Gunns were rather hardfeatured than otherwise, and that such very low dresses as they wore might have been attributed to vanity if their shoulders had been pretty, but that, being as they were, it was not reasonable to suppose that they showed their necks from a love of display, but rather from some obligation not inconsistent with sense and modesty. She felt convinced, as she opened her box, that this must be her aunt Osgood's opinion, for Miss

Nancy's mind resembled her aunt's to a degree that everybody said was surprising, considering the kinship was on Mr. Osgood's side; and though you might not have supposed it from the formality of their greeting, there was a devoted attachment and mutual admiration between aunt and niece. Even Miss Nancy's refusal of her cousin Gilbert Osgood (on the ground solely that he was her cousin), though it had grieved her aunt greatly, had not in the least cooled the preference which had determined her to leave Nancy several of her hereditary ornaments, let Gilbert's future wife be whom she might.[1]

Three of the ladies quickly retired, but the Miss Gunns were quite content that Mrs. Osgood's inclination to remain with her niece gave them also a reason for staying to see the rustic beauty's toilette. And it was really a pleasure—from the first opening of the bandbox, where everything smelt of lavender and rose-leaves, to the clasping of the small coral necklace that fitted closely round her little white neck. Everything belonging to Miss Nancy was of delicate purity and nattiness: not a crease was where it had no business to be, not a bit of her linen professed whiteness without fulfilling its profession; the very pins on her pincushion were stuck in after a pattern from which she was careful to allow no aberration; and as for her own person, it gave the same idea of perfect unvarying neatness as the body of a little bird. It is true that her light-brown hair was cropped behind like a boy's, and was dressed in

front in a number of flat rings, that lay quite away
from her face; but there was no sort of coiffure that
could make Miss Nancy's cheek and neck look otherwise than pretty; and when at last she stood complete in her silvery twilled silk, her lace tucker, her
coral necklace, and coral ear-drops, the Miss Gunns
could see nothing to criticize except her hands, which
bore the traces of butter-making, cheese-crushing,
and even still coarser work. But Miss Nancy was
not ashamed of that, for while she was dressing she
narrated to her aunt how she and Priscilla had
packed their boxes yesterday, because this morning
was baking morning, and since they were leaving
home, it was desirable to make a good supply of meat-
pies for the kitchen; and as she concluded this judi-
cious remark, she turned to the Miss Gunns that she
might not commit the rudeness of not including them
in the conversation. The Miss Gunns smiled stiffly,
and thought what a pity it was that these rich country people, who could afford to buy such good clothes
(really Miss Nancy's lace and silk were very costly),
should be brought up in utter ignorance and vul-
garity. She actually said "mate" for "meat,"
" 'appen" for "perhaps," and "oss" for "horse,"
which, to young ladies living in good Lytherly society, who habitually said 'orse, even in domestic
privacy, and only said 'appen on the right occasions,
was necessarily shocking. Miss Nancy, indeed, had
never been to any school higher than Dame Tedman's:[1] her acquaintance with profane literature

hardly went beyond the rhymes she had worked in her large sampler under the lamb and the shepherdess; and in order to balance an account, she was obliged to effect her subtraction by removing visible metallic shillings and six-pences from a visible metallic total. There is hardly a servant-maid in these days who is not better informed than Miss Nancy; yet she had the essential attributes of a lady—high veracity, delicate honor in her dealings, deference to others, and refined personal habits,—and lest these should not suffice to convince grammatical fair ones that her feelings can at all resemble theirs, I will add that she was slightly proud and exacting, and as constant in her affection towards a baseless opinion as towards an erring lover.

The anxiety about sister Priscilla, which had grown rather active by the time the coral necklace was clasped, was happily ended by the entrance of that cheerful-looking lady herself, with a face made blowsy by cold and damp. After the first questions and greetings, she turned to Nancy, and surveyed her from head to foot—then wheeled her round, to ascertain that the back view was equally faultless.

"What do you think o' *these* gowns, aunt Osgood?" said Priscilla, while Nancy helped her to unrobe.

"Very handsome indeed, niece," said Mrs. Osgood, with a slight increase of formality. She always thought niece Priscilla too rough.

"I'm obliged to have the same as Nancy, you

know, for all I'm five years older, and it makes me look yellow; for she never *will* have anything without I have mine just like it, because she wants us to look like sisters. And I tell her, folks 'ull think it's my weakness makes me fancy as I shall look pretty in what she looks pretty in. For I *am* ugly—there's no denying that: I feature my father's family. But, law! I don't mind, do you?'' Priscilla here turned to the Miss Gunns, rattling on in too much pre-occupation with the delight of talking, to notice that her candor was not appreciated. ''The pretty uns do for fly-catchers—they keep the men off us. I've no opinion o' the men, Miss Gunn—I don't know what *you* have. And as for fretting and stewing about what *they*'ll think of you from morning till night, and making your life uneasy about what they're doing when they're out o' your sight—as I tell Nancy, it's a folly no woman need be guilty of, if she's got a good father and a good home: let her leave it to them as have got no fortin, and can't help themselves. As I say, Mr. Have-your-own-way is the best husband, and the only one I'd ever promise to obey. I know it isn't pleasant, when you've been used to living in a big way, and managing hogsheads and all that, to go and put your nose in by some-body else's fireside, or to sit down by yourself to a scrag or a knuckle; but, thank God! my father's a sober man and likely to live; and if you've got a man by the chimney-corner, it doesn't matter if he's childish—the business needn't be broke up.''

The delicate process of getting her narrow gown over her head without injury to her smooth curls, obliged Miss Priscilla to pause in this rapid survey of life, and Mrs. Osgood seized the opportunity of rising and saying—

"Well, niece, you'll follow us. The Miss Gunns will like to go down."

"Sister," said Nancy, when they were alone, "you've offended the Miss Gunns, I'm sure."

"What have I done, child?" said Priscilla, in some alarm.

"Why, you asked them if they minded about being ugly—you're so very blunt."

"Law, did I? Well, it popped out: it's a mercy I said no more, for I'm a bad un to live with folks when they don't like the truth. But as for being ugly, look at me, child, in this silver-colored silk— I told you how it 'ud be—I look as yellow as a daffadil. Anybody 'ud say you wanted to make a mawkin of me."

"No, Priscy, don't say so. I begged and prayed of you not to let us have the silk if you'd like another better. I was willing to have *your* choice, you know I was," said Nancy, in anxious self-vindication.

"Nonsense, child! you know you'd set your heart on this; and reason good, for you're the color o' cream. It 'ud be fine doings for you to dress yourself to suit *my* skin. What I find fault with, is that notion o' yours as I must dress myself just like you. But you do as you like with me—you always did, from when first you begun to walk. If you wanted to go the field's length, the field's length you'd go; and there was no whipping you, for you looked as prim and innicent as a daisy all the while.''

"Priscy,'' said Nancy, gently, as she fastened a coral necklace, exactly like her own, round Priscilla's neck, which was very far from being like her own, ''I'm am sure I'm willing to give way as far as is right, but who shouldn't dress alike if it isn't sisters? Would you have us go about looking as if we were no kin to one another—us that have got no mother and not another sister in the world? I'd do what was right, if I dressed in a gown dyed with cheese-coloring; and I'd rather you'd choose, and let me wear what pleases you.''

"There you go again! You'd come round to the same thing if one talked to you from Saturday night till Saturday morning. It'll be fine fun to see how you'll master your husband and never raise your voice above the singing o' the kettle all the while. I like to see the men mastered!''

"Don't talk *so*, Priscy,'' said Nancy, blushing. "You know I don't mean ever to be married.''

"Oh, you never mean a fiddle-stick's end!'' said Priscilla, as she arranged her discarded dress, and closed her bandbox. "Who shall *I* have to work for when father's gone, if you are to go and take notions in your head and be an old maid, because some folks are no better than they should be? I haven't a bit o' patience with you—sitting on an addled egg forever, as if there was never a fresh un in the world. One old maid's enough out o' two sisters; and I shall do credit to a single life, for God A'mighty meant me for it. Come, we can go down now. I'm as ready as a mawkin *can* be—there's nothing awanting to frighten the crows, now I've got my ear-droppers in.''

As the two Miss Lammeters walked into the large parlor together, any one who did not know the character of both might certainly have supposed that the reason why the square-shouldered, clumsy, high-featured Priscilla wore a dress the facsimile of her pretty sister's, was either the mistaken vanity of the one, or the malicious contrivance of the other in order to set off her own rare beauty. But the good-natured self-forgetful cheeriness and common-sense of Priscilla would soon have dissipated the one suspicion; and the modest calm of Nancy's speech and manners told clearly of a mind free from all disavowed devices.

Places of honor had been kept for the Miss Lammeters near the head of the principal tea-table in the wainscoted parlor, now looking fresh and pleasant with handsome branches of holly, yew, and laurel, from the abundant growths of the old garden; and Nancy felt an inward flutter, that no firmness of purpose could prevent, when she saw Mr. Godfrey Cass advancing to lead her to a seat between himself and Mr. Crackenthorp, while Priscilla was called to the opposite side between her father and the Squire.

It certainly did make some difference to Nancy that
the lover she had given up was the young man of
quite the highest consequence in the parish—at home
in a venerable and unique [1] parlor, which was the
extremity of grandeur in her experience, a parlor
where *she* might one day have been mistress, with
the consciousness that she was spoken of as "Madam
Cass," the Squire's wife. These circumstances exalted her inward drama in her own eyes, and deepened the emphasis with which she declared to herself
that not the most dazzling rank should induce her to
marry a man whose conduct showed him careless of
his character, but that, "love once, love always,"
was the motto of a true and pure woman, and no
man should ever have any right over her which would
be a call on her to destroy the dried flowers that she
treasured, and always would treasure, for Godfrey
Cass's sake. And Nancy was capable of keeping
her word to herself under very trying conditions.
Nothing but a becoming blush betrayed the moving
thoughts that urged themselves upon her as she accepted the seat next to Mr. Crackenthorp; for she
was so instinctively neat and adroit in all her actions, and her pretty lips met each other with such
quiet firmness, that it would have been difficult for
her to appear agitated.

It was not the Rector's practice to let a charming
blush pass without an appropriate compliment. He
was not in the least lofty or aristocratic, but simply
a merry-eyed, small-featured, gray-haired man, with

his chin propped by an ample, many-creased white neckcloth which seemed to predominate over every other point in his person, and somehow to impress its peculiar character on his remarks; so that to have considered his amenities apart from his cravat would have been a severe, and perhaps a dangerous, effort of abstraction.

"Ha, Miss Nancy," he said, turning his head within his cravat and smiling down pleasantly upon her, "when anybody pretends this has been a severe winter, I shall tell them I saw the roses blooming on New Year's Eve—eh, Godfrey, what do *you* say?"

Godfrey made no reply, and avoided looking at Nancy very markedly; for though these complimentary personalities were held to be in excellent taste in old-fashioned Raveloe society, reverent love has a politeness of its own which it teaches to men otherwise of small schooling. But the Squire was rather impatient at Godfrey's showing himself a dull spark in this way. By this advanced hour of the day, the Squire was always in higher spirits than we have seen him in at the breakfast-table, and felt it quite pleasant to fulfill the hereditary duty of being noisily jovial and patronizing: the large silver snuff-box [1] was in active service and was offered without fail to all neighbors from time to time, however often they might have declined the favor. At present, the Squire had only given an express welcome to the heads of families as they appeared; but always as the evening deepened, his hospitality rayed out more

widely, till he had tapped the youngest guests on the
back and shown a peculiar fondness for their presence, in the full belief that they must feel their lives
made happy by their belonging to a parish where
there was such a hearty man as Squire Cass to invite
them and wish them well. Even in this early stage
of the jovial mood, it was natural that he should wish
to supply his son's deficiencies by looking and speaking for him.

"Ay, ay," he began, offering his snuff-box to Mr.
Lammeter, who for the second time bowed his head
and waved his hand in stiff rejection of the offer,
"us old fellows may wish ourselves young to-night,
when we see the mistletoe-bough in the White Parlor.
It's true, most things are gone back'ard in these last
thirty years—the country's going down since the old
king fell ill. But when I look at Miss Nancy here,
I begin to think the lasses keep up their quality;—
ding me if I remember a sample to match her, not
when I was a fine young fellow, and thought a deal
about my pigtail.[1] No offense to you, madam," he
added, bending to Mrs. Crackenthorp, who sat by
him, "I didn't know *you* when you were as young
as Miss Nancy here."

Mrs. Crackenthorp—a small blinking woman, who
fidgeted incessantly with her lace, ribbons, and gold
chain, turning her head about and making subdued
noises, very much like a guinea-pig that twitches its
nose and soliloquizes in all company indiscriminately

—now blinked and fidgeted towards the Squire, and said, "Oh no—no offense."

This emphatic compliment of the Squire's to Nancy was felt by others besides Godfrey to have a diplomatic significance; and her father gave a slight additional erectness to his back, as he looked across the table at her with complacent gravity. That grave and orderly senior was not going to bate [1] a jot of his dignity by seeming elated at the notion of a match between his family and the Squire's: he was gratified by any honor paid to his daughter; but he must see an alteration in several ways before his consent would be vouchsafed. His spare but healthy person, and high-featured firm face, that looked as if it had never been flushed by excess, was in strong contrast, not only with the Squire's, but with the appearance of the Raveloe farmers generally—in accordance with a favorite saying of his own, that "breed was stronger than pasture."

"Miss Nancy's wonderful like what her mother was, though; isn't she, Kimble?" said the stout lady of that name, looking round for her husband.

But Doctor Kimble (country apothecaries in old days enjoyed that title without authority of diploma), being a thin and agile man, was flitting about the room with his hands in his pockets, making himself agreeable to his feminine patients, with medical impartiality, and being welcomed everywhere as a doctor by hereditary right—not one of those miserable

apothecaries who canvass for practice in strange
neighborhoods, and spend all their income in starv-
ing their one horse, but a man of substance, able to
keep an extravagant table like the best of his patients.
Time out of mind the Raveloe doctor had been a
Kimble; Kimble was inherently a doctor's name;
and it was difficult to contemplate firmly the melancholy fact that the actual Kimble had no son, so that
his practice might one day be handed over to a suc-
cessor with the incongruous name of Taylor or
Johnson. But in that case the wiser people in Raveloe would employ Dr. Blick of Flitton—as less unnatural.

"Did you speak to me, my dear?" said the au-
thentic doctor, coming quickly to his wife's side; but,
as if foreseeing that she would be too much out of
breath to repeat her remark, he went on immediately
—"Ha, Miss Priscilla, the sight of you revives the
taste of that super-excellent pork-pie. I hope the
batch isn't near an end."

"Yes, indeed, it is, doctor," said Priscilla; "but
I'll answer for it the next shall be as good. My
pork-pies don't turn out well by chance."

"Not as your doctoring does, eh, Kimble?—because folks forget to take your physic, eh?" said the
Squire, who regarded physic and doctors as many
loyal churchmen regard the church and the clergy—
tasting a joke against them when he was in health,
but impatiently eager for their aid when anything

was the matter with him. He tapped his box, and looked round with a triumphant laugh.

"Ah, she has a quick wit, my friend Priscilla has," said the doctor, choosing to attribute the epigram to a lady rather than allow a brother-in-law that advantage over him. "She saves a little pepper to sprinkle over her talk—that's the reason why she never puts too much into her pies. There's my wife, now, she never has an answer at her tongue's end; but if I offend her, she's sure to scarify my throat with black pepper the next day, or else give me the colic with watery greens. That's an awful tit-for-tat." Here the vivacious doctor made a pathetic grimace.

"Did you ever hear the like?" said Mrs. Kimble, laughing above her double chin with much good-humor, aside to Mrs. Crackenthorp, who blinked and nodded, and amiably intended to smile, but the intention lost itself in small twitchings and noises.

"I suppose that's the sort of tit-for-tat adopted in your profession, Kimble, if you've a grudge against a patient," said the Rector.

"Never do have a grudge against our patients," said Mr. Kimble, "except when they leave us; and then, you see, we haven't the chance of prescribing for 'em. Ha, Miss Nancy," he continued, suddenly skipping to Nancy's side, "you won't forget your promise? You're to save a dance for me, you know."

"Come, come, Kimble, don't you be too for'ard," said the Squire. "Give the young uns fair-play. There's my son Godfrey'll be wanting to have a round with you if you run off with Miss Nancy. He's bespoke her for the first dance, I'll be bound. Eh, sir! what do you say?" he continued, throwing himself backward, and looking at Godfrey. "Haven't you asked Miss Nancy to open the dance with you?"

Godfrey, sorely uncomfortable under this significant insistence about Nancy, and afraid to think where it would end by the time his father had set his usual hospitable example of drinking before and after supper, saw no course open but to turn to Nancy and say, with as little awkwardness as possible—

"No; I've not asked her yet, but I hope she'll consent—if somebody else hasn't been before me."

"No, I've not engaged myself," said Nancy, quietly, though blushingly. (If Mr. Godfrey founded any hopes on her consenting to dance with him, he would soon be undeceived; but there was no need for her to be uncivil.)

"Then I hope you've no objections to dancing with me," said Godfrey, beginning to lose the sense that there was anything uncomfortable in this arrangement.

"No, no objections," said Nancy, in a cold tone.

"Ah, well, you are a lucky fellow, Godfrey," said uncle Kimble; "but you're my godson, so I won't stand in your way. Else I'm not so very old, eh, my dear?'' he went on, skipping to his wife's side again. "You wouldn't mind my having a second after you were gone—not if I cried a good deal first?"

"Come, come, take a cup o' tea and stop your tongue, do,'' said good-humored Mrs. Kimble, feeling some pride in a husband who must be regarded as so clever and amusing by the company generally. If he had only not been irritable at cards!

While safe, well-tested personalities were enlivening the tea in this way, the sound of the fiddle approaching within a distance at which it could be heard distinctly, made the young people look at each other with sympathetic impatience for the end of the meal.

"Why, there's Solomon in the hall,'' said the Squire, "and playing my fav'rite tune, *I* believe— 'The flaxen-headed plowboy'—he's for giving us a hint as we aren't enough in a hurry to hear him play. Bob,'' he called out to his third long-legged son, who was at the other end of the room, "open the door, and tell Solomon to come in. He shall give us a tune here.''

Bob obeyed, and Solomon walked in, fiddling as he walked, for he would on no account break off in the middle of a tune.

"Here, Solomon,'' said the Squire, with loud patronage. "Round here, my man. Ah, I knew it was 'The flaxen-headed plowboy:' there's no finer tune.''

Solomon Macey, a small hale old man, with an abundant crop of long white hair reaching nearly to

his shoulders, advanced to the indicated spot, bowing
reverently while he fiddled, as much as to say that he
respected the company though he respected the key-
note more. As soon as he had repeated the tune
and lowered his fiddle, he bowed again to the Squire
and the Rector, and said, "I hope I see your honor
and your reverence well, and wishing you health and
long life and a happy New Year. And wishing the
same to you, Mr. Lammeter, sir; and to the other
gentlemen, and the madams, and the young lasses."

As Solomon uttered the last words, he bowed in
all directions solicitously, lest he should be wanting
in due respect. But thereupon he immediately began to prelude, and fell into the tune which he knew
would be taken as a special compliment by Mr. Lammeter.

"Thank ye, Solomon, thank ye," said Mr. Lammeter when the fiddle paused again. "That's 'Over
the hills and far away,' that is. My father used to
say to me, whenever we heard that tune, 'Ah, lad, *I*
come from over the hills and far away.' There's
a many tunes I don't make head or tail of; but that
speaks to me like the blackbird's whistle. I suppose
it's the name: there's a deal in the name of a tune."

But Solomon was already impatient to prelude
again, and presently broke with much spirit into
"Sir Roger de Coverley,"[1] at which there was a
sound of chairs pushed back, and laughing voices.

"Ay, ay, Solomon, we know what that means,"
said the Squire, rising. "It's time to begin the

dance, eh? Lead the way, then, and we'll all follow you."

So Solomon, holding his white head on one side, and playing vigorously, marched forward at the head of the gay procession into the White Parlor, where the mistletoe-bough was hung, and multitudinous tallow candles made rather a brilliant effect, gleaming from among the berried holly-boughs, and reflected in the old-fashioned oval mirrors fastened in the panels of the white wainscot. A quaint procession! Old Solomon, in his seedy clothes and long white locks, seemed to be luring that decent company by the magic scream of his fiddle—luring discreet matrons in turban-shaped caps, nay, Mrs. Crackenthorp herself, the summit of whose perpendicular feather was on a level with the Squire's shoulder—luring fair lasses complacently conscious of very short waists and skirts blameless of front-folds—luring burly fathers in large variegated waistcoats, and ruddy sons, for the most part shy and sheepish, in short nether garments and very long coat-tails.

Already Mr. Macey and a few other privileged villagers, who were allowed to be spectators on these great occasions, were seated on benches placed for them near the door; and great was the admiration and satisfaction in that quarter when the couples had formed themselves for the dance, and the Squire led off with Mrs. Crackenthorp, joining hands with the Rector and Mrs. Osgood. That was as it should

be—that was what everybody had been used to—and
the charter [1] of Raveloe seemed to be renewed by the
ceremony. It was not thought of as an unbecoming
levity for the old and middle-aged people to dance a
little before sitting down to cards, but rather as part
of their social duties. For what were these if not
to be merry at appropriate times, interchanging
visits and poultry with due frequency, paying each
other old-established compliments in sound tra-
ditional phrases, passing well-tried personal jokes,
urging your guests to eat and drink too much out of
hospitality, and eating and drinking too much in
your neighbor's house to show that you liked your
cheer? And the parson naturally set an example in
these social duties. For it would not have been possible for the Raveloe mind, without a peculiar revelation, to know that a clergyman should be a pale-
faced memento of solemnities, instead of a reason-
ably faulty man whose exclusive authority to read
prayers and preach, to christen, marry, and bury
you, necessarily co-existed with the right to sell you
the ground to be buried in and to take tithe in kind;
on which last point, of course, there was a little
grumbling, but not to the extent of irreligion—not
of deeper significance than the grumbling at the
rain, which was by no means accompanied with a
spirit of impious defiance, but with a desire that the
prayer for fine weather might be read forthwith.

There was no reason, then, why the Rector's dancing should not be received as part of the fitness of

things quite as much as the Squire's, or why, on the other hand, Mr. Macey's official respect should restrain him from subjecting the parson's performance to that criticism with which minds of extraordinary acuteness must necessarily contemplate the doings of their fallible fellow-men.

"The Squire's pretty springe,[1] considering his weight," said Mr. Macey, "and he stamps uncommon well. But Mr. Lammeter beats 'em all for shapes: you see he holds his head like a sodger, and he isn't so cushiony as most o' the oldish gentlefolks—they run fat in general; and he's got a fine leg. The parson's nimble enough, but he hasn't got much of a leg: it's a bit too thick down'ard, and his knees might be a bit nearer wi'out damage; but he might do worse, he might do worse. Though he hasn't that grand way o' waving his hand as the Squire has."

"Talk o' nimbleness, look at Mrs. Osgood," said Ben Winthrop, who was holding his son Aaron between his knees. "She trips along with her little steps, so as nobody can see how she goes—it's like as if she had little wheels to her feet. She doesn't look a day older nor last year: she's the finest-made woman as is, let the next be where she will."

"I don't heed how the women are made," said Mr. Macey, with some contempt. "They wear nayther coat nor breeches: you can't make much out o' their shapes."

"Fayder," said Aaron, whose feet were busy beating out the tune, "how does that big cock's-feather stick in Mrs. Crackenthorp's head? Is there a little hole for it, like in my shuttle-cock?''

''Hush, lad, hush; that's the way the ladies dress theirselves, that is. said the father, adding, however, in an undertone to Mr. Macey, ''It does make her look funny, though—partly like a short-necked bottle wi' a long quill in it. Hey, by jingo, there's the young Squire leading off now, wi' Miss Nancy for partners! There's a lass for you!—like a pink-and-white posy—there's nobody 'ud think as anybody could be so pritty. I shouldn't wonder if she's Madam Cass some day, arter all—and nobody more rightfuller, for they'd make a fine match. You can find nothing against Master Godfrey's shapes, Macey, I'll bet a penny.''

Mr. Macey screwed up his mouth, leaned his head further on one side, and twirled his thumbs with a presto movement as his eyes followed Godfrey up the dance. At last he summed up his opinion.

''Pretty well down'ard, but a bit too round i' the shoulderblades. And as for them coats as he gets from the Flitton tailor, they're a poor cut to pay double money for.''

''Ah, Mr. Macey, you and me are two folks,'' said Ben, slightly indignant at this carping. ''When I've got a pot o' good ale, I like to swaller it, and do my inside good, i'stead o' smelling and staring at it to see if I can't find fault wi' the brewing. I should like you to pick me out a finer-limbed young fellow nor Master Godfrey—one as 'ud knock you down easier, or's more pleasanter looksed when he s pıert and merry.''

"Tchuh!'' said Mr. Macey, provoked to increased severity, ''he isn't come to his right color yet: he's partly like a slack-baked pie. And I doubt he's got a soft place in his head, else why should he be turned round the finger by that offal Dunsey as nobody's seen o' late, and let him kill that fine hunting hoss as was the talk o' the country? And one while he was allays after Miss Nancy, and then it all went off again, like a smell o' hot porridge, as I may say. That wasn't my way when *I* went a-coorting.''

"Ah, but mayhap Miss Nancy hung off like, and your lass didn't,'' said Ben.

"I should say she didn't,'' said Mr. Macey, significantly. "Before I said 'sniff,' I took care to know as she'd say 'snaff,' and pretty quick too. I wasn't a-going to open *my* mouth, like a dog at a fly, and snap it to again, wi' nothing to swaller.''

"Well, I think Miss Nancy's a-coming round again,'' said Ben, ''for Master Godfrey doesn't look so down-hearted to-night. And I see he's for taking her away to sit down, now they're at the end o' the dance: that looks like sweethearting, that does.''

The reason why Godfrey and Nancy had left the dance was not so tender as Ben imagined. In the close press of couples a slight accident had happened to Nancy's dress, which, while it was short enough to show her neat ankle in front, was long enough behind to be caught under the stately stamp of the

Squire's foot, so as to rend certain stitches at the waist, and cause much sisterly agitation in Priscilla's mind, as well as serious concern in Nancy's. One's thoughts may be much occupied with love-struggles, but hardly so as to be insensible to a disorder in the general framework of things. Nancy had no sooner completed her duty in the figure they were dancing than she said to Godfrey, with a deep blush, that she must go and sit down till Priscilla could come to her; for the sisters had already exchanged a short whisper and an open-eyed glance full of meaning. No reason less urgent than this could have prevailed on Nancy to give Godfrey this opportunity of sitting apart with her. As for Godfrey, he was feeling so happy and oblivious under the long charm of the country-dance with Nancy, that he got rather bold on the strength of her confusion, and was capable of leading her straight away, without leave asked, into the adjoining small parlor, where the card-tables were set.

"Oh no, thank you," said Nancy, coldly, as soon as she perceived where he was going, "not in there. I'll wait here till Priscilla's ready to come to me. I'm sorry to bring you out of the dance and make myself troublesome."

"Why, you'll be more comfortable here by yourself," said the artful Godfrey: "I'll leave you here till your sister can come." He spoke in an indifferent tone.

That was an agreeable proposition, and just what

Nancy desired; why, then, was she a little hurt that
Mr. Godfrey should make it? They entered, and she
seated herself on a chair against one of the card-
tables, as the stiffest and most unapproachable position she could choose.

"Thank you, sir," she said immediately. "I
needn't give you any more trouble. I'm sorry you've
had such an unlucky partner."

"That's very ill-natured of you," said Godfrey,
standing by her without any sign of intended departure, "to be sorry you've danced with me."

"Oh no, sir, I don't mean to say what's ill-natured
at all," said Nancy, looking distractingly prim and
pretty. "When gentlemen have so many pleasures,
one dance can matter but very little."

"You know that isn't true. You know one dance
with you matters more to me than all the other pleasures in the world."

It was a long, long while since Godfrey had said
anything so direct as that, and Nancy was startled.
But her instinctive dignity and repugnance to any
show of emotion made her sit perfectly still, and only
throw a little more decision into her voice, as she
said—

"No, indeed, Mr. Godfrey, that's not known to
me, and I have very good reasons for thinking different. But if it's true, I don't wish to hear it."

"Would you never forgive me, then Nancy—never
think well of me, let what would happen—would you
never think the present made amends for the past?

Not if I turned a good fellow, and gave up everything you didn't like?''

Godfrey was half conscious that this sudden opportunity of speaking to Nancy alone had driven him
beside himself; but blind feeling had got the mastery
of his tongue. Nancy really felt much agitated by
the possibility Godfrey's words suggested, but
this very pressure of emotion that she was in danger
of finding too strong for her roused all her power of
self-command.

"I should be glad to see a good change in anybody,
Mr. Godfrey,'' she answered, with the slightest discernible difference of tone, "but it 'ud be better if
no change was wanted.''

"You're very hard-hearted, Nancy,'' said Godfrey, pettishly. "You might encourage me to be a
better fellow. I'm very miserable—but you've no
feeling.''

"I think those have the least feeling that act wrong
to begin with,'' said Nancy, sending out a flash in
spite of herself. Godfrey was delighted with that
little flash, and would have liked to go on and make
her quarrel with him; Nancy was so exasperatingly
quiet and firm. But she was not indifferent to him
yet.

The entrance of Priscilla, bustling forward and
saying, "Dear heart alive, child, let us look at this
gown,'' cut off Godfrey's hopes of a quarrel.

"I suppose I must go now,'' he said to Priscilla.

"It's no matter to me whether you go or stay,''

said that frank lady, searching for something in her pocket, with a preoccupied brow.

"Do *you* want me to go?" said Godfrey, looking at Nancy, who was now standing up by Priscilla's order.

"As you like," said Nancy, trying to recover all her former coldness, and looking down carefully at the hem of her gown.

"Then I like to stay," said Godfrey, with a reckless determination to get as much of this joy as he could to-night, and think nothing of the morrow.

CHAPTER XII

WHILE Godfrey Cass was taking draughts of forgetfulness from the sweet presence of Nancy, willingly losing all sense of that hidden bond which at other moments galled and fretted him so as to mingle irritation with the very sunshine, Godfrey's wife was walking with slow uncertain steps through the snow-covered Raveloe lanes, carrying her child in her arms.

This journey on New Year's Eve was a premeditated act of vengeance which she had kept in her heart ever since Godfrey, in a fit of passion, had told her he would sooner die than acknowledge her as his wife. There would be a great party at the Red House on New Year's Eve, she knew: her husband would be smiling and smiled upon, hiding *her* existence in the darkest corner of his heart. But she would mar his pleasure: she would go in her dingy rags, with her faded face, once as handsome as the best, with her little child that had its father's hair and eyes, and disclose herself to the Squire as his eldest son's wife. It is seldom that the miserable can help regarding their misery as a wrong inflicted by those who are less miserable. Molly knew that the cause of her dingy rags was not her husband's neglect, but the demon Opium to whom she was enslaved, body and soul, except in the lingering mother's tenderness that refused to give him her hungry child. She knew this well; and yet, in the moments of wretched unbenumbed consciousness, the sense of her want and degradation transformed itself continually into bitterness towards Godfrey. *He* was well off; and if she had her rights she would be well off too. The belief that he repented his marriage, and suffered from it, only aggravated her vindictiveness. Just and self-reproving thoughts do not come to us too thickly, even in the purest air and with the best lessons of heaven and earth; how should those white-winged delicate messengers make their way to Molly's poisoned chamber, inhabited by no higher memories than those of a barmaid's paradise of pink ribbons and gentlemen's jokes?

She had set out at an early hour, but had lingered on the road, inclined by her indolence to believe that if she waited under a warm shed the snow would cease to fall. She had waited longer than she knew, and now that she found herself belated in the snow-hidden ruggedness of the long lanes, even the animation of a vindictive purpose could not keep her spirit from failing. It was seven o'clock, and by this time she was not very far from Raveloe, but she was not familiar enough with those monotonous lanes to know how near she was to her journey's end. She needed comfort, and she knew but one comforter— the familiar demon in her bosom; but she hesitated a moment, after drawing out the black remnant, before she raised it to her lips. In that moment the mother's love pleaded for painful consciousness rather than oblivion—pleaded to be left in aching weariness, rather than to have the encircling arms benumbed so that they could not feel the dear burden. In another moment Molly had flung something away, but it was not the black remnant—it was an empty phial. And she walked on again under the breaking cloud, from which there came now and then the light of a quickly veiled star, for a freezing wind had sprung up since the snowing had ceased. But she walked always more and more drowsily, and clutched more and more automatically the sleeping child at her bosom.

Slowly the demon was working his will, and cold and weariness were his helpers. Soon she felt nothing but a supreme immediate longing that curtained off all futurity—the longing to lie down and sleep. She had arrived at a spot where her footsteps were no longer checked by a hedgerow, and she had wandered vaguely, unable to distinguish any objects, notwithstanding the wide whiteness around her, and the growing starlight. She sank down against a straggling furze bush, an easy pillow enough; and the bed of snow, too, was soft. She did not feel that the bed was cold, and did not heed whether the child would wake and cry for her. But her arms had not yet relaxed their instinctive clutch; and the little one slumbered on as gently as if it had been rocked in a lace-trimmed cradle.

But the complete torpor came at last: the fingers lost their tension, the arms unbent; then the little head fell away from the bosom, and the blue eyes opened wide on the cold starlight. At first there was a little peevish cry of "mammy," and an effort to regain the pillowing arm and bosom; but mammy's ear was deaf, and the pillow seemed to be slipping away backward. Suddenly, as the child rolled downward on its mother's knees, all wet with snow, its eyes were caught by a bright glancing light on the white ground, and, with the ready transition of infancy, it was immediately absorbed in watching the bright living thing running towards it, yet never arriving. That bright living thing must be caught; and in an instant the child had slipped on all fours, and held out one little hand to catch the gleam. But the gleam would not be caught in that way, and now the head was held up to see where the cunning gleam came from. It came from a very bright place; and the little one, rising on its legs, toddled through the snow, the old grimy shawl in which it was wrapped trailing behind it, and the queer little bonnet dangling at its back—toddled on to the open door of Silas Marner's cottage, and right up to the warm hearth, where there was a bright fire of logs and sticks, which had thoroughly warmed the old sack (Silas's greatcoat) spread out on the bricks to dry. The little one, accustomed to be left to itself for long hours without notice from its mother, squatted down on the sack, and spread its tiny hands towards the blaze, in perfect contentment, gurgling and making many inarticulate communications to the cheerful fire, like a new-hatched gosling beginning to find itself comfortable. But presently the warmth had a lulling effect, and the little golden head sank down on the old sack, and the blue eyes were veiled by their delicate half-transparent lids.

But where was Silas Marner while this strange visitor had come to his hearth? He was in the cottage, but he did not see the child. During the last few weeks, since he had lost his money, he had contracted the habit of opening his door and looking out from time to time, as if he thought that his money might be somehow coming back to him, or that some trace, some news of it, might be mysteriously on the road, and be caught by the listening ear or the straining eye. It was chiefly at night, when he was not occupied in his loom, that he fell into this repetition of an act for which he could have assigned no definite purpose, and which can hardly be understood except by those who have undergone a bewildering separation from a supremely loved object. In the evening twilight, and later whenever the night was not dark, Silas looked out on that narrow prospect round the Stone-pits, listening and gazing, not with hope, but with mere yearning and unrest.

This morning he had been told by some of his neighbors that it was New Year's Eve, and that he must sit up and hear the old year rung out and the new rung in, because that was good luck, and

might bring his money back again.[1] This was only
a friendly Raveloe-way of jesting with the half-
crazy oddities of a miser, but it had perhaps helped
to throw Silas into a more than usually excited state.
Since the on-coming of twilight he had opened his
door again and again, though only to shut it immediately at seeing all distance veiled by the falling
snow. But the last time he opened it the snow had
ceased, and the clouds were parting here and there.
He stood and listened, and gazed for a long while—
there was really something on the road coming
towards him then, but he caught no sign of it; and
the stillness and the wide trackless snow seemed to
narrow his solitude, and touched his yearning with
the chill of despair. He went in again, and put his
right hand on the latch of the door to close it—but
he did not close it : he was arrested, as he had been
already since his loss, by the invisible wand of cat-
alepsy, and stood like a graven image, with wide but
sightless eyes, holding open his door, powerless to re-
sist either the good or evil that might enter there.

When Marner's sensibility returned, he continued the action which had been arrested, and closed
his door, unaware of the chasm in his consciousness,
unaware of any intermediate change, except that the
light had grown dim, and that he was chilled and
faint. He thought he had been too long standing at
the door and looking out. Turning towards the
hearth, where the two logs had fallen apart, and sent
forth only a red uncertain glimmer, he seated him-

self on his fireside chair, and was stooping to push his logs together, when, to his blurred vision, it seemed as if there were gold on the floor in front of the hearth. Gold!—his own gold—brought back to him as mysteriously as it had been taken away! He felt his heart begin to beat violently, and for a few moments he was unable to stretch out his hand and grasp the restored treasure. The heap of gold seemed to glow and get larger beneath his agitated gaze. He leaned forward at last, and stretched forth his hand; but instead of the hard coin with the familiar resisting outline, his fingers encountered soft warm curls. In utter amazement, Silas fell on his knees and bent his head low to examine the marvel: it was a sleeping child—a round, fair thing, with soft yellow rings all over its head. Could this be his little sister come back to him in a dream—his little sister whom he had carried about in his arms for a year before she died, when he was a small boy without shoes or stockings? That was the first thought that darted across Silas's blank wonderment. *Was* it a dream? He rose to his feet again, pushed his logs together, and, throwing on some dried leaves and sticks, raised a flame; but the flame did not disperse the vision—it only lit up more distinctly the little round form of the child, and its shabby clothing. It was very much like his little sister. Silas sank into his chair powerless, under the double presence of an inexplicable surprise and a hurrying influx of memories. How and when had the child come in without his knowledge? He had never been beyond the door. But along with that question, and almost thrusting it away, there was a vision of the old home and the old streets leading to Lantern Yard—and within that vision another, of the thoughts which had been present with him in those far-off scenes. The thoughts were strange to him now, like old friendships impossible to revive; and yet he had a dreamy feeling that this child was somehow a message come to him from that far-off life: it stirred fibers that had never been moved in Raveloe—old quiverings of tenderness —old impressions of awe at the presentiment of some Power presiding over his life; for his imagination had not yet extricated itself from the sense of mystery in the child's sudden presence, and had formed no conjectures of ordinary natural means by which the event could have been brought about.

But there was a cry on the hearth: the child had awaked, and Marner stooped to lift it on his knee. It clung round his neck, and burst louder and louder into that mingling of inarticulate cries with "mammy" by which little children express the bewilderment of waking. Silas pressed it to him, and almost unconsciously uttered sounds of hushing tenderness, while he bethought himself that some of his porridge, which had got cool by the dying fire, would do to feed the child with if it were only warmed up a little.

He had plenty to do through the next hour. The porridge, sweetened with some dry brown sugar from an old store which he had refrained from using for himself, stopped the cries of the little one, and made her lift her blue eyes with a wide quiet gaze at Silas, as he put the spoon into her mouth. Presently she slipped from his knee and began to toddle about, but with a pretty stagger that made Silas jump up and follow her lest she should fall against anything that would hurt her. But she only fell in a sitting posture on the ground, and began to pull at her boots, looking up at him with a crying face as if the boots hurt her. He took her on his knee again, but it was some time before it occurred to Silas's dull bachelor mind that the wet boots were the grievance, pressing on her warm ankles. He got them off with difficulty, and baby was at once happily occupied with the primary mystery of her own toes, inviting Silas, with much chuckling, to consider the mystery too. But the wet boots had at last suggested to Silas that the child had been walking on the snow, and this roused him from his entire oblivion of any ordinary means by which it could have entered or been brought into his house. Under the prompting of this new idea, and without waiting to form conjectures, he raised the child in his arms, and went to the door. As soon as he had opened it, there was the cry of "mammy" again, which Silas had not heard since the child's first hungry waking. Bending forward, he could just discern the marks made by the little feet on the virgin snow, and he followed their track to the furze bushes. "Mammy!" the little one cried again and again, stretching itself forward so as almost to escape from Silas's arms, before he himself was aware that there was something more than the bush before him—that there was a human body, with the head sunk low in the furze, and half-covered with the shaken snow.

CHAPTER XIII

It was after the early supper-time at the Red House, and the entertainment was in that stage when bashfulness itself had passed into easy jollity, when gentlemen, conscious of unusual accomplishments, could at length be prevailed on to dance a hornpipe, and when the Squire preferred talking loudly, scattering snuff, and patting his visitor's backs, to sitting longer at the whist-table—a choice exasperating to uncle Kimble, who, being always volatile in sober business hours, became intense and bitter over cards and brandy, shuffled before his adversary's deal with a glare of suspicion, and turned up a mean trump-card with an air of inexpressible disgust, as if in a world where such things could happen one might as well enter on a course of reckless profligacy. When the evening had advanced to this pitch of freedom and enjoyment, it was usual for the servants, the heavy-duties of supper being well over, to get their share of amusement by coming to look on at the dancing; so that the back regions of the house were left in solitude.

There were two doors by which the White Parlor was entered from the hall, and they were both standing open for the sake of air; but the lower one was

crowded [with the servants and villagers, and only
the upper doorway was left free. Bob Cass was fig-
uring in a hornpipe, and his father, very proud of
this lithe son, whom he repeatedly declared to be
just like himself in his young days in a tone that implied this to be the very highest stamp of juvenile
merit, was the center of a group who had placed themselves opposite the performer, not far from the upper
door. Godfrey was standing a little way off, not to
admire his brother's dancing, but to keep sight of
Nancy, who was seated in the group, near her father.
He stood aloof, because he wished to avoid suggesting
himself as a subject for the Squire's fatherly jokes
in connection with matrimony and Miss Nancy Lammeter's beauty, which were likely to become more
and more explicit. But he had the prospect of dancing with her again when the hornpipe was concluded,
and in the meanwhile it was very pleasant to get
long glances at her quite unobserved.

But when Godfrey was lifting his eyes from one
of those long glances, they encountered an object as
startling to him at that moment as if it had been an
apparition from the dead. It *was* an apparition
from that hidden life which lies, like a dark by-street,
behind the goodly ornamented façade that meets the
sunlight and the gaze of respectable admirers. It
was his own child carried in Silas Marner's arms.
That was his instantaneous impression, unaccom-
panied by doubt, though he had not seen the child for
months past; and when the hope was rising that he

might possibly be mistaken, Mr. Crackenthorp and Mr. Lammeter had already advanced to Silas, in astonishment at this strange advent. Godfrey joined them immediately, unable to rest without hearing every word—trying to control himself, but conscious that if any one noticed him, they must see that he was white-lipped and trembling.

But now all eyes at that end of the room were bent on Silas Marner; the Squire himself had risen, and asked angrily. "How's this?—what's this?—what do you do coming in here in this way?"

"I'm come for the doctor—I want the doctor," Silas had said, in the first moment, to Mr. Crackenthorp.

"Why, what's the matter, Marner?" said the Rector. "The doctor's here; but say quietly what you want him for."

"It's a woman," said Silas, speaking low, and half-breathlessly, just as Godfrey came up. "She's dead, I think—dead in the snow at the Stone-pits—not far from my door."

Godfrey felt a great throb: there was one terror in his mind at that moment: it was, that the woman might *not* be dead. That was an evil terror—an ugly inmate to have found a nestling-place in Godfrey's kindly disposition; but no disposition is a security from evil wishes to a man whose happiness hangs on duplicity.

"Hush, hush!" said Mr. Crackenthorp. "Go out

into the hall there. I'll fetch the doctor to you. Found a woman in the snow—and thinks she's dead," he added, speaking low, to the Squire. "Better say as little about it as possible: it will shock the ladies. Just tell them a poor woman is ill from cold and hunger. I'll go and fetch Kimble."

By this time, however, the ladies had pressed forward, curious to know what could have brought the solitary linen-weaver there under such strange circumstances, and interested in the pretty child, who, half alarmed and half attracted by the brightness and the numerous company, now frowned and hid her face, now lifted up her head again and looked round placably, until a touch or a coaxing word brought back the frown, and made her bury her face with new determination.

"What child is it?" said several ladies at once, and, among the rest, Nancy Lammeter, addressing Godfrey.

"I don't know—some poor woman's who has been found in the snow, I believe," was the answer Godfrey wrung from himself with a terrible effort. ("After all, *am* I certain?" he hastened to add, in anticipation of his own conscience.)

"Why, you'd better leave the child here, then, Master Marner," said good-natured Mrs. Kimble, hesitating, however, to take those dingy clothes into contact with her own ornamented satin bodice. "I'll tell one o' the girls to fetch it."

"No—no—I can't part with it, I can't let it go,"
said Silas, abruptly. "It's come to me—I've a right
to keep it."

The proposition to take the child from him had
come to Silas quite unexpectedly, and his speech,
uttered under a strong sudden impulse, was almost
like a revelation to himself: a minute before, he had
no distinct intention about the child.

"Did you ever hear the like?" said Mrs. Kimble,
in mild surprise, to her neighbor.

"Now, ladies, I must trouble you to stand aside,"
said Mr. Kimble, coming from the card-room, in
some bitterness at the interruption, but drilled by
the long habit of his profession into obedience to unpleasant calls, even when he was hardly sober.

"It's a nasty business turning out now, eh, Kimble?" said the Squire. "He might ha' gone for
your young fellow—the 'prentice, there—what's his
name?"

"Might? ay—what's the use of talking about
might?" growled uncle Kimble, hastening out with
Marner, and followed by Mr. Crackenthorp and Godfrey. "Get me a pair of thick boots, Godfrey, will
you? And stay, let somebody run to Winthrop's
and fetch Dolly—she's the best woman to get. Ben
was here himself before supper; is he gone?"

"Yes, sir, I met him," said Marner; "but I
couldn't stop to tell him anything, only I said I was
going for the doctor, and he said the doctor was at
the Squire's. And I made haste and ran, and there

was nobody to be seen at the back o' the house, and so I went in to where the company was."

The child, no longer distracted by the bright light and the smiling women's faces, began to cry and call for "mammy," though always clinging to Marner, who had apparently won her thorough confidence. Godfrey had come back with the boots and felt the cry as if some fiber were drawn tight within him.[1]

"I'll go," he said, hastily, eager for some movement; "I'll go and fetch the woman—Mrs. Winthrop."

"Oh, pooh—send somebody else," said uncle Kimble, hurrying away with Marner.

"You'll let me know if I can be of any use, Kimble," said Mr. Crackenthorp. But the doctor was out of hearing.

Godfrey, too, had disappeared: he was gone to snatch his hat and coat, having just reflection enough to remember that he must not look like a madman; but he rushed out of the house into the snow without heeding his thin shoes.

In a few minutes he was on his rapid way to the Stone-pits by the side of Dolly, who, though feeling that she was entirely in her place in encountering cold and snow on an errand of mercy, was much concerned at a young gentleman's getting his feet wet under a like impulse.

"You'd a deal better go back, sir," said Dolly, with respectful compassion. "You've no call to catch cold; and I'd ask you if you'd be so good as tell my husband to come, on your way back—he's at the Rainbow, I doubt—if you found him anyway sober enough to be o' use. Or else, there's Mrs. Snell 'ud happen send the boy up to fetch and carry, for there may be things wanted from the doctor's."

"No, I'll stay, now I'm once out—I'll stay outside here," said Godfrey, when they came opposite Marner's cottage. "You can come and tell me if I can do anything."

"Well, sir, you're very good: you've a tender heart," said Dolly, going to the door.

Godfrey was too painfully preoccupied to feel a twinge of self-reproach at this undeserved praise. He walked up and down, unconscious that he was plunging ankle-deep in snow, unconscious of everything but trembling suspense about what was going on in the cottage, and the effect of each alternative on his future lot. No, not quite unconscious of everything else. Deeper down, and half-smothered by passionate desire and dread there was the sense that he ought not to be waiting on these alternatives; that he ought to accept the consequences of his deeds, own the miserable wife, and fulfil the claims of the helpless child. But he had not moral courage enough to contemplate that active renunciation of Nancy as possible for him: he had only conscience and heart enough to make him forever uneasy under the weakness that forbade the renunciation. And at this moment his mind leaped away from all restraint towards the sudden prospect of deliverance from his long bondage.

"Is she dead?" said the voice that predominated over every other within him. "If she is, I may marry Nancy; and then I shall be a good fellow in future, and have no secrets, and the child—shall be taken care of somehow." But across that vision came the other possibility—"She may live, and then it's all up with me."

Godfrey never knew how long it was before the door of the cottage opened and Mr. Kimble came out. He went forward to meet his uncle, prepared to suppress the agitation he must feel, whatever news he was to hear.

"I waited for you, as I'd come so far," he said, speaking first.

"Pooh, it was nonsense for you to come out: why didn't you send one of the men? There's nothing to be done. She's dead—has been dead for hours, I should say."

"What sort of woman is she?" said Godfrey, feeling the blood rush to his face.

"A young woman, but emaciated, with long black hair. Some vagrant—quite in rags. She's got a wedding-ring on, however. They must fetch her away to the workhouse to-morrow. Come, come along."

"I want to look at her," said Godfrey. "I think I saw such a woman yesterday. I'll overtake you in a minute or two."

Mr. Kimble went on, and Godfrey turned back to
the cottage. He cast only one glance at the dead
face on the pillow, which Dolly had smoothed with
decent care; but he remembered that last look at his
unhappy hated wife so well, that at the end of sixteen years every line in the worn face was present
to him when he told the full story of this night.

He turned immediately towards the hearth, where
Silas Marner sat lulling the child. She was perfectly
quiet now, but not asleep—only soothed by sweet
porridge and warmth into that wide-gazing calm
which makes us older human beings, with our inward turmoil, feel a certain awe in the presence of a
little child, such as we feel before some quiet majesty
or beauty in the earth or sky—before a steady glowing planet, or a full-flowered eglantine, or the bending trees over a silent pathway. The wide-open blue
eyes looked up at Godfrey's without any uneasiness
or sign of recognition: the child could make no visible
audible claim on its father; and the father felt a
strange mixture of feelings, a conflict of regret and
joy, that the pulse of that little heart had no response
for the half-jealous yearning in his own, when the
blue eyes turned away from him slowly, and fixed
themselves on the weaver's queer face, which was
bent low down to look at them, while the small hand
began to pull Marner's withered cheek with loving
disfiguration.

"You'll take the child to the parish [1] to-morrow?"
asked Godfrey, speaking as indifferently as he could.

"Who says so?" said Marner, sharply. "Will they make me take her?"

"Why, you wouldn't like to keep her, should you —and old bachelor like you?"

"Till anybody shows they've a right to take her away from me," said Marner. "The mother's dead, and I reckon it's got no father: it's a lone thing— and I'm a lone thing. My money's gone, I don't know where—and this is come from I don't know where. I know nothing—I'm partly mazed."

"Poor little thing!" said Godfrey. "Let me give something towards finding it clothes."

He had put his hand in his pocket and found half-a-guinea, and, thrusting it into Silas's hand, he hurried out of the cottage to overtake Mr. Kimble.

"Ah, I see it's not the same woman I saw," he said, as he came up. "It's a pretty little child: the old fellow seems to want to keep it; that's strange for a miser like him. But I gave him a trifle to help him out: the parish isn't likely to quarrel with him for the right to keep the child."

"No; but I've seen the time when I might have quarreled with him for it myself. It's too late now, though. If the child ran into the fire, your aunt's too fat to overtake it: she could only sit and grunt like an alarmed sow. But what a fool you are, Godfrey, to come out in your dancing shoes and stockings in this way—and you one of the beaux of the evening and at your own house! What do you mean by such freaks, young fellow? Has Miss Nancy been cruel, and do you want to spite her by spoiling your pumps?''

"Oh, everything has been disagreeable to-night. I was tired to death of jigging and gallanting, and that bother about the hornpipes. And I'd got to dance with the other Miss Gunn," said Godfrey, glad of the subterfuge his uncle had suggested to him.

The prevarication and white lies which a mind that keeps itself ambitiously pure is as uneasy under as a great artist under the false touches that no eye detects but his own, are worn as lightly as mere trimmings when once the actions have become a lie.

Godfrey reappeared in the White Parlor with dry feet, and, since the truth must be told, with a sense of relief and gladness that was too strong for painful thoughts to struggle with. For could he not venture now, whenever opportunity offered, to say the tenderest things to Nancy Lammeter—to promise her and himself that he would always be just what she would desire to see him? There was no danger that his dead wife would be recognized: those were not days of active inquiry and wide report; and as for the registry of their marriage, that was a long way off, buried in unturned pages, away from every one's interest but his own. Dunsey might betray him if he came back; but Dunsey might be won to silence.

And when events turn out so much better for a man than he has had reason to dread, is it not a proof that his conduct has been less foolish and

blameworthy than it might otherwise have appeared?
When we are treated well, we naturally begin to
think that we are not altogether unmeritorious, and
that it is only just we should treat ourselves well,
and not mar our own good fortune. Where, after
all, would be the use of his confessing the past to
Nancy Lammeter, and throwing away his happiness?
—nay, hers? for he felt some confidence that she
loved him. As for the child, he would see that it
was cared for: he would never forsake it; he would
do everything but own it. Perhaps it would be just
as happy in life without being owned by its father,
seeing that nobody could tell how things would turn
out, and that—is there any other reason wanted?—
well, then, that the father would be much happier
without owning the child.

CHAPTER XIV

THERE was a pauper's burial that week in Raveloe, and up Kench Yard at Batherly it was known
that the dark-haired woman with the fair child, who
had lately come to lodge there, was gone away again.
That was all the express note taken that Molly had
disappeared from the eyes of men. But the unwept
death which, to the general lot, seemed as trivial as
the summer-shed leaf, was charged with the force of
destiny to certain human lives that we know of,
shaping their joys and sorrows even to the end.

Silas Marner's determination to keep the "tramp's
child" was matter of hardly less surprise and iterated
talk in the village than the robbery of his money.
That softening of feeling towards him which dated
from his misfortune, that merging of suspicion and
dislike in a rather contemptuous pity for him as
lone and crazy, was now accompanied with a more
active sympathy, especially among the women. Notable mothers, who knew what it was to keep children
"whole and sweet;" lazy mothers, who knew what it
was to be interrupted in folding their arms and
scratching their elbows by the mischievous propen-
sities of children just firm on their legs, were equally
interested in conjecturing how a lone man would

218

manage with a two-year-old child on his hands, and were equally ready with their suggestions; the notable chiefly telling him what he had better do, and the lazy ones being emphatic in telling him what he would never be able to do.

Among the notable mothers, Dolly Winthrop was the one whose neighborly offices were the most acceptable to Marner, for they were rendered without any show of bustling instruction. Silas had shown her the half-guinea given to him by Godfrey, and had asked her what he should do about getting some clothes for the child.

"Eh, Master Marner," said Dolly, "there's no call to buy, no more nor a pair o' shoes; for I've got the little petticoats as Aaron wore five years ago, and it's ill spending the money on them baby-clothes, for the child 'ull grow like grass i' May, bless it—that it will."

And the same day Dolly brought her bundle, and displayed to Marner, one by one, the tiny garments in their due order of succession, most of them patched and darned, but clean and neat as fresh-sprung herbs. This was the introduction to a great ceremony with soap and water, from which Baby came out in new beauty, and sat on Dolly's knee, handling her toes and chuckling and patting her palms together with an air of having made several discoveries about herself, which she communicated by alternate sounds of "gug-gug-gug," and "mammy." The "mammy" was not a cry of need or uneasiness: Baby had been used to utter it without expecting either tender sound or touch to follow.

"Anybody 'ud think the angils in heaven couldn't be prettier," said Dolly, rubbing the golden curls and kissing them. "And to think of its being covered wi' them dirty rags—and the poor mother froze to death; but there's Them as took care of it, and brought it to your door, Master Marner. The door was open, and it walked in over the snow, like as if it had been a little starved robin. Didn't you say the door was open?"

"Yes," said Silas, meditatively. "Yes—the door was open. The money's gone I don't know where, and this is come from I don't know where."

He had not mentioned to any one his unconsciousness of the child's entrance, shrinking from questions which might lead to the fact he himself suspected —namely, that he had been in one of his trances.

"Ah," said Dolly, with soothing gravity, "it's like the night and the morning, and the sleeping and the waking, and the rain and the harvest—one goes and the other comes, and we know nothing how nor where. We may strive and scrat and fend,[1] but it's little we can do arter all—the big things come and go wi' no striving o' our'n—they do, that they do; and I think you're in the right on it to keep the little un, Master Marner, seeing as it's been sent to you, though there's folks as thinks different. You'll happen to be a bit moithered [1] with it while it's so little; but I'll come, and welcome, and see to it for you: I've a bit o' time to spare most days, for when one gets up betimes i' the morning the clock seems to stan' still tow'r ten, afore it's time to go about the victual. So, as I say, I'll come and see to the child for you, and welcome."

"Thank you—kindly," said Silas, hesitating a little. "I'll be glad if you'll tell me things. But," he added uneasily, leaning forward to look at Baby with some jealousy, as she was resting her head backward against Dolly's arm, and eying him contentedly from a distance—"but I want to do things for it myself, else it may get fond o' somebody else, and not fond o' me. I've been used to fending for myself in the house—I can learn, I can learn."

"Eh, to be sure," said Dolly, gently. "I've seen men as are wonderful handy wi' children. The men are awk'ard and contrairy mostly, God help 'em— but when the drink's out of 'em, they aren't unsensible, though they're bad for leeching [1] and bandaging—so fiery and unpatient. You see this goes first, next the skin," proceeded Dolly, taking up the little shirt, and putting it on.

"Yes," said Marner, docilely, bringing his eyes very close. that they might be initiated in the mysteries; whereupon Baby seized his head with both her small arms, and put her lips against his face with purring noises.

"See there," said Dolly, with a woman's tender tact, "she's fondest o' you. She wants to go o' your lap, I'll be bound. Go, then; take her, Master

Marner; you can put the things on, and then you
can say as you've done for her from the first of her
coming to you.''

Marner took her on his lap, trembling with an
emotion mysterious to himself, at something unknown dawning on his life. Thought and feeling
were so confused within him, that if he had tried to
give them utterance, he could only have said that
the child was come instead of the gold—that the
gold had turned into the child. He took the garments from Dolly, and put them on under her
teaching interrupted, of course, by Baby's gymnas-
tics.

''There, then! why, you take to it quite easy, Master Marner,'' said Dolly; ''but what shall you do
when you're forced to sit in your loom? For she'll
get busier and mischievouser every day—she will,
bless her. It's lucky as you've got that high hearth
i'stead of a grate, for that keeps the fire more out
of her reach: but if you've got anything as can be
split or broke, or as is fit to cut her fingers off, she'll
be at it—and it is but right you should know.''

Silas meditated a little while in some perplexity.
''I'll tie her to the leg o' the loom,'' he said at last
—''tie her with a good long strip o' something.''

''Well, mayhap that'll do, as it's a little gell, for
they're easier persuaded to sit i' one place nor the
lads. I know what the lads are; for I've had four
—four I've had, God knows—and if you was to take
and tie 'em up, they'd make a fighting and a crying

as if you was ringing the pigs. But I'll bring you my little chair, and some bits o' red rag and things for her to play wi'; and she'll sit and chatter to 'em as if they was alive. Eh, if it wasn't a sin to the lads to wish 'em made different, bless 'em, I should ha' been glad for one of 'em to be a little gell; and to think as I could ha' taught her to scour, and mend, and the knitting, and everything. But I can teach 'em this little un, Master Marner, when she gets old enough.''

''But she'll be *my* little un,'' said Marner, rather hastily. ''She'll be nobody else's.''

''No, to be sure; you'll have a right to her, if you're a father to her, and bring her up according. But,'' added Dolly, coming to a point which she had determined beforehand to touch upon, ''you must bring her up like christened folks's children, and take her to church, and let her learn her catechise, as my little Aaron can say off—the 'I believe,' and everything, and 'hurt nobody by word or deed,'— as well as if he was the clerk. That's what you must do, Master Marner, if you'd do the right thing by the orphin child.''

Marner's pale face flushed suddenly under a new anxiety. His mind was too busy trying to give some definite bearing to Dolly's words for him to think of answering her.

''And it's my belief,'' she went on, ''as the poor little creature has never been christened, and it's nothing but right as the parson should be spoke to;

and if you was noways unwilling, I'd talk to Mr.
Macey about it this very day. For if the child ever
went anyways wrong, and you hadn't done your
part by it, Master Marner—'noculation,[1] and everything to save it from harm— it 'ud be a thorn i'
your bed forever o' this side the grave; and I can't
think as it 'ud be easy lying down for anybody when
they'd got to another world, if they hadn't done
their part by the helpless children as come wi'out
their own asking.''

Dolly herself was disposed to be silent for some
time now, for she had spoken from the depths of her
own simple belief, and was much concerned to know
whether her words would produce the desired effect
on Silas. He was puzzled and anxious, for Dolly's
word ''christened'' conveyed no distinct meaning to
him. He had only heard of baptism, and had only
seen the baptism of grown-up men and women.

''What is it as you mean by 'christened'?'' he said
at last, timidly. ''Won't folks be good to her without it?''

''Dear, dear! Master Marner,'' said Dolly, with
gentle distress and compassion. ''Had you never no
father nor mother as taught you to say your prayers,
and as there's good words and good things to keep us
from harm?''

''Yes,'' said Silas, in a low voice; ''I know a deal
about that—used to, used to. But your ways are
different: my country was a good way off.'' He
paused a few moments, and then added, more de-

cidedly, "But I want to do everything as can be done for the child. And whatever's right for it i' this country, and you think 'll do it good, I'll act according, if you'll tell me."

"Well, then, Master Marner," said Dolly inwardly rejoiced, "I'll ask Mr. Macey to speak to the parson about it; and you must fix on a name for it, because it must have a name giv' it when it's christened."

"My mother's name was Hephzibah," said Silas, "and my little sister was named after her."

"Eh, that's a hard name," said Dolly. "I partly think it isn't a christened name."

"It's a Bible name," said Silas, old ideas recurring.

"Then I've no call to speak again' it," said Dolly, rather startled by Silas's knowledge on this head; "but you see I'm no scholard, and I'm slow at catching the words. My husband says I'm allays like as if I was putting the haft for the handle—that's what he says—for he's very sharp. God help him. But it was awk'ard calling your little sister by such a hard name, when you'd got nothing big to say, like—wasn't it, Master Marner?"

"We called her Eppie," said Silas.

"Well, if it was noways wrong to shorten the name, it 'ud be a deal handier. And so I'll go now, Master Marner, and I'll speak about the christening afore dark; and I wish you the best o' luck, and it's my belief as it'll come to you, if you do what's right by the orphin child;—and there's the 'nocula-

tion to be seen to; and as to washing its bits o'
things, you need look to nobody but me, for I can do
'em wi' one hand when I've got my suds about.
Eh, the blessed angil! You'll let me bring my Aaron
one o' these days, and he'll show her his little cart
as his father's made for him, and the black-and-
white pup as he's got a-rearing.''

Baby *was* christened, the Rector deciding that a
double baptism was the lesser risk to incur; and on
this occasion Silas, making himself as clean and tidy
as he could, appeared for the first time within the
church, and shared in the observances held sacred
by his neighbors. He was quite unable, by means
of anything he heard or saw, to identify the Raveloe
religion with his old faith; if he could at any time
in his previous life have done so, it must have been
by the aid of a strong feeling ready to vibrate with
sympathy, rather than by a comparison of phrases
and ideas: and now for long years that feeling had
been dormant. He had no distinct idea about the
baptism and the church-going, except that Dolly had
said it was for the good of the child; and in this way,
as the weeks grew to months, the child created fresh
and fresh links between his life and the lives from
which he had hitherto shrunk continually into narrower isolation. Unlike the gold which needed nothing, and must be worshiped in close-locked solitude
—which was hidden away from the daylight, was
deaf to the song of birds, and started to no human
tones—Eppie was a creature of endless claims and

ever-growing desires, seeking and loving sunshine,
and living sounds, and living movements; making
trial of everything, with trust in new joy, and stirring
the human kindness in all eyes that looked on her.
The gold had kept his thoughts in an ever-repeated
circle, leading to nothing beyond itself; but Eppie
was an object compacted of changes and hopes that
forced his thoughts onward, and carried them far
away from their old eager pacing towards the same
blank limit—carried them away to the new things
that would come with the coming years, when Eppie
would have learned to understand how her father
Silas cared for her; and made him look for images
of that time in the ties and charities that bound
together the families of his neighbors. The gold
had asked that he should sit weaving longer and
longer, deafened and blinded more and more to all
things except the monotony of his loom and the
repetition of his web; but Eppie called him away
from his weaving, and made him think all its pauses
a holiday, reawakening his senses with her fresh life,
even to the old winter-flies that came crawling forth
in the early spring sunshine, and warming him into
joy because *she* had joy.

And when the sunshine grew strong and lasting,
so that the buttercups were thick in the meadows,
Silas might be seen in the sunny mid-day, or in the
late afternoon when the shadows were lengthening
under the hedgerows, strolling out with uncovered
head to carry Eppie beyond the Stone-pits to where

the flowers grew, till they reached some favorite bank where he could sit down, while Eppie toddled to pluck the flowers, and make remarks to the winged things that murmured happily above the bright petals, calling "Dad-dad's" attention continually by bringing him the flowers. Then she would turn her ear to some sudden bird-note, and Silas learned to please her by making signs of hushed stillness, that they might listen for the note to come again: so that when it came, she set up her small back and laughed with gurgling triumph. Sitting on the banks in this way, Silas began to look for the once familiar herbs again; and as the leaves, with their unchanged outline and markings, lay on his palm, there was a sense of crowding remembrances from which he turned away timidly, taking refuge in Eppie's little world, that lay lightly on his enfeebled spirit.

As the child's mind was growing into knowledge, his mind was growing into memory: as her life unfolded, his soul, long stupefied in a cold narrow prison, was unfolding too, and trembling gradually into full consciousness.

It was an influence which must gather force with every new year: the tones that stirred Silas's heart grew articulate, and called for more distinct answers; shapes and sounds grew clearer for Eppie's eyes and ears, and there was more that "Dad-dad" was imperatively required to notice and account for. Also, by the time Eppie was three years old, she developed a fine capacity for mischief, and for de-

vising ingenious ways of being troublesome, which
found much exercise, not only for Silas's patience,
but for his watchfulness and penetration. Sorely
was poor Silas puzzled on such occasions by the in-
compatible demands of love. Dolly Winthrop told
him that punishment was good for Eppie, and that,
as for rearing a child without making it tingle a little
in soft and safe places now and then, it was not to
be done.

"To be sure, there's another thing you might do,
Master Marner," added Dolly meditatively: "you
might shut her up once i' the coal-hole. That was
what I did wi' Aaron; for I was that silly wi' the
youngest lad, as I could never bear to smack him.
Not as I could find i' in my heart to let him stay
i' the coal-hole more nor a minute, but it was enough
to colly him all over, so as he must be new washed
and dressed, and it was as good as a rod to him—
that was. But I put it upo' your conscience, Master
Marner, as there's one of 'em you must choose—
ayther smacking or the coal-hole—else she'll get so
masterful, there'll be no holding her."

Silas was impressed with the melancholy truth of
this last remark; but his force of mind failed before
the only two penal methods open to him, not only
because it was painful to him to hurt Eppie, but
because he trembled at a moment's contention with
her, lest she should love him the less for it. Let
even an affectionate Goliath get himself tied to a small
tender thing, dreading to hurt it by pulling, and

dreading still more to snap the cord, and which of
the two, pray, will be master? It was clear that
Eppie, with her short toddling steps, must lead
father Silas a pretty dance on any fine morning when
circumstances favored mischief.

For example. He had wisely chosen a broad strip
of linen as a means of fastening her to his loom
when he was busy: it made a broad belt round her
waist, and was long enough to allow of her reaching
the truckle-bed and sitting down on it, but not long
enough for her to attempt any dangerous climbing.
One bright summer's morning Silas had been more
engrossed than usual in "setting up" a new piece of
work, an occasion on which his scissors were in
requisition. These scissors, owing to an especial warning of Dolly's had been kept carefully out of Eppie's
reach; but the click of them had had a peculiar
attraction for her ear, and watching the results of
that click, she had derived the philosophic lesson
that the same cause would produce the same effect.
Silas had seated himself in his loom, and the noise
of weaving had begun; but he had left his scissors
on a ledge which Eppie's arm was long enough to
reach; and now, like a small mouse, watching her
opportunity, she stole quietly from her corner, secured
the scissors, and toddled to the bed again, setting up
her back as a mode of concealing the fact. She had
a distinct intention as to the use of the scissors; and
having cut the linen strip in a jagged but effectual
manner, in two moments she had run out at the open

door where the sunshine was inviting her, while poor
Silas believed her to be a better child than usual.
It was not until he happened to need his scissors
that the terrible fact burst upon him: Eppie had
run out by herself—had perhaps fallen into the
Stone-pit. Silas, shaken by the worst fear that could
have befallen him, rushed out, calling "Eppie!" and
ran eagerly about the unenclosed space, exploring
the dry cavities into which she might have fallen,
and then gazing with questioning dread at the smooth
red surface of the water. The cold drops stood on
his brow. How long had she been out? There was
one hope—that she had crept through the stile and
got into the fields, where he habitually took her to
stroll. But the grass was high in the meadow, and
there was no descrying her, if she were there, except
by a close search that would be a trespass on Mr.
Osgood's crop. Still, that misdemeanor must be committed; and poor Silas, after peering all round the
hedgerows, traversed the grass, beginning with per-
turbed vision to see Eppie behind every group of red
sorrel, and to see her moving always farther off as
he approached. The meadow was searched in vain;
and he got over the stile into the next field, looking
with dying hope towards a small pond which was
now reduced to its summer shallowness, so as to leave
a wide margin of good adhesive mud. Here, however, sat Eppie, discoursing cheerfully to her own
small boot, which she was using as a bucket to con-
vey the water into a deep hoof-mark, while her little

naked foot was planted comfortably on a cushion of
olive-green mud. A red-headed calf was observing
her with alarmed doubt through the opposite hedge.

Here was clearly a case of aberration [1] in a christened child which demanded severe treatment; but
Silas, overcome with convulsive joy at finding his
treasure again, could do nothing but snatch her up,
and cover her with half-sobbing kisses. It was not
until he had carried her home, and had begun to
think of the necessary washing, that he recollected
the need that he should punish Eppie, and "make
her remember." The idea that she might run away
again and come to harm, gave him unusual resolution, and for the first time he determined to try the
coal-hole—a small closet near the hearth.

"Naughty, naughty Eppie," he suddenly began,
holding her on his knee, and pointing to her muddy
feet and clothes—"naughty to cut with the scissors
and run away. Eppie must go into the coal-hole
for being naughty. Daddy must put her in the coal-
hole."

He half expected that this would be shock enough,
and that Eppie would begin to cry. But instead
of that, she began to shake herself on his knee, as if
the proposition opened a pleasing novelty. Seeing
that he must proceed to extremities, he put her into
the coal-hole, and held the door closed, with a trembling sense that he was using a strong measure.
For a moment there was silence, but then came a
little cry, "Opy, opy!" and Silas let her out again,

saying, "Now Eppie 'ull never be naughty again, else she must go in the coal-hole—a black naughty place."

The weaving must stand still a long while this morning, for now Eppie must be washed, and have clean clothes on; but it was to be hoped that this punishment would have a lasting effect, and save time in future—though, perhaps, it would have been better if Eppie had cried more.

In half an hour she was clean again, and Silas having turned his back to see what he could do with the linen band, threw it down again, with the reflection that Eppie would be good without fastening for the rest of the morning. He turned round again, and was going to place her in her little chair near the loom, when she peeped out at him with black face and hands again, and said, "Eppie in de toal-hole!"

This total failure of the coal-hole discipline shook Silas's belief in the efficacy of punishment. "She'd take it all for fun," he observed to Dolly, "if I didn't hurt her, and that I can't do, Mrs. Winthrop. If she makes me a bit o' trouble, I can bear it. And she's got no tricks but what she'll grow out of."

"Well, that's partly true, Master Marner," said Dolly, sympathetically; "and if you can't bring your mind to frighten her off touching things, you must do what you can to keep 'em out o' her way. That's what I do wi' the pups as the lads are allays a-rearing. They *will* worry and gnaw—worry and gnaw they will, if it was one's Sunday cap as hung anywhere so as they could drag it. They know no difference, God help 'em: it's the pushing o' the teeth as sets 'em on, that's what it is.''

So Eppie was reared without punishment, the burden of her misdeeds being borne vicariously[1] by father Silas. The stone hut was made a soft nest for her, lined with downy patience: and also in the world that lay beyond the stone hut she knew nothing of frowns and denials.

Notwithstanding the difficulty of carrying her and his yarn or linen at the same time, Silas took her with him in most of his journeys to the farm-houses, unwilling to leave her behind at Dolly Winthrop's, who was always ready to take care of her; and little curly-headed Eppie, the weaver's child, became an object of interest at several outlying homesteads, as well as in the village. Hitherto he had been treated very much as if he had been a useful gnome or brownie—a queer and unaccountable creature, who must necessarily be looked at with wondering curiosity and repulsion, and with whom one would be glad to make all greetings and bargains as brief as possible, but who must be dealt with in a propitiatory way, and occasionally have a present of pork or garden stuff to carry home with him, seeing that without him there was no getting the yarn woven. But now Silas met with open smiling faces and cheerful questioning, as a person whose satisfactions and difficulties could be understood. Everywhere he

must sit a little and talk about the child, and words
of interest were always ready for him: "Ah, Master
Marner, you'll be lucky if she takes the measles soon
and easy!"—or, "Why, there isn't many lone men
'ud ha' been wishing to take up with a little un like
that: but I reckon the weaving makes you handier
than men as do out-door work—you're partly as
handy as a woman, for weaving comes next to spinning." Elderly masters and mistresses, seated ob-
servantly in large kitchen arm-chairs, shook their
heads over the difficulties attendant on rearing children, felt Eppie's round arms and legs, and pronounced them remarkably firm, and told Silas, that,
if she turned out well (which, however, there was
no telling), it would be a fine thing for him to have
a steady lass to do for him when he got helpless.
Servant maidens were fond of carrying her out to
look at the hens and chickens, or to see if any cherries
could be shaken down in the orchard; and the small
boys and girls approached her slowly, with cautious
movement and steady gaze, like little dogs face to
face with one of their own kind, till attraction had
reached the point at which the soft lips were put out
for a kiss. No child was afraid of approaching
Silas when Eppie was near him: there was no repulsion around him now, either for young or old;
for the little child had come to link him once more
with the whole world. There was love between him
and the child that blent them into one, and there was
love between the child and the world—from men

and women with parental looks and tones, to the
red lady-birds and the round pebbles.

Silas began now to think of Raveloe life entirely
in relation to Eppie: she must have everything that
was a good in Raveloe; and he listened docilely, that
he might come to understand better what this life
was, from which, for fifteen years, he had stood aloof
as from a strange thing, wherewith he could have
no communion: as some man who has a precious plant
to which he would give a nurturing home in a new
soil, thinks of the rain, and the sunshine, and all
influences, in relation to his nursling, and asks in-
dustriously for all knowledge that will help him to
satisfy the wants of the searching roots, or to guard
leaf and bud from invading harm. The disposition
to hoard had been utterly crushed at the very first
by the loss of his long-stored gold: the coins he earned
afterwards seemed as irrelevant as stones brought to
complete a house suddenly buried by an earthquake;
the sense of bereavement was too heavy upon him
for the old thrill of satisfaction to arise again at the
touch of the newly-earned coin. And now something
had come to replace his hoard which gave a growing
purpose to the earnings, drawing his hope and joy
continually onward beyond the money.

In old days there were angels who came and took
men by the hand and led them away from the city
of destruction. We see no white-winged angels now.
But yet men are led away from threatening destruc-

tion: a hand is put into theirs, which leads them forth gently towards a calm and bright land, so that they look no more backward; and the hand may be a little child's.

CHAPTER XV

THERE was one person, as you will believe, who watched with keener though more hidden interest than any other, the prosperous growth of Eppie under the weaver's care. He dared not do anything that would imply a stronger interest in a poor man's adopted child than could be expected from the kindliness of the young Squire, when a chance meeting suggested a little present to a simple old fellow whom others noticed with goodwill; but he told himself that the time would come when he might do something towards furthering the welfare of his daughter without incurring suspicion. Was he very uneasy in the meantime at his inability to give his daughter her birthright? I cannot say that he was. The child was being taken care of, and would very likely be happy, as people in humble stations often were—happier, perhaps, than those brought up in luxury.

That famous ring[1] that pricked its owner when he forgot duty and followed desire—I wonder if it pricked very hard when he set out on the chase, or whether it pricked but lightly then, and only pierced to the quick when the chase had long been ended, and hope, folding her wings, looked backward and became regret?

Godfrey Cass's cheek and eye were brighter than ever now. He was so undivided in his aims, that he seemed like a man of firmness. No Dunsey had come back: people had made up their minds that he was gone for a soldier, or gone "out of the country," and no one cared to be specific in their inquiries on a subject delicate to a respectable family. Godfrey had ceased to see the shadow of Dunsey across his path; and the path now lay straight forward to the accomplishment of his best, longest-cherished wishes. Everybody said Mr. Godfrey had taken the right turn; and it was pretty clear what would be the end of things, for there were not many days in the week that he was not seen riding to the Warrens. Godfrey himself, when he was asked jocosely if the day had been fixed, smiled with the pleasant consciousness of a lover who could say "yes," if he liked. He felt a reformed man, delivered from temptation; and the vision of his future life seemed to him as a promised land for which he had no cause to fight. He saw himself with all his happiness centered on his own hearth, while Nancy would smile on him as he played with the children.

And that other child, not on the hearth—he would not forget it; he would see that it was well provided for. That was a father's duty.[1]

PART II

CHAPTER XVI

It was a bright autumn Sunday, sixteen years after Silas Marner had found his new treasure on the hearth. The bells of the old Raveloe church were ringing the cheerful peal which told that the morning service was ended; and out of the arched doorway in the tower came slowly, retarded by friendly greetings and questions, the richer parishioners who had chosen this bright Sunday morning as eligible [1] for church-going. It was the rural fashion of that time for the more important members of the congregation to depart first, while their humbler neighbors waited and looked on, stroking their bent heads or dropping their curtsies to any large ratepayer [2] who turned to notice them.

Foremost among these advancing groups of well-clad people, there are some whom we shall recognize, in spite of Time, who has laid his hand on them all. The tall blond man of forty is not much changed in feature from the Godfrey Cass of six-and-twenty: he is only fuller in flesh, and has only lost the indefinable look of youth—a loss which is marked even when the eye is undulled and the wrinkles are not yet come.

241

Perhaps the pretty woman, not much younger than he, who is leaning on his arm, is more changed than her husband: the lovely bloom that used to be always on her cheek now comes but fitfully, with the fresh morning air or with some strong surprise; yet to all who love human faces best for what they tell of human experience, Nancy's beauty has a heightened interest. Often the soul is ripened into fuller goodness while age has spread an ugly film, so that mere glances can never divine the preciousness of the fruit. But the years have not been so cruel to Nancy. The firm yet placid mouth, the clear veracious glance of the brown eyes, speak now of a nature that has been tested and has kept its highest qualities; and even the costume, with its dainty neatness and purity, has more significance now the coquetries of youth can have nothing to do with it.

Mr. and Mrs. Godfrey Cass (any higher title has died away from Raveloe lips, since the old Squire was gathered to his fathers and his inheritance was divided) have turned round to look for the tall aged man and the plainly dressed woman who are a little behind—Nancy having observed that they must wait for "father and Priscilla"—and now they all turn into a narrower path leading across the churchyard to a small gate opposite the Red House. We will not follow them now; for may there not be some others in this departing congregation whom we should like to see again—some of those who are not likely to be handsomely clad, and whom we may not recog-

nize so easily as the master and mistress of the Red
House?

But it is impossible to mistake Silas Marner. His
large brown eyes seem to have gathered a longer
vision, as is the way with eyes that have been short-
sighted in early life, and they have a less vague, a
more answering gaze; but in everything else one
sees signs of a frame much enfeebled by the lapse of
the sixteen years. The weaver's bent shoulders and
white hair give him almost the look of advanced age,
though he is not more than five-and-fifty; but there is
the freshest blossom of youth close by his side—a
blond dimpled girl of eighteen, who has vainly tried
to chastise her curly auburn hair into smoothness
under her brown bonnet: the hair ripples as obsti-
nately as a brooklet under the March breeze, and the
little ringlets burst away from the restraining comb
behind and show themselves below the bonnet-crown.
Eppie cannot help being rather vexed about her hair,
for there is no other girl in Raveloe who has hair at
all like it, and she thinks hair ought to be smooth.
She does not like to be blameworthy even in small
things: you see how neatly her prayer-book is folded
in her spotted handkerchief.

That good-looking young fellow, in a new fustian
suit, who walks behind her, is not quite sure upon the
question of hair in the abstract, when Eppie puts it
to him, and thinks that perhaps straight hair is the
best in general, but he doesn't want Eppie's hair to
be different. She surely divines that there is some

one behind her who is thinking about her very particularly, and mustering courage to come to her side as soon as they are out in the lane, else why should she look rather shy, and take care not to turn away her head from her father Silas, to whom she keeps murmuring little sentences as to who was at church, and who was not at church, and how pretty the red mountain-ash is over the Rectory wall!

"I wish *we* had a little garden, father, with double daisies in, like Mrs. Winthrop's," said Eppie, when they were out in the lane; "only they say it 'ud take a deal of digging and bringing fresh soil—and you couldn't do that, could you, father? Anyhow, I shouldn't like you to do it, for it 'ud be too hard work for you."

"Yes, I could do it, child, if you want a bit o' garden: these long evenings, I could work at taking in a little bit o' the waste, just enough for a root or two o' flowers for you; and again, i' the morning, I could have a turn wi' the spade before I sat down to the loom. Why didn't you tell me before as you wanted a bit o' garden?"

"*I* can dig it for you, Master Marner," said the young man in fustian, who was now by Eppie's side, entering into the conversation without the trouble of formalities. "It'll be play to me after I've done my day's work, or any odd bits o' time when the work's slack. And I'll bring you some soil from Mr. Cass's garden—he'll let me, and willing."

"Eh, Aaron, my lad, are you there?" said Silas;

"I wasn't aware of you; for when Eppie's talking o' things, I see nothing but what she's a-saying. Well, if you could help me with the digging, we might get her a bit o' garden all the sooner."

"Then, if you think well and good," said Aaron, "I'll come to the Stone-pits this afternoon, and we'll settle what land's to be taken in, and I'll get up an hour earlier i' the morning, and begin on it."

"But not if you don't promise me not to work at the hard digging, father," said Eppie. "For I shouldn't ha' said anything about it," she added, half-bashfully half-roguishly, "only Mrs. Winthrop said as Aaron 'ud be so good, and—"

"And you might ha' known it without mother telling you," said Aaron. "And Master Marner knows too, I hope, as I'm able and willing to do a turn o' work for him, and he won't do me the unkindness to anyways take it out o' my hands."

"There, now, father, you won't work in it till it's all easy," said Eppie, "and you and me can mark out the beds, and make holes and plant the roots. It'll be a deal livelier at the Stone-pits when we've got some flowers, for I always think the flowers can see us and know what we're talking about. And I'll have a bit o' rosemary, and bergamot, and thyme, because they're so sweet-smelling; but there's no lavender only in the gentlefolks' gardens, I think."

"That's no reason why you shouldn't have some," said Aaron, "for I can bring you slips of anything; I'm forced to cut no end of 'em when I'm gardening, and throw 'em away mostly. There's a big bed o' lavender at the Red House: the missis is very fond of it.''

''Well,'' said Silas, gravely, ''so as you don't make free for us, or ask for anything as is worth much at the Red House: for Mr. Cass's been so good to us, and built us up the new end o' the cottage, and given us beds and things, as I couldn't abide to be imposin' for garden-stuff or anything else.''

''No, no, there's no imposin','' said Aaron; ''there's never a garden in all the parish but what there's endless waste in it for want o' somebody as could use everything up. It's what I think to myself sometimes, as there need nobody run short o' victuals if the land was made the most on, and there was never a morsel but what could find its way to a mouth. It sets one thinking o' that—gardening does. But I must go back now, else mother 'ull be in trouble as I aren't there.''

''Bring her with you this afternoon, Aaron,'' said Eppie; ''I shouldn't like to fix about the garden, and her not know everything from the first— should *you*, father?''

''Ay, bring her if you can, Aaron,'' said Silas; ''she's sure to have a word to say as 'll help us to set things on their right end.''

Aaron turned back up the village, while Silas and Eppie went on up the lonely sheltered lane.

''Oh, daddy!'' she began, when they were in privacy, clasping and squeezing Silas's arm, and skipping round to give him an energetic kiss. "My little old daddy! I'm so glad. I don't think I shall want anything else when we've got a little garden; and I knew Aaron would dig it for us," she went on with roguish triumph—"I knew that very well."

"You're a deep little puss, you are," said Silas, with the mild passive happiness of love-crowned age in his face; "but you'll make yourself fine and beholden to Aaron."

"Oh no, I shan't," said Eppie, laughing and frisking; "he likes it."

"Come, come, let me carry your prayer-book, else you'll be dropping it, jumping i' that way."

Eppie was now aware that her behavior was under observation, but it was only the observation of a friendly donkey, browsing with a log fastened to his foot—a meek donkey, not scornfully critical of human trivialities, but thankful to share in them, if possible, by getting his nose scratched; and Eppie did not fail to gratify him with her usual notice, though it was attended with the inconvenience of his following them, painfully, up to the very door of their home.

But the sound of a sharp bark inside, as Eppie put the key in the door, modified the donkey's views, and he limped away again without bidding. The sharp bark was the sign of an excited welcome that was awaiting them from a knowing brown terrier, who, after dancing at their legs in a hysterical manner, rushed with a worrying noise at a tortoise-shell

kitten under the loom, and then rushed back with a
sharp bark again, as much as to say, "I have done
my duty by this feeble creature, you perceive;"
while the lady-mother of the kitten sat sunning her
white bosom in the window, and looked round with a
sleepy air of expecting caresses, though she was not
going to take any trouble for them.

The presence of this happy animal life was not
the only change which had come over the interior of
the stone cottage. There was no bed now in the
living-room, and the small space was well filled with
decent furniture, all bright and clean enough to satisfy Dolly Winthrop's eye. The oaken table and
three-cornered oaken chair were hardly what was
likely to be seen in so poor a cottage: they had come,
with the beds and other things, from the Red House;
for Mr. Godfrey Cass, as every one said in the village, did very kindly by the weaver; and it was
nothing but right a man should be looked on and
helped by those who could afford it, when he had
brought up an orphan child, and been father and
mother to her—and had lost his money too, so as he
had nothing but what he worked for week by week,
and when the weaving was going down too—for
there was less and less flax spun—and Master Marner
was none so young. Nobody was jealous of the
weaver, for he was regarded as an exceptional person, whose claims on neighborly help were not to be
matched in Raveloe. Any superstition that remained concerning him had taken an entirely new

color; and Mr. Macey, now a very feeble old man of fourscore and six, never seen except in his chimney-corner or sitting in the sunshine at his door-sill, was of opinion that when a man had done what Silas had done by an orphan child, it was a sign that his money would come to light again, or leastwise that the robber would be made to answer for it—for, as Mr. Macey observed of himself, his faculties were as strong as ever.

Silas sat down now and watched Eppie with a satisfied gaze as she spread the clean cloth, and set on it the potato-pie, warmed up slowly in a safe Sunday fashion, by being put into a dry pot over a slowly-dying fire, as the best substitute for an oven. For Silas would not consent to have a grate and oven added to his conveniences: he loved the old brick hearth as he had loved his brown pot—and was it not there when he had found Eppie? The gods of the hearth exist for us still; and let all new faith be tolerant of that fetichism, lest it bruise its own roots.

Silas ate his dinner more silently than usual, soon laying down his knife and fork, and watching half-abstractedly Eppie's play with Snap and the cat, by which her own dining was made rather a lengthy business. Yet it was a sight that might well arrest wandering thoughts: Eppie, with the rippling radiance of her hair and the whiteness of her rounded chin and throat set off by the dark-blue cotton gown, laughing merrily as the kitten held on with her four claws to one shoulder, like a design for a jug-handle,

while Snap on the right hand and Puss on the other
put up their paws towards a morsel which she held
out of the reach of both—Snap occasionally de-
sisting in order to remonstrate with the cat by a
cogent worrying growl on the greediness and futility
of her conduct; till Eppie relented, caressed them
both, and divided the morsel between them.

But at last Eppie, glancing at the clock, checked
the play, and said, "Oh, daddy, you're wanting to
go into the sunshine to smoke your pipe. But I must
clear away first, so as the house may be tidy when
godmother comes. I'll make haste—I won't be
long."

Silas had taken to smoking a pipe daily during the
last two years, having been strongly urged to it by
the sages of Raveloe, as a practice "good for the fits;"
and this advice was sanctioned by Dr. Kimble, on the
ground that it was as well to try what could do no
harm—a principle which was made to answer for a
great deal of work in that gentleman's medical practice. Silas did not highly enjoy smoking, and often
wondered how his neighbors could be so fond of it;
but a humble sort of acquiescence in what was held
to be good, had become a strong habit of that new self
which had been developed in him since he had found
Eppie on his hearth: it had been the only clew his
bewildered mind could hold by in cherishing this
young life that had been sent to him out of the darkness into which his gold had departed. By seeking
what was needful for Eppie, by sharing the effect

that everything produced on her, he had himself
come to appropriate the forms of custom and belief
which were the mold of Raveloe life; and as, with
reawakening sensibilities, memory also reawakened,
he had begun to ponder over the elements of his old
faith, and blend them with his new impressions, till
he recovered a consciousness of unity [1] between his
past and present. The sense of presiding goodness
and the human trust which come with all pure peace
and joy, had given him a dim impression that there
had been some error, some mistake, which had thrown
that dark shadow over the days of his best years;
and as it grew more and more easy to him to open
his mind to Dolly Winthrop, he gradually communicated to her all he could describe of his early life.
The communication was necessarily a slow and difficult process, for Silas's meager power of explanation was not aided by any readiness of interpreta-
tion in Dolly, whose narrow outward experience
gave her no key to strange customs, and made every
novelty a source of wonder that arrested them at
every step of the narrative. It was only by fragments, and at intervals which left Dolly time to re-
volve what she had heard till it acquired some familiarity for her, that Silas at last arrived at the
climax of the sad story—the drawing of lots, and its
false testimony concerning him; and this had to be
repeated in several interviews, under new questions
on her part as to the nature of this plan for detect-
ing the guilty and clearing the innocent.

"And yourn's the same Bible, you're sure o' that, Master Marner—the Bible as you brought wi' you from that country—it's the same as what they've got at church, and what Eppie's a-learning to read in?"

"Yes," said Silas, "every bit the same; and there's drawing o' lots in the Bible, mind you," he added in a lower tone.

"Oh dear, dear," said Dolly in a grieved voice, as if she were hearing an unfavorable report of a sick man's case. She was silent for some minutes; at last she said—

"There's wise folks, happen, as know how it all is; the parson knows, I'll be bound; but it takes big words to tell them things, and such as poor folks can't make much out on. I can never rightly know the meaning o' what I hear at church, only a bit here and there, but I know it's good words—I do. But what lies upo' your mind—it's this, Master Marner: as, if Them above had done the right thing by you, They'd never ha' let you be turned out for a wicked thief when you was innicent."

"Ah!" said Silas, who had now come to understand Dolly's phraseology, "that was what fell on me like as if it had been red-hot iron; because, you see, there was nobody as cared for me or clave to me above nor below. And him as I'd gone out and in wi' for ten year and more, since when we was lads and went halves—mine own familiar friend in whom I trusted, had lifted up his heel again' me, and worked to ruin me."

"Eh, but he was a bad un—I can't think as there's another such," said Dolly. "But I'm o'ercome, Master Marner; I'm like, as if I'd waked and didn't know whether it was night or morning. I feel somehow as sure as I do when I've laid something up though I can't just put my hand on it, as there was a rights in what happened to you, if one could but make it out; and you'd no call to lose heart as you did. But we'll talk on it again; for sometimes things come into my head when I'm leeching or poulticing, or such, as I could never think on when I was sitting still."

Dolly was too useful a woman not to have many opportunities of illumination of the kind she alluded to, and she was not long before she recurred to the subject.

"Master Marner," she said, one day that she came to bring home Eppie's washing, "I'v been sore puzzled for a good bit wi' that trouble o' yourn and the drawing o' lots: and it got twisted back'ards and for'ards, as I didn't know which end to lay hold on. But it come to me all clear like, that night when I was sitting up wi' poor Bessy Fawkes, as is dead and left her children behind, God help 'em—it come to me as clear as daylight; but whether I've got hold on it now, or can anyways bring it to my tongue's end, that I don't know. For I've often a deal inside me as 'll never come out; and for what you talk o' your folks in your old country niver saying prayers by heart nor saying 'em out of a book, they must be wonderful

cliver; for if I didn't know 'Our Father,' and little
bits o' good words as I can carry out o' church wi'
me, I might down o' my knees every night, but
nothing could I say."

"But you can mostly say something as I can make
sense on, Mrs. Winthrop," said Silas.

"Well, then, Master Marner, it come to me summat
like this: I can make nothing o' the drawing o' lots
and the answer coming wrong; it 'ud mayhap take
the parson to tell that, and he could only tell us i'
big words. But what come to me as clear as the daylight, it was when I was troubling over poor Bessy
Fawkes, and it allays comes into my head when I'm
sorry for folks, and feel as I can't do a power to
help 'em, not if I was to get up i' the middle o' the
night—it comes into my head as Them above has
got a deal tenderer heart nor what I've got—for I
can't be anyways better nor Them as made me; and
if anything looks hard to me, it's because there's
things I don't know on; and for the matter o' that,
there may be plenty o' things I don't know on, for
it's little as I know—that it is. And so, while I was
thinking o' that, you come into my mind, Master Marner, and it all come pouring in:—if *I* felt i' my inside what was the right and just thing by you, and
them as prayed and drawed the lots, all but that
wicked un, if *they*'d ha' done the right thing by you
if they could, isn't there Them as was at the making
on us, and knows better and has a better will? And
that's all as ever I can be sure on, and everything

else is a big puzzle to me when I think on it. For
there was the fever come and took off them as were
full-growed, and left the helpless children; and
there's the breaking o' limbs; and them as 'ud do
right and be sober have to suffer by them as are contrairy—eh, there's trouble i' this world, and there's
things as we can niver make out the rights on. And
all as we've got to do is to trusten, Master Marner—
to do the right thing as fur as we know, and to
trusten. For if us as knows so little can see a bit o'
good and rights, we may be sure as there's a good and
a rights bigger nor what we can know—I feel it i'
my own inside as it must be so. And if you could
but ha' gone on trustening, Master Marner, you
wouldn't ha' run away from your fellow-creaturs
and been so lone."

"Ah, but that 'ud ha' been hard," said Silas, in an
undertone; "it 'ud ha' been hard to trusten then."

"And so it would," said Dolly, almost with compunction; "them things are easier said nor done;
and I'm partly ashamed o' talking."

"Nay, nay," said Silas, "you're i' the right, Mrs.
Winthrop—you're i' the right. There's good i' this
world—I've a feeling o' that now; and it makes a
man feel as there's a good more nor he can see, i'
spite o' the trouble and the wickedness. That drawing o' the lots is dark; but the child was sent to me:
there's dealings with us—there's dealings."

This dialogue took place in Eppie's earlier years,
when Silas had to part with her for two hours every

day, that she might learn to read at the dame school, after he had vainly tried himself to guide her in that first step to learning. Now that she was grown up, Silas had often been led, in those moments of quiet outpouring which come to people who live together in perfect love, to talk with *her* too of the past, and how and why he had lived a lonely man until she had been sent to him. For it would have been impossible for him to hide from Eppie that she was not his own child: even if the most delicate reticence on the point could have been expected from Raveloe gossips in her presence, her own questions about her mother could not have been parried, as she grew up, without that complete shrouding of the past which would have made a painful barrier between their minds. So Eppie had long known how her mother had died on the snowy ground, and how she herself had been found on the hearth by her father Silas, who had taken her golden curls for his lost guineas brought back to him. The tender and peculiar love with which Silas had reared her in almost inseparable companionship with himself, aided by the seclusion of their dwelling, had preserved her from the lowering influences of the village talk and habits, and had kept her mind in that freshness which is sometimes falsely supposed to be an invariable attribute of rusticity. Perfect love has a breath of poetry which can exalt the relations of the least-instructed human beings; and this breath of poetry had surrounded Eppie from the time when she had followed the bright gleam that beckoned her to Silas's hearth; so that it is not surprising if, in other things besides her delicate prettiness, she was not quite a common village maiden, but had a touch of refinement and fervor which came from no other teaching than that of tenderly-nurtured unvitiated feeling. She was too childish and simple for her imagination to rove into questions about her unknown father; for a long while it did not even occur to her that she must have had a father; and the first time that the idea of her mother having had a husband presented itself to her, was when Silas showed her the wedding-ring which had been taken from the wasted finger, and had been carefully preserved by him in a little lacquered box shaped like a shoe. He delivered this box into Eppie's charge when she had grown up, and she often opened it to look at the ring: but still she thought hardly at all about the father of whom it was the symbol. Had she not a father very close to her, who loved her better than any real fathers in the village seemed to love their daughters? On the contrary, who her mother was, and how she came to die in that forlornness, were questions that often pressed on Eppie's mind. Her knowledge of Mrs. Winthrop, who was her nearest friend next to Silas, made her feel that a mother must be very precious; and she had again and again asked Silas to tell her how her mother looked, whom she was like, and how he had found her against the furze bush, led towards it by the little footsteps and the outstretched arms.

The furze bush was there still; and this afternoon, when Eppie came out with Silas into the sunshine, it was the first object that arrested her eyes and thoughts.

"Father," she said, in a tone of gentle gravity, which sometimes came like a sadder, slower cadence across her playfulness, "we shall take the furze bush into the garden; it'll come into the corner, and just against it I'll put snowdrops and crocuses, 'cause Aaron says they won't die out, but'll always get more and more."

"Ah, child," said Silas, always ready to talk when he had his pipe in his hand, apparently enjoying the pauses more than the puffs, "it wouldn't do to leave out the furze bush; and there's nothing prettier to my thinking, when it's yallow with flowers. But it's just come into my head what we're to do for a fence —mayhap Aaron can help us to a thought; but a fence we must have, else the donkeys and things 'ull come and trample everything down. And fencing's hard to be got at, by what I can make out."

"Oh, I'll tell you, daddy," said Eppie, clasping her hands suddenly, after a minute's thought. "There's lots o' loose stones about, some of 'em not big, and we might lay 'em atop of one another, and make a wall. You and me could carry the smallest, and Aaron 'ud carry the rest—I know he would."

"Eh, my precious un," said Silas, "there isn't enough stones to go all round; and as for you carrying, why, wi' your little arms you couldn't carry a stone no bigger than a turnip. You're dillicate made, my dear," he added, with a tender intonation —"that's what Mrs. Winthrop says."

"Oh, I'm stronger than you think, daddy," said Eppie; "and if there wasn't stones enough to go all round, why they'll go part o' the way, and then it'll be easier to get sticks and things for the rest. See here, round the big pit, what a many stones!"

She skipped forward to the pit, meaning to lift one of the stones and exhibit her strength, but she started back in surprise.

"Oh, father, just come and look here," she exclaimed—"come and see how the water's gone down since yesterday. Why, yesterday the pit was ever so full!"

"Well, to be sure," said Silas, coming to her side. "Why, that's the draining they've begun on, since harvest, i' Mr. Osgood's fields, I reckon. The foreman said to me the other day, when I passed by 'em, 'Master Marner,' he said, 'I shouldn't wonder if we lay your bit o' waste as dry as a bone.' It was Mr. Godfrey Cass, he said, had gone into the draining: he'd been taking these fields o' Mr. Osgood."

"How odd it'll seem to have the old pit dried up!" said Eppie, turning away, and stooping to lift rather a large stone. "See, daddy, I can carry this quite well," she said, going along with much energy for a few steps, but presently letting it fall.

"Ah, you're fine and strong, aren't you?" said Silas, while Eppie shook her aching arms and laughed. "Come, come, let us go and sit down on the bank against the stile there, and have no more lifting. You might hurt yourself, child. You'd need have somebody to work for you—and my arm isn't over strong."

Silas uttered the last sentence slowly, as if it implied more than met the ear; and Eppie, when they sat down on the bank, nestled close to his side, and, taking hold caressingly of the arm that was not over strong, held it on her lap, while Silas puffed again dutifully at the pipe, which occupied his other arm. An ash in the hedgerow behind made a fretted screen from the sun, and threw happy playful shadows all about them.

"Father," said Eppie, very gently, after they had been sitting in silence a little while, "if I was to be married, ought I to be married with my mother's ring?"

Silas gave an almost imperceptible start, though the question fell in with the under-current of thought in his own mind, and then said, in a subdued tone, "Why, Eppie, have you been a-thinking on it?"

"Only this last week, father," said Eppie, ingenuously, "since Aaron talked to me about it."

"And what did he say?" said Silas, still in the same subdued way, as if he were anxious lest he should fall into the slightest tone that was not for Eppie's good.

"He said he should like to be married, because he was a-going in four-and-twenty, and had got a deal of gardening work, now Mr. Mott's given up; and he goes twice a-week regular to Mr. Cass's and once to Mr. Osgood's, and they're going to take him on at the Rectory.''

"And who is it as he's wanting to marry?'' said Silas, with rather a sad smile.

"Why, me, to be sure, daddy,'' said Eppie, with dimpling laughter. kissing her father's cheek; "as if he'd want to marry anybody else!''

"And you mean to have him, do you?'' said Silas.

"Yes, some time,'' said Eppie, "I don't know when. Everybody's married some time, Aaron says. But I told him that wasn't true: for, I said, look at father —he's never been married.''

"No, child,'' said Silas, "your father was a lone man till you was sent to him.''

"But you'll never be lone again, father,'' said Eppie, tenderly. "That was what Aaron said—'I could never think o' taking you away from Master Marner, Eppie.' And I said, 'It 'ud be no use if you did, Aaron.' And he wants us all to live together, so as you needn't work a bit, father, only what's for your own pleasure; and he'd be as good as a son to you— that was what he said.''

"And should you like that, Eppie?'' said Silas, looking at her.

"I shouldn't mind it, father,'' said Eppie, quite simply. "And I should like things to be so you needn't work much. But if it wasn't for that, I'd sooner things didn't change. I'm very happy: I like Aaron to be fond of me, and come and see us often, and behave pretty to you—he always *does* behave pretty to you, doesn't he, father?''

"Yes, child, nobody could behave better," said Silas, emphatically. "He's his mother's lad."

"But I don't want any change," said Eppie. "I should like to go on a long, long while, just as we are. Only Aaron does want a change; and he made me cry a bit—only a bit—because he said I didn't care for him, for if I cared for him I should want us to be married, as he did."

"Eh, my blessed child," said Silas, laying down his pipe as if it were useless to pretend to smoke any longer, "you're o'er young to be married. We'll ask Mrs. Winthrop—we'll ask Aaron's mother what *she* thinks: if there's a right thing to do, she'll come at it. But there's this to be thought on, Eppie: things *will* change, whether we like it or no; things won't go on for a long while just as they are and no difference. I shall get older and helplesser, and be a burden on you, belike, if I don't go away from you altogether. Not as I mean you'd think me a burden—I know you wouldn't— but it 'ud be hard upon you; and when I look for'ard to that, I like to think as you'd have somebody else besides me— somebody young and strong, as'll outlast your own life, and take care on you to the end." Silas paused, and, resting his wrists on his knees, lifted his hands up and down meditatively as he looked on the ground.

"Then, would you like me to be married, father?" said Eppie, with a little trembling in her voice.

"I'll not be the man to say no, Eppie," said Silas, emphatically; "but we'll ask your godmother. She'll wish the right thing by you and her son too."

"There they come then," said Eppie. "Let us go and meet 'em. Oh the pipe! won't you have it lit again, father?" said Eppie, lifting that medicinal appliance from the ground.

"Nay, child," said Silas, "I've done enough for to-day. I think, mayhap, a little of it does me more good than so much at once."

CHAPTER XVII

While Silas and Eppie were seated on the bank discoursing in the fleckered shade of the ash-tree, Miss Priscilla Lammeter was resisting her sister's arguments, that it would be better to take tea at the Red House, and let her father have a long nap, than drive home to the Warrens so soon after dinner. The family party (of four only) were seated round the table in the dark wainscoted parlor, with the Sunday dessert before them, of fresh filberts, apples, and pears, duly ornamented with leaves by Nancy's own hand before the bells had rung for church.

A great change has come over the dark wainscoted parlor since we saw it in Godfrey's bachelor days, and under the wifeless reign of the old Squire. Now all is polish, on which no yesterday's dust is ever allowed to rest, from the yard's width of oaken boards round the carpet, to the old Squire's gun and whips and walking-sticks, ranged on the stag's antlers above the mantelpiece. All other signs of sporting and out-door occupation Nancy has removed to another room; but she has brought into the Red House the habit of filial reverence, and preserves sacredly in a place of honor these relics of her husband's departed father. The tankards are on the side-table

still, but the bossed silver is undimmed by handling,
and there are no dregs to send forth unpleasant suggestions: the only prevailing scent is of the lavender
and rose-leaves that fill the vases of Derbyshire spar.
All is purity and order in this once dreary room, for,
fifteen years ago, it was entered by a new presiding
spirit.

"Now, father," said Nancy, "*is* there any call for
you to go home to tea? Mayn't you just as well stay
with us?—such a beautiful evening as it's likely to
be."

The old gentleman had been talking with Godfrey
about the increasing poor-rate [1] and the ruinous
times, and had not heard the dialogue between his
daughters.

"My dear, you must ask Priscilla," he said, in the
once firm voice, now become rather broken. "She
manages me and the farm too."

"And reason good as I should manage you, father,"
said Priscilla, "else you'd be giving yourself your
death with rheumatism. And as for the farm, if
anything turns out wrong, as it can't but do in these
times, there's nothing kills a man so soon as having
nobody to find fault with but himself. It's a deal
the best way o' being master, to let somebody else
do the ordering, and keep the blaming in your own
hands. It 'ud save many a man a stroke, *I* believe."

"Well, well, my dear," said her father, with a
quiet laugh, "I didn't say you don't manage for
everybody's good."

"Then manage so as you may stay tea, Priscilla," said Nancy, putting her hand on her sister's arm affectionately. "Come now; and we'll go round the garden while father has his nap."

"My dear child, he'll have a beautiful nap in the gig, for I shall drive. And as for staying tea, I can't hear of it; for there's this dairymaid, now she knows she's to be married, turned Michaelmas, she'd as lief pour the new milk into the pig-trough as into the pans. That's the way with 'em all: it's as if they thought the world 'ud be new-made because they're to be married. So come and let me put my bonnet on, and there'll be time for us to walk round the garden while the horse is being put in."

When the sisters were treading the neatly-swept garden-walks, between the bright turf that contrasted pleasantly with the dark cones and arches and wall-like hedges of yew, Priscilla said—

"I'm as glad as anything at your husband's making that exchange o' land with cousin Osgood, and beginning the dairying. It's a thousand pities you didn't do it before; for it'll give you something to fill your mind. There's nothing like a dairy if folks want a bit o' worrit to make the days pass. For as for rubbing furniture, when you can once see your face in a table there's nothing else to look for; but there's always something fresh with the dairy; for even in the depths o' winter there's some pleasure in conquering the butter, and making it come whether or no. My dear," added Priscilla, pressing her sister's hand affectionately as they walked side by side. "you'll never be low when you've got a dairy."

"Ah, Priscilla," said Nancy, returning the pressure with a grateful glance of her clear eyes, "but it won't make up to Godfrey: a dairy's not so much to a man. And it's only what he cares for that ever makes me low. I'm contented with the blessings we have, if he could be contented."

"It drives me past patience," said Priscilla, impetuously, "that way o' the men—always wanting and wanting, and never easy with what they've got: they can't sit comfortable in their chairs when they've neither ache nor pain, but either they must stick a pipe in their mouths, to make 'em better than well, or else they must be swallowing something strong, though they're forced to make haste before the next meal comes in. But joyful be it spoken, our father was never that sort o' man. And if it had pleased God to make you ugly, like me, so as the men wouldn't ha' run after you, we might have kept to our own family, and had nothing to do with folks as have got uneasy blood in their veins."

" Oh don't say so, Priscilla," said Nancy, repenting that she had called forth this outburst; "nobody has any occasion to find fault with Godfrey. It's natural he should be disappointed at not having any children: every man likes to have somebody to work for and lay by for, and he always counted so on making a fuss with 'em when they were little.

There's many another man 'ud hanker more than he does. He's the best of husbands.''

"Oh, I know," said Priscilla, smiling sarcastically, "I know the way o' wives; they set one on to abuse their husbands, and then they turn round on one and praise 'em as if they wanted to sell 'em. But father'll be waiting for me; we must turn now.''

The large gig with the steady old gray was at the front door, and Mr. Lammeter was already on the stone steps, passing the time in recalling to Godfrey what very fine points Speckle had when his master used to ride him.

"I always *would* have a good horse, you know," said the old gentleman, not liking that spirited time to be quite effaced from the memory of his juniors.

"Mind you bring Nancy to the Warrens before the week's out, Mr. Cass," was Priscilla's parting injunction, as she took the reins, and shook them gently, by way of friendly incitement to Speckle.

"I shall just take a turn to the fields against the Stone-pits, Nancy, and look at the draining," said Godfrey.

"You'll be in again by tea-time, dear?''

"Oh yes, I shall be back in an hour.''

It was Godfrey's custom on a Sunday afternoon to do a little contemplative farming in a leisurely walk. Nancy seldom accompanied him; for the women of her generation—unless, like Priscilla, they took to outdoor management—were not given to much walking beyond their own house and garden, finding sufficient exercise in domestic duties. So, when Priscilla was not with her, she usually sat with Mant's Bible [1] before her, and after following the text with her eyes for a little while, she would gradually permit them to wander as her thoughts had already insisted on wandering.

But Nancy's Sunday thoughts were rarely quite out of keeping with the devout and reverential intention implied by the book spread open before her. She was not theologically instructed enough to discern very clearly the relation between the sacred documents of the past which she opened without method, and her own obscure, simple life; but the spirit of rectitude, and the sense of responsibility for the effect of her conduct on others, which were strong elements in Nancy's character, had made it a habit with her to scrutinize her past feelings and actions with self-questioning solicitude. Her mind not being courted by a great variety of subjects, she filled the vacant moments by living inwardly, again and again, through all her remembered experience, especially through the fifteen years of her married time, in which her life and its significance had been doubled. She recalled the small details, the words, tones, and looks, in the critical scenes which had opened a new epoch for her by giving her a deeper insight into the relations and trials of life, or which had called on her for some little effort of forbearance, or of painful adherence to an imagined or real duty—asking herself continually whether she had been in any re-

spect blamable. This excessive rumination [1] and
self-questioning is perhaps a morbid habit inevitable
to a mind of much moral sensibility when shut out
from its due share of outward activity and of practical claims on its affections—inevitable to a noble-
hearted, childless woman, when her lot is narrow. "I
can do so little—have I done it all well?" is the per-
petually recurring thought; and there are no voices
calling her away from that soliloquy, no peremptory
demands to divert energy from vain regret or superfluous scruple.

There was one main thread of painful experience
in Nancy's married life, and on it hung certain deep-
ly-felt scenes, which were the oftenest revived in
retrospect. The short dialogue with Priscilla in the
garden had determined the current of retrospect in
that frequent direction this particular Sunday afternoon. The first wandering of her thought from the
text, which she still attempted dutifully to follow
with her eyes and silent lips, was into an imaginary
enlargement of the defense she had set up for her
husband against Priscilla's implied blame. The vin-
dication of the loved object is the best balm affection
can find for its wounds:—"A man must have so
much on his mind," is the belief by which a wife
often supports a cheerful face under rough answers and unfeeling words. And Nancy's deepest
wounds had all come from the perception that the
absence of children from their hearth was dwelt on in

her husband's mind as a privation to which he could not reconcile himself.

Yet sweet Nancy might have been expected to feel still more keenly the denial of a blessing to which she had looked forward with all the varied expectations and preparations, solemn and prettily trivial, which fill the mind of a loving woman when she expects to become a mother. Was there not a drawer filled with the neat work of her hands, all unworn and untouched, just as she had arranged it there fourteen years ago—just, but for one little dress, which had been made the burial-dress? But under this immediate personal trial Nancy was so firmly unmurmuring, that years ago she had suddenly renounced the habit of visiting this drawer, lest she should in this way be cherishing a longing for what was not given.

Perhaps it was this very severity towards any indulgence of what she held to be sinful regret in herself, that made her shrink from applying her own standard to her husband. "It is very different—it is much worse for a man to be disappointed in that way: a woman can always be satisfied with devoting herself to her husband, but a man wants something that will make him look forward more—and sitting by the fire is so much duller to him than to a woman." And always, when Nancy reached this point in her meditations—trying, with predetermined sympathy, to see everything as Godfrey saw it—there came a renewal of self-questioning. *Had* she done everything in her power to lighten Godfrey's privation? Had she really been right in the resistance which had cost her so much pain six years ago, and again four years ago—the resistance to her husband's wish that they should adopt a child? Adoption was more remote from the ideas and habits of that time than of our own; still Nancy had her opinion on it. It was as necessary to her mind to have an opinion on all topics, not exclusively masculine, that had come under her notice, as for her to have a precisely marked place for every article of her personal property: and her opinions were always principles to be unwaveringly acted on. They were firm, not because of their basis, but because she held them with a tenacity inseparable from her mental action. On all the duties and proprieties of life, from filial behavior to the arrangements of the evening toilet, pretty Nancy Lammeter, by the time she was three-and-twenty, had her unalterable little code, and had formed every one of her habits in strict accordance with that code. She carried these decided judgments within her in the most unobtrusive way: they rooted themselves in her mind, and grew there as quietly as grass. Years ago, we know, she insisted on dressing like Priscilla, because "it was right for sisters to dress alike," and because "she would do what was right if she wore a gown dyed with cheese-coloring." That was a trivial but typical instance of the mode in which Nancy's life was regulated.

It was one of those rigid principles, and no petty egoistic feeling, which had been the ground of Nancy's difficult resistance to her husband's wish. To adopt a child, because children of your own had been denied you, was to try and choose your lot in spite of Providence: the adopted child, she was convinced, would never turn out well, and would be a curse to those who had wilfully and rebelliously sought what it was clear that, for some high reason, they were better without. When you saw a thing was not meant to be, said Nancy, it was a bounden duty to leave off so much as wishing for it. And so far, perhaps, the wisest of men could scarcely make more than a verbal improvement in her principle. But the conditions under which she held it apparent that a thing was not meant to be, depended on a more peculiar mode of thinking. She would have given up making a purchase at a particular place if, on three successive times, rain, or some other cause of Heaven's sending, had formed an obstacle; and she would have anticipated a broken limb or other heavy misfortune to any one who persisted in spite of such indications.

"But why should you think the child would turn out ill?" said Godfrey, in his remonstrances. "She has thriven as well as child can do with the weaver; and *he* adopted her. There isn't such a pretty little girl anywhere else in the parish, or one fitter for the station we could give her. Where can be the likelihood of her being a curse to anybody?"

"Yes, my dear Godfrey," said Nancy, who was sitting with her hands tightly clasped together, and with yearning, regretful affection in her eyes. "The child may not turn out ill with the weaver. But, then, he didn't go to seek her, as we should be doing. It will be wrong: I feel sure it will. Don't you remember what that lady we met at the Royston Baths told us about the child her sister adopted? That was the only adopting I ever heard of: and the child was transported when it was twenty-three. Dear Godfrey, don't ask me to do what I know is wrong: I should never be happy again. I know it's very hard for *you*—it's easier for me—but it's the will of Providence."

It might seem singular that Nancy—with her religious theory pieced together out of narrow social traditions, fragments of church doctrine imperfectly understood, and girlish reasonings on her small experience—should have arrived by herself at a way of thinking so nearly akin to that of many devout people whose beliefs are held in the shape of a system quite remote from her knowledge: singular, if we did not know that human beliefs, like all other natural growths, elude the barriers of system.

Godfrey had from the first specified Eppie, then about twelve years old, as a child suitable for them to adopt. It had never occurred to him that Silas would rather part with his life than with Eppie. Surely the weaver would wish the best to the child he had taken so much trouble with, and would be glad that such good fortune should happen to her: she would always be very grateful to him, and he would be well provided for to the end of his life— provided for as the excellent part he had done by the child deserved. Was it not an appropriate thing for people in a higher station to take a charge off the hands of a man in a lower? It seemed an eminently appropriate thing to Godfrey, for reasons that were known only to himself; and by a common fallacy, he imagined the measure would be easy because he had private motives for desiring it. This was rather a coarse mode of estimating Silas's relation to Eppie; but we must remember that many of the impressions which Godfrey was likely to gather concerning the laboring people around him would favor the idea that deep affections can hardly go along with callous palms and scant means; and he had not had the opportunity, even if he had had the power, of entering intimately into all that was exceptional in the weaver's experience. It was only the want of adequate knowledge that could have made it possible for Godfrey deliberately to entertain an unfeeling project: his natural kindness had outlived that blighting time of cruel wishes, and Nancy's praise of him as a husband was not founded entirely on a wilful illusion.

"I was right," she said to herself, when she had recalled all their scenes of discussion—"I feel I was right to say him nay, though it hurt me more than anything; but how good Godfrey has been about it! Many men would have been very angry with me for

standing out against their wishes; and they might
have thrown out that they'd had ill-luck in marrying
me; but Godfrey has never been the man to say me
an unkind word. It's only what he can't hide:
everything seems so blank to him, I know; and the
land—what a difference it 'ud make to him, when he
goes to see after things, if he'd children growing up
that he was doing it all for! But I won't murmur;
and perhaps if he'd married a woman who'd have
had children, she'd have vexed him in other ways."

This possibility was Nancy's chief comfort; and to
give it greater strength, she labored to make it impossible that any other wife should have had more
perfect tenderness. She had been *forced* to vex him
by that one denial. Godfrey was not insensible to
her loving effort, and did Nancy no injustice as to
the motives of her obstinacy. It was impossible to
have lived with her fifteen years and not be aware
that an unselfish clinging to the right, and a sincerity
clear as the flower-born dew, were her main characteristics; indeed, Godfrey felt this so strongly, that
his own more wavering nature, too averse to facing
difficulty to be unvaryingly simple and truthful, was
kept in a certain awe of this gentle wife who watched
his looks with a yearning to obey them. It seemed
to him impossible that he should ever confess to her
the truth about Eppie: she would never recover from
the repulsion the story of his earlier marriage would
create, told to her now, after that long concealment.
And the child, too, he thought, must become an ob-

ject of repulsion: the very sight of her would be painful. The shock to Nancy's mingled pride and ignorance of the world's evil might even be too much for her delicate frame. Since he had married her with that secret on his heart, he must keep it there to the last. Whatever else he did, he could not make an irreparable breach between himself and this long-loved wife.

Meanwhile, why could he not make up his mind to the absence of children from a hearth brightened by such a wife? Why did his mind fly uneasily to that void, as if it were the sole reason why life was not thoroughly joyous to him? I suppose it is the way with all men and women who reach middle age without the clear perception that life never *can* be thoroughly joyous: under the vague dulness of the gray hours, dissatisfaction seeks a definite object, and finds it in the privation of an untried good. Dissatisfaction seated musingly on a childless hearth, thinks with envy of the father whose return is greeted by young voices—seated at the meal where the little heads rise one above another like nursery plants, it sees a black care hovering behind every one of them, and thinks the impulses by which men abandon freedom, and seek for ties, are surely nothing but a brief madness. In Godfrey's case there were further reasons why his thoughts should be continually solicited by this one point in his lot: his conscience, never thoroughly easy about Eppie, now gave his childless home the aspect of a retribution; [1] and as the time passed on, under Nancy's refusal to adopt her, any retrieval of his error became more and more difficult.

On this Sunday afternoon it was already four years since there had been any allusion to the subject between them, and Nancy supposed that it was forever buried.

"I wonder if he'll mind it less or more as he gets older," she thought; "I'm afraid more. Aged people feel the miss of children: what would father do without Priscilla? And if I die, Godfrey will be very lonely—not holding together with his brothers much. But I won't be over-anxious, and trying to make things out beforehand: I must do my best for the present."

With that last thought Nancy roused herself from her revery, and turned her eyes again towards the forsaken page. It had been forsaken longer than she imagined, for she was presently surprised by the appearance of the servant with the tea-things. It was, in fact, a little before the usual time for tea; but Jane had her reasons.

"Is your master come into the yard, Jane?"

"No'm, he isn't," said Jane, with a slight emphasis, of which, however, her mistress took no notice.

"I don't know whether you've seen 'em, 'm," continued Jane, after a pause, "but there's folks making haste all one way, afore the front window. I doubt something's happened. There's niver a man to be seen i' the yard, else I'd send and see. I've been up into the top attic, but there's no seeing anything for trees. I hope nobody's hurt, that's all.''

"Oh, no, I dare say there's nothing much the matter,'' said Nancy. "It's perhaps Mr. Snell's bull got out again, as he did before.''

"I wish he mayn't gore anybody then, that's all,'' said Jane, not altogether despising a hypothesis which covered a few imaginary calamities.

"That girl is always terrifying me,'' thought Nancy; "I wish Godfrey would come in.''

She went to the front window and looked as far as she could see along the road, with an uneasiness which she felt to be childish, for there were now no such signs of excitement as Jane had spoken of, and Godfrey would not be likely to return by the village road, but by the fields. She continued to stand, however, looking at the placid churchyard with the long shadows of the gravestones across the bright green hillocks, and at the glowing autumn colors of the Rectory trees beyond. Before such calm external beauty the presence of a vague fear is more distinctly felt—like a raven flapping its slow wings across the sunny air. Nancy wished more and more that Godfrey would come in.

CHAPTER XVIII

Some one opened the door at the other end of the room, and Nancy felt that it was her husband. She turned from the window with gladness in her eyes, for the wife's chief dread was stilled.

"Dear, I'm so thankful you're come," she said, going towards him. "I began to get—"

She paused abruptly, for Godfrey was laying down his hat with trembling hands, and turned towards her with a pale face and a strange unanswering glance, as if he saw her indeed, but saw her as part of a scene invisible to herself. She laid her hand on his arm, not daring to speak again; but he left the touch unnoticed, and threw himself into his chair.

Jane was already at the door with the hissing urn.

"Tell her to keep away, will you?" said Godfrey; and when the door was closed again he exerted himself to speak more distinctly.

"Sit down, Nancy—there," he said, pointing to a chair opposite him. "I came back as soon as I could, to hinder anybody's telling you but me. I've had a great shock—but I care most about the shock it'll be to you."

"It isn't father and Priscilla?" said Nancy, with

quivering lips, clasping her hands together tightly on her lap.

"No, it's nobody living," said Godfrey, unequal to the considerate skill with which he would have wished to make his revelation. "It's Dunstan—my brother Dunstan, that we lost sight of sixteen years ago. We've found him—found his body—his skeleton."

The deep dread Godfrey's look had created in Nancy made her feel these words a relief. She sat in comparative calmness to hear what else he had to tell. He went on:

"The Stone-pit has gone dry suddenly—from the draining, I suppose; and there he lies—has lain for sixteen years, wedged between two great stones. There's his watch and seals, and there's my gold-handled hunting-whip,[1] with my name on: he took it away, without my knowing, the day he went hunting on Wildfire, the last time he was seen."

Godfrey paused: it was not so easy to say what came next.

"Do you think he drowned himself?" said Nancy, almost wondering that her husband should be so deeply shaken by what had happened all those years ago to an unloved brother, of whom worse things had been augured.

"No, he fell in," said Godfrey, in a low but distinct voice, as if he felt some deep meaning in the fact. Presently he added: "Dunstan was the man that robbed Silas Marner."

The blood rushed to Nancy's face and neck at this

surprise and shame, for she had been bred up to regard even a distant kinship with crime as a dishonor.

"Oh, Godfrey!" she said, with compassion in her tone, for she had immediately reflected that the dishonor must be felt still more keenly by her husband.

"There was the money in the pit," he continued— "all the weaver's money. Everything's been gathered up, and they're taking the skeleton to the Rainbow. But I came back to tell you: there was no hindering it; you must know."

He was silent, looking on the ground for two long minutes. Nancy would have said some words of comfort under this disgrace, but she refrained, from an instinctive sense that there was something behind —that Godfrey had something else to tell her. Presently he lifted his eyes to her face, and kept them fixed on her, as he said—

"Everything comes to light, Nancy, sooner or later. When God Almighty wills it, our secrets are found out. I've lived with a secret on my mind, but I'll keep it from you no longer. I wouldn't have you know it by somebody else, and not by me—I wouldn't have you find it out after I'm dead. I'll tell you now. It's been 'I will' and 'I won't' with me all my life [1]—I'll make sure of myself now."

Nancy's utmost dread had returned. The eyes of the husband and wife met with awe in them, as at a crisis which suspended affection.

"Nancy," said Godfrey, slowly, "when I married

you, I hid something from you—something I ought
to have told you. That woman Marner found dead
in the snow—Eppie's mother—that wretched woman
—was my wife: Eppie is my child.''

He paused, dreading the effect of his confession.
But Nancy sat quite still, only that her eyes dropped
and ceased to meet his. She was pale and quiet as a
meditative statue, clasping her hands on her lap.

''You'll never think the same of me again,'' said
Godfrey, after a little while, with some tremor in
his voice.

She was silent.

''I oughtn't to have left the child unowned: I
oughtn't to have kept it from you. But I couldn't
bear to give you up, Nancy. I was led away into
marrying her—I suffered for it.''

Still Nancy was silent, looking down; and he almost
expected that she would presently get up and say
she would go to her father's. How could she have
any mercy for faults that must seem so black to her,
with her simple severe notions?

But at last she lifted up her eyes to his again and
spoke. There was no indignation in her voice—
only deep regret.

''Godfrey, if you had but told me this six years
ago, we could have done some of our duty by the
child. Do you think I'd have refused to take her in,
if I'd known she was yours?''

At that moment Godfrey felt all the bitterness of
an error that was not simply futile,[1] but had defeated

its own end. He had not measured this wife with whom he had lived so long. But she spoke again, with more agitation.

"And—oh, Godfrey—if we'd had her from the first, if you'd taken to her as you ought, she'd have loved me for her mother—and you'd have been happier with me: I could better have bore my little baby dying, and our life might have been more what we used to think it 'ud be."

The tears fell, and Nancy ceased to speak.

"But you wouldn't have married me then, Nancy, if I'd told you," said Godfrey, urged, in the bitterness of his self-reproach, to prove to himself that his conduct had not been utter folly. "You may think you would now, but you wouldn't then. With your pride and your father's, you'd have hated having anything to do with me after the talk there'd have been."

"I can't say what I should have done about that, Godfrey. I should never have married anybody else. But I wasn't worth doing wrong for—nothing is in this world.[1] Nothing is so good as it seems beforehand [2]—not even our marrying wasn't, you see." There was a faint sad smile on Nancy's face as she said the last words.

"I'm a worse man than you thought I was, Nancy," said Godfrey, rather tremulously. "Can you forgive me ever?"

"The wrong to me is but little, Godfrey: you've made it up to me—you've been good to me for fifteen

years. It's another you did the wrong to; and I
doubt it can never be all made up for."

"But we can take Eppie now," said Godfrey. "I
won't mind the world knowing at last. I'll be plain
and open for the rest o' my life."

"It'll be different coming to us, now she's grown
up," said Nancy, shaking her head sadly. "But it's
your duty to acknowledge her and provide for her;
and I'll do my part by her, and pray to God Almighty to make her love me."

"Then we'll go together to Silas Marner's this very
night, as soon as everything's quiet at the Stone-
pits."

CHAPTER XIX

BETWEEN eight and nine o'clock that evening, Eppie and Silas were seated alone in the cottage. After the great excitement the weaver had undergone from the events of the afternoon, he had felt a longing for this quietude, and had even begged Mrs. Winthrop and Aaron, who had naturally lingered behind every one else, to leave him alone with his child. The excitement had not passed away:[1] it had only reached that stage when the keenness of the susceptibility makes external stimulus intolerable[2]—when there is no sense of weariness, but rather an intensity of inward life, under which sleep is an impossibility. Any one who has watched such moments in other men remembers the brightness of the eyes and the strange definiteness that comes over coarse features from that transient influence. It is as if a new fineness of ear for all spiritual voices had sent wonder-working vibrations through the heavy mortal frame—as if "beauty born of murmuring sound"[3] had passed into the face of the listener.

Silas's face showed that sort of transfiguration, as he sat in his arm-chair and looked at Eppie. She had drawn her own chair towards his knees, and leaned forward, holding both his hands, while she looked up at him. On the table near them, lit by a candle, lay the recovered gold[1]—the old long-loved gold, ranged in orderly heaps, as Silas used to range it in the days when it was his only joy. He had been telling her how he used to count it every night, and how his soul was utterly desolate till she was sent to him.

"At first, I'd a sort o' feeling come across me now and then," he was saying in a subdued tone, "as if you might be changed into the gold again; for sometimes, turn my head which way I would, I seemed to see the gold; and I thought I should be glad if I could feel it, and find it was come back. But that didn't last long. After a bit, I should have thought it was a curse come again, if it had drove you from me, for I'd got to feel the need o' your looks and your voice and the touch o' your little fingers. You didn't know then, Eppie, when you were such a little un—you didn't know what your old father Silas felt for you."

"But I know now, father," said Eppie. "If it hadn't been for you, they'd have taken me to the workhouse, and there'd have been nobody to love me."

"Eh, my precious child, the blessing was mine. If you hadn't been sent to save me, I should ha' gone to the grave in my misery. The money was taken away from me in time; and you see it's been kept—kept till it was wanted for you. It's wonderful—our life is wonderful."[2]

Silas sat in silence a few minutes, looking at the money. "It takes no hold of me now," he said, ponderingly—"the money doesn't. I wonder if it ever could again—I doubt it might, if I lost you, Eppie. I might come to think I was forsaken again, and lose the feeling that God was good to me."

At that moment there was a knocking at the door; and Eppie was obliged to rise without answering Silas. Beautiful she looked, with the tenderness of gathering tears in her eyes and a slight flush on her cheeks, as she stepped to open the door. The flush deepened when she saw Mr. and Mrs. Godfrey Cass. She made her little rustic curtsy, and held the door wide for them to enter.

"We're disturbing you very late, my dear," said Mrs. Cass, taking Eppie's hand, and looking in her face with an expression of anxious interest and admiration. Nancy herself was pale and tremulous.

Eppie, after placing chairs for Mr. and Mrs. Cass, went to stand against Silas, opposite to them.

"Well, Marner," said Godfrey, trying to speak with perfect firmness, "it's a great comfort to me to see you with your money again, that you've been deprived of so many years. It was one of my family did you the wrong—the more grief to me—and I feel bound to make up to you for it in every way. Whatever I can do for you will be nothing but paying a debt, even if I looked no further than the robbery. But there are other things I'm beholden [1]—shall be beholden to you for, Marner."

Godfrey checked himself. It had been agreed between him and his wife that the subject of his fatherhood should be approached very carefully, and that, if possible, the disclosure should be reserved for the future, so that it might be made to Eppie gradually. Nancy had urged this, because she felt strongly the painful light in which Eppie must inevitably see the relation between her father and mother.

Silas, always ill at ease when he was being spoken to by "betters," such as Mr. Cass—tall, powerful, florid men, seen chiefly on horseback—answered with some constraint—

"Sir, I've a deal to thank you for a'ready. As for the robbery, I count it no loss to me. And if I did, you couldn't help it: you aren't answerable for it."

"You may look at it in that way, Marner, but I never can; and I hope you'll let me act according to my own feeling of what's just. I know you're easily contented: you've been a hard-working man all your life."

"Yes, sir, yes," said Marner, meditatively. "I should ha' been bad off without my work:[1] it was what I held by when everything else was gone from me."

"Ah," said Godfrey, applying Marner's words simply to his bodily wants, "it was a good trade for you in this country, because there's been a great deal of linen-weaving to be done. But you're getting rather past such close work, Marner: it's time you laid by and had some rest. You look a good deal pulled down, though you're not an old man, *are* you?"

"Fifty-five, as near as I can say, sir," said Silas.

"Oh, why, you may live thirty years longer—look at old Macey! And that money on the table, after all, is but little. It won't go far either way—whether it's put out to interest, or you were to live on it as long as it would last: it wouldn't go far if you'd nobody to keep but yourself, and you've had two to keep for a good many years now."

"Eh, sir," said Silas, unaffected by anything Godfrey was saying, "I'm in no fear o' want. We shall do very well—Eppie and me 'ull do well enough. There's few working-folks have got so much laid by as that. I don't know what it is to gentlefolks, but I look upon it as a deal—almost too much. And as for us, it's little we want."

"Only the garden, father," said Eppie, blushing up to the ears the moment after.

"You love a garden, do you, my dear?" said Nancy, thinking that this turn in the point of view might help her husband. "We should agree in that: I give a deal of time to the garden."

"Ah, there's plenty of gardening at the Red House," said Godfrey, surprised at the difficulty he found in approaching a proposition which had seemed so easy to him in the distance. "You've done a good part by Eppie, Marner, for sixteen years. It 'ud be a great comfort to you to see her well provided for, wouldn't it? She looks blooming and healthy, but not fit for any hardships: she doesn't look like a strapping girl come of working parents. You'd like to see her taken care of by those who can leave her well off, and make a lady of her; she's more fit for it than for a rough life, such as she might come to have in a few years' time."

A slight flush came over Marner's face, and disappeared, like a passing gleam. Eppie was simply wondering Mr. Cass should talk so about things that seemed to have nothing to do with reality, but Silas was hurt and uneasy.

"I don't take your meaning, sir," he answered, not having words at command to express the mingled feelings with which he had heard Mr. Cass's words.

"Well, my meaning is this, Marner," said Godfrey, determined to come to the point. "Mrs. Cass and I, you know, have no children—nobody to be the better for our good home and everything else we have— more than enough for ourselves. And we should like to have somebody in the place of a daughter to us— we should like to have Eppie, and treat her in every way as our own child. It 'ud be a great comfort to you in your old age, I hope, to see her fortune made in that way, after you've been at the trouble of bringing her up so well. And it's right you should have every reward for that. And Eppie, I'm sure, will always love you and be grateful to you: she'd come and see you very often, and we should all be on the look-out to do everything we could towards making you comfortable."

A plain man like Godfrey Cass, speaking under some embarrassment, necessarily blunders on words that are coarser than his intentions, and that are likely to fall gratingly on susceptible feelings.[1] While he had been speaking, Eppie had quietly passed her arm behind Silas's head, and let her hand rest against it caressingly: she felt him trembling violently. He was silent for some moments when Mr. Cass had ended—powerless under the conflict of emotions, all alike painful. Eppie's heart was swelling at the sense that her father was in distress; and she was just going to lean down and speak to him, when one struggling dread at last gained the mastery over every other in Silas, and he said, faintly—

"Eppie, my child, speak. I won't stand in your way.[2] Thank Mr. and Mrs. Cass."

Eppie took her hand from her father's head, and came forward a step. Her cheeks were flushed, but not with shyness this time: the sense that her father was in doubt and suffering banished that sort of self-consciousness. She dropped a low curtsy, first to Mrs. Cass and then to Mr. Cass, and said—

"Thank you, ma'am—thank you, sir. But I can't leave my father, nor own anybody nearer than him. And I don't want to be a lady—thank you all the same" (here Eppie dropped another curtsy). "I couldn't give up the folks I've been used to."

Eppie's lip began to tremble a little at the last words. She retreated to her father's chair again, and held him round the neck: while Silas, with a subdued sob, put up his hand to grasp hers.

The tears were in Nancy's eyes, but her sympathy with Eppie was, naturally, divided with distress on her husband's account. She dared not speak, wondering what was going on in her husband's mind.

Godfrey felt an irritation inevitable to almost all of us when we encounter an unexpected obstacle. He had been full of his own penitence and resolution to retrieve his error as far as the time was left to him; he was possessed with all-important feelings, that were to lead to a predetermined course of action which he had fixed on as the right, and he was not prepared to enter with lively appreciation into other people's feelings counteracting his virtuous resolves. The agitation with which he spoke again was not quite unmixed with anger.

"But I've a claim on you, Eppie—the strongest of all claims. It's my duty, Marner, to own Eppie as my child, and provide for her. She's my own child: her mother was my wife. I've a natural claim on her that must stand before every other."

Eppie had given a violent start, and turned quite pale. Silas, on the contrary, who had been relieved, by Eppie's answer, from the dread lest his mind should be in opposition to hers, felt the spirit of resistance in him set free, not without a touch of parental fierceness. "Then, sir," he answered, with an accent of bitterness that had been silent in him since

the memorable day when his youthful hope had per-
ished—"then, sir, why didn't you say so sixteen year
ago, and claim her before I'd come to love her, i'stead
o' coming to take her from me now, when you might
as well take the heart out o' my body? God gave
her to me because you turned your back upon her,
and He looks upon her as mine: you've no right to
her! When a man turns a blessing from his door,
it falls to them as take it in."

"I know that, Marner. I was wrong. I've repented of my conduct in that matter," said Godfrey,
who could not help feeling the edge of Silas's
words.

"I'm glad to hear it, sir," said Marner, with
gathering excitement; "but repentance doesn't alter
what's been going on for sixteen year. Your coming now and saying 'I'm her father,' doesn't alter
the feelings inside us. It's me she's been calling her
father ever since she could say the word."

"But I think you might look at the thing more
reasonable, Marner," said Godfrey, unexpectedly
awed by the weaver's direct truth-speaking. "It
isn't as if she was to be taken quite away from you,
so that you'd never see her again. She'll be very
near you, and come to see you very often. She'll
feel just the same towards you."

"Just the same?" said Marner, more bitterly than
ever. "How'll she feel just the same for me as she
does now, when we eat o' the same bit, and drink o'
the same cup, and think o' the same things from one

day's end to another? Just the same? That's idle talk. You'd cut us i' two.''

Godfrey, unqualified by experience to discern the pregnancy of Marner's simple words, felt rather angry again. It seemed to him that the weaver was very selfish (a judgment readily passed by those who have never tested their own power of sacrifice) to oppose what was undoubtedly for Eppie's welfare; and he felt himself called upon, for her sake, to assert his authority.

''I should have thought, Marner,'' he said, severely —''I should have thought your affection for Eppie would make you rejoice in what was for her good, even if it did call upon you to give up something. You ought to remember your own life's uncertain, and she's at an age now when her lot may soon be fixed in a way very different from what it would be in her father's home: she may marry some low working-man, and then, whatever I might do for her, I couldn't make her well-off. You're putting yourself in the way of her welfare; and though I'm sorry to hurt you after what you've done, and what I've left undone, I feel now it's my duty to insist on taking care of my own daughter. I want to do my duty.''

It would be difficult to say whether it were Silas or Eppie that was more deeply stirred by this last speech of Godfrey's. Thought had been very busy in Eppie as she listened to the contest between her old long-loved father and this new unfamiliar father who had suddenly come to fill the place of that black featureless shadow which had held the ring and placed it on her mother's finger. Her imagination had darted backward in conjectures, and forward in previsions, of what this revealed fatherhood implied; and there were words in Godfrey's last speech which helped to make the previsions especially definite. Not that these thoughts, either of past or future, determined her resolution—*that* was determined by the feelings which vibrated to every word Silas had uttered; but they raised, even apart from these feelings, a repulsion towards the offered lot and the newly-revealed father.

Silas, on the other hand, was again stricken in conscience, and alarmed lest Godfrey's accusation should be true—lest he should be raising his own will as an obstacle to Eppie's good. For many moments he was mute, struggling for the self-conquest necessary to the uttering of the difficult words. They came out tremulously.

"I'll say no more. Let it be as you will. Speak to the child. I'll hinder nothing."

Even Nancy, with all the acute sensibility of her own affections, shared her husband's view, that Marner was not justifiable in his wish to retain Eppie, after her real father had avowed himself. She felt that it was a very hard trial for the poor weaver, but her code allowed no question that a father by blood must have a claim above that of any foster-father. Besides, Nancy, used all her life to plenteous circumstances and the privileges of "respectability," [1] could not enter into the pleasures which early nurture and habit connect with all the little aims and efforts of the poor who are born poor: to her mind Eppie, in being restored to her birthright, was entering on a too long withheld but unquestionable good. Hence she heard Silas's last words with relief, and thought, as Godfrey did, that their wish was achieved.

"Eppie, my dear," said Godfrey, looking at his daughter, not without some embarrassment, under the sense that she was old enough to judge him, "it'll always be our wish that you should show your love and gratitude to one who's been a father to you so many years, and we shall want to help you to make him comfortable in every way. But we hope you'll come to love us as well; and though I haven't been what a father should ha' been to you all these years, I wish to do the utmost in my power for you for the rest of my life, and provide for you as my only child. And you'll have the best of mothers in my wife—that'll be a blessing you haven't known since you were old enough to know it."

"My dear, you'll be a treasure to me," said Nancy, in her gentle voice. "We shall want for nothing when we have our daughter."

Eppie did not come forward and curtsy, as she had done before. She held Silas's hand in hers, and grasped it firmly—it was a weaver's hand, with a palm and finger-tips that were sensitive to such pressure—while she spoke with colder decision than before.

"Thank you, ma'am—thank you, sir, for your offers—they're very great, and far above my wish. For I should have no delight i' life any more if I was forced to go away from my father, and knew he was sitting at home, a-thinking of me and feeling lone. We've been used to be happy together every day, and I can't think o' no happiness without him. And he says he'd nobody i' the world till I was sent to him, and he'd have nothing when I was gone. And he's took care of me and loved me from the first, and I'll cleave to him as long as he lives, and nobody shall ever come between him and me."

"But you must make sure, Eppie," said Silas, in a low voice—"you must make sure as you won't ever be sorry, because you've made your choice to stay among poor folks, and with poor clothes and things, when you might ha' had everything o' the best."

His sensitiveness on this point had increased as he listened to Eppie's words of faithful affection.

"I can never be sorry, father," said Eppie. "I shouldn't know what to think on or to wish for with fine things about me, as I haven't been used to. And it 'ud be poor work for me to put on things, and ride in a gig, and sit in a place at church, as 'ud make them as I'm fond of think me unfitting company for 'em. What could *I* care for then?"

Nancy looked at Godfrey with a pained questioning glance. But his eyes were fixed on the floor, where he was moving the end of his stick, as if he were pondering on something absently. She thought there was a word which might perhaps come better from her lips than from his.

"What you say is natural, my dear child—it's natural you should cling to those who've brought you up," she said, mildly; "but there's a duty you owe to your lawful father. There's perhaps something to be given up on more sides than one. When your father opens his home to you, I think it's right you shouldn't turn your back on it."

"I can't feel as I've got any father but one," said Eppie, impetuously, while the tears gathered. "I've always thought of a little home where he'd sit i' the corner, and I should fend and do everything for him : I can't think o' no other home. I wasn't brought up to be a lady, and I can't turn my mind to it. I like the working-folks, and their victuals, and their ways. And," she ended passionately, while the tears fell, "I'm promised to marry a working-man, as'll live with father, and help me to take care of him."

Godfrey looked up at Nancy with a flushed face and smarting dilated eyes. This frustration of a purpose towards which he had set out under the exalted consciousness that he was about to compensate in some degree for the greatest demerit of his life, made him feel the air of the room stifling.

"Let us go," he said, in an under-tone.

"We won't talk of this any longer now," said Nancy, rising. "We're your well-wishers, my dear

—and yours too, Marner. We shall come and see you again. It's getting late now.''

In this way she covered her husband's abrupt departure, for Godfrey had gone straight to the door, unable to say more.

CHAPTER XX

NANCY and Godfrey walked home under the star-light in silence. When they entered the oaken parlor, Godfrey threw himself into his chair, while Nancy laid down her bonnet and shawl, and stood on the hearth near her husband, unwilling to leave him even for a few minutes, and yet fearing to utter any word lest it might jar on his feeling. At last Godfrey turned his head towards her, and their eyes met, dwelling in that meeting without any movement on either side. That quiet mutual gaze of a trusting husband and wife is like the first moment of rest or refuge from a great weariness or a great danger—not to be interfered with by speech or action which would distract the sensations from the fresh enjoy-ment of repose.

But presently he put out his hand, and as Nancy placed hers within it, he drew her towards him, and said—

"That's ended!"

She bent to kiss him, and then said, as she stood by his side, "Yes, I'm afraid we must give up the hope of having her for a daughter. It wouldn't be right to want to force her to come to us against her

will. We can't alter her bringing up and what's
come of it.''

"No," said Godfrey, with a keen decisiveness of
tone, in contrast with his usually careless and un-
emphatic speech—"there's debts we can't pay like
money debts, by paying extra for the years that have
slipped by. While I've been putting off and putting
off, the trees have been growing—it's too late now.
Marner was in the right in what he said about a
man's turning away a blessing from his door: it falls
to somebody else. I wanted to pass for childless once,
Nancy—I shall pass for childless now against my
wish."

Nancy did not speak immediately, but after a little
while she asked—"You won't make it known, then,
about Eppie's being your daughter?''

"No: where would be the good to anybody?—only
harm. I must do what I can for her in the state of
life she chooses. I must see who it is she's thinking
of marrying.''

"If it won't do any good to make the thing known,''
said Nancy, who thought she might now allow herself
the relief of entertaining a feeling which she had
tried to silence before, "I should be very thankful
for father and Priscilla never to be troubled with
knowing what was done in the past, more than about
Dunsey: it can't be helped, their knowing that.''

"I shall put it in my will—I think I shall put it
in my will. I shouldn't like to leave anything to be
found out, like this about Dunsey,'' said Godfrey,

meditatively. "But I can't see anything but difficulties that 'ud come from telling it now. I must do
what I can to make her happy in her own way. I've
a notion," he added, after a moment's pause, "it's
Aaron Winthrop she meant she was engaged to. I
remember seeing him with her and Marner going
away from church."

"Well, he's very sober and industrious," said
Nancy, trying to view the matter as cheerfully as
possible.

Godfrey fell into thoughtfulness again. Presently
he looked up at Nancy sorrowfully, and said—

"She's a very pretty, nice girl, isn't she, Nancy?"

"Yes, dear; and with just your hair and eyes: I
wondered it had never struck me before."

"I think she took a dislike to me at the thought of
my being her father: I could see a change in her
manner after that."

"She couldn't bear to think of not looking on
Marner as her father," said Nancy, not wishing to
confirm her husband's painful impression.

"She thinks I did wrong by her mother as well as
by her. She thinks me worse than I am. But she
must think it: she can never know all. It's part of
my punishment, Nancy, for my daughter to dislike
me. I should never have got into that trouble if I'd
been true to you—if I hadn't been a fool. I'd no
right to expect anything but evil could come of that
marriage—and when I shirked doing a father's part
too."

Nancy was silent: her spirit of rectitude would not let her try to soften the edge of what she felt to be a just compunction. He spoke again after a little while, but the tone was rather changed: there was tenderness mingled with the previous self-reproach.

"And I got *you*, Nancy, in spite of all; and yet I've been grumbling and uneasy because I hadn't something else—as if I deserved it."

"You've never been wanting to me, Godfrey," said Nancy, with quiet sincerity. "My only trouble would be gone if you resigned yourself to the lot that's been given us."

"Well, perhaps it isn't too late to mend a bit there. Though it *is* too late to mend some things, say what they will."

CHAPTER XXI

The next morning, when Silas and Eppie were seated at their breakfast, he said to her—

"Eppie, there's a thing I've had on my mind to do this two year, and now the money's been brought back to us, we can do it. I've been turning it over and over in the night, and I think we'll set out to-morrow, while the fine days last. We'll leave the house and everything for your godmother to take care on, and we'll make a little bundle o' things and set out."

"Where to go, daddy?" said Eppie, in much surprise.

"To my old country [1]—to the town where I was born—up Lantern Yard. I want to see Mr. Paston, the minister: something may ha' come out to make 'em know I was innicent o' the robbery. And Mr. Paston was a man with a deal o' light—I want to speak to him about the drawing o' the lots. And I should like to talk to him about the religion o' this country-side, for I partly think he doesn't know on it."

Eppie was very joyful, for there was the prospect not only of wonder and delight at seeing a strange country, but also of coming back to tell Aaron all about it. Aaron was so much wiser than she was

about most things—it would be rather pleasant to
have this little advantage over him. Mrs. Winthrop,
though possessed with a dim fear of dangers attendant
on so long a journey, and requiring many assurances
that it would not take them out of the region of
carriers' carts and slow wagons, was nevertheless
well pleased that Silas should revisit his own country,
and find out if he had been cleared from that false
accusation.

"You'd be easier in your mind for the rest o'
your life, Master Marner," said Dolly—"that you
would. And if there's any light to be got up the
Yard as you talk on, we've need of it i' this world,
and I'd be glad on it myself, if you could bring it
back."

So on the fourth day from that time, Silas and
Eppie, in their Sunday clothes, with a small bundle
tied in a blue linen handkerchief, were making their
way through the streets of a great manufacturing
town. Silas, bewildered by the changes thirty years
had brought over his native place, had stopped several
persons in succession to ask them the name of this
town, that he might be sure he was not under a mistake about it.

"Ask for Lantern Yard, father—ask this gentleman with the tassels on his shoulders a-standing at
the shop door; he isn't in a hurry like the rest," said
Eppie, in some distress at her father's bewilderment,
and ill at ease, besides, amidst the noise, the movement, and the multitude of strange indifferent faces.

"Eh, my child, he won't know anything about it," said Silas; "gentlefolks didn't ever go up the Yard. But happen somebody can tell me which is the way to Prison Street, where the jail is. I know the way out o' that as if I'd seen it yesterday."

With some difficulty, after many turnings and new inquiries, they reached Prison Street; and the grim walls of the jail, the first object that answered to any image in Silas's memory, cheered him with the certitude, which no assurance of the town's name had hitherto given him, that he was in his native place.

"Ah," he said, drawing a long breath, "there's the jail, Eppie; that's just the same: I aren't afraid now. It's the third turning on the left hand from the jail doors—that's the way we must go."

"Oh, what a dark ugly place!" said Eppie. "How it hides the sky! It's worse than the workhouse. I'm glad you don't live in this town now, father. Is Lantern Yard like this street?"

"My precious child," said Silas, smiling, "it isn't a big street like this. I never was easy i' this street myself, but I was fond o' Lantern Yard. The shops here are all altered, I think—I can't make 'em out; but I shall know the turning, because it's the third."

"Here it is," he said, in a tone of satisfaction, as they came to a narrow alley. "And then we must go to the left again, and then straight for'ard for a bit, up Shoe Lane: and then we shall be at the entry next to the o'erhanging window, where there's the

nick in the road for the water to run. Eh, I can see
it all.''

"Oh, father, I'm like as if I was stifled," said
Eppie. "I couldn't ha' thought as any folks lived i'
this way, so close together. How pretty the Stone-
pits 'ull look when we get back!''

"It looks comical to *me*, child, now—and smells
bad. I can't think as it usened to smell so.''

Here and there a sallow, begrimed face looked out
from a gloomy doorway at the strangers, and increased Eppie's uneasiness, so that it was a longed-for
relief when they issued from the alleys into Shoe
Lane, where there was a broader strip of sky.

"Dear heart!" said Silas, "why, there's people
coming out o' the Yard as if they'd been to chapel
at this time o' day—a weekday noon!''

Suddenly he started and stood still with a look of
distressed amazement, that alarmed Eppie. They
were before an opening in front of a large factory,
from which men and women were streaming for their
mid-day meal.

"Father," said Eppie, clasping his arm, "what's
the matter?''

But she had to speak again and again before Silas
could answer her.

"It's gone, child," he said, at last, in strong agitation—"Lantern Yard's gone. It must ha' been
here, because here's the house with the o'erhanging
window—I know that—it's just the same; but they've

made this new opening; and see that big factory! It's all gone—chapel and all.''

"Come into that little brush-shop and sit down, father—they'll let you sit down,'' said Eppie, always on the watch lest one of her father's strange attacks should come on. "Perhaps the people can tell you all about it.''

But neither from the brush-maker, who had come to Shoe Lane only ten years ago, when the factory was already built, nor from any other source within his reach, could Silas learn anything of the old Lantern Yard friends, or of Mr. Paston the minister.

"The old place is all swep' away,'' Silas said to Dolly Winthrop on the night of his return—"the little graveyard and everything. The old home's gone; I've no home but this now. I shall never know whether they got at the truth o' the robbery, nor whether Mr. Paston could ha' given me any light about the drawing o' the lots. It's dark to me, Mrs. Winthrop, that is; I doubt it'll be dark to the last.''

"Well, yes, Master Marner,'' said Dolly, who sat with a placid listening face, now bordered by gray hairs; "I doubt it may. It's the will o' Them above as a many things should be dark to us; but there's some things as I've never felt i' the dark about, and they're mostly what comes i' the day's work. You were hard done by that once, Master Marner, and it seems as you'll never know the rights of it; but that doesn't hinder there *being* a rights, Master Marner, for all it's dark to you and me.''

"No," said Silas, "no; that doesn't hinder. Since the time the child was sent to me and I've come to love her as myself, I've had light enough to trusten by; and now she says she'll never leave me, I think I shall trusten till I die.''

CONCLUSION

THERE was one time of the year which was held in Raveloe to be especially suitable for a wedding. It was when the great lilacs and laburnums in the old-fashioned gardens showed their golden and purple wealth above the lichen-tinted walls, and when there were calves still young enough to want bucketfuls of fragrant milk. People were not so busy then as they must become when the full cheese-making and the mowing had set in; and besides, it was a time when a light bridal dress could be worn with comfort and seen to advantage.

Happily the sunshine fell more warmly than usual on the lilac tufts the morning that Eppie was married, for her dress was a very light one. She had often thought, though with a feeling of renunciation, that the perfection of a wedding-dress would be a white cotton, with the tiniest pink sprig at wide intervals; so that when Mrs. Godfrey Cass begged to provide one, and asked Eppie to choose what it should be, previous meditation had enabled her to give a decided answer at once.

Seen at a little distance as she walked across the churchyard and down the village, she seemed to be attired in pure white, and her hair looked like the

dash of gold on a lily. One hand was on her husband's arm, and with the other she clasped the hand
of her father Silas.

"You won't be giving me away, father," she had
said before they went to church; "you'll only be taking Aaron to be a son to you."

Dolly Winthrop walked behind with her husband;
and there ended the little bridal procession.

There were many eyes to look at it, and Miss Priscilla Lammeter was glad that she and her father had
happened to drive up to the door of the Red House
just in time to see this pretty sight. They had come
to keep Nancy company to-day, because Mr. Cass had
had to go away to Lytherley, for special reasons.
That seemed to be a pity, for otherwise he might have
gone, as Mr. Crackenthorp and Mr. Osgood certainly
would, to look on at the wedding-feast which he had
ordered at the Rainbow, naturally feeling a great interest in the weaver who had been wronged by one
of his own family.

"I could ha' wished Nancy had had the luck to
find a child like that and bring her up," said Priscilla to her father, as they sat in the gig; "I should
ha' had something young to think of then, besides the
lambs and the calves."

"Yes, my dear, yes," said Mr. Lammeter; "one
feels that as one gets older. Things look dim to old
folks: they'd need have some young eyes about 'em,
to let 'em know the world's the same as it used to be."

Nancy came out now to welcome her father and

sister; and the wedding group had passed on beyond the Red House to the humbler part of the village.

Dolly Winthrop was the first to divine that old Mr. Macey, who had been set in his arm-chair outside his own door, would expect some special notice as they passed, since he was too old to be at the wedding-feast.

"Mr. Macey's looking for a word from us," said Dolly; "he'll be hurt if we pass him and say nothing—and him so racked with rheumatiz."

So they turned aside to shake hands with the old man. He had looked forward to the occasion, and had his premeditated speech.

"Well, Master Marner," he said, in a voice that quavered a good deal, "I've lived to see my words come true. I was the first to say there was no harm in you, though your looks might be again' you; and I was the first to say you'd get your money back. And it's nothing but rightful as you should. And I'd ha' said the 'Amens,' and willing, at the holy matrimony; but Tookey's done it a good while now, and I hope you'll have none the worse luck."

In the open yard before the Rainbow the party of guests were already assembled, though it was still nearly an hour before the appointed feast-time. But by this means they could not only enjoy the slow advent of their pleasure; they had also ample leisure to talk of Silas Marner's strange history, and arrive by due degrees at the conclusion that he had brought a blessing on himself by acting like a father to a lone motherless child. Even the farrier did not negative this sentiment: on the contrary, he took it up as peculiarly his own, and invited any hardy person present to contradict him. But he met with no contradiction; and all differences among the company were merged in a general agreement with Mr. Snell's sentiment, that when a man has deserved his good luck, it was the part of his neighbors to wish him joy.

As the bridal group approached, a hearty cheer was raised in the Rainbow yard; and Ben Winthrop, whose jokes had retained their acceptable flavor, found it agreeable to turn in there and receive congratulations; not requiring the proposed interval of quiet at the Stone-pits before joining the company.

Eppie had a larger garden than she had ever expected there now; and in other ways there had been alterations at the expense of Mr. Cass, the landlord, to suit Silas's larger family. For he and Eppie had declared that they would rather stay at the Stone-pits than go to any new home. The garden was fenced with stones on two sides, but in front there was an open fence, through which the flowers shone with answering gladness, as the four united people came within sight of them.

"Oh, father," said Eppie, "what a pretty home ours is! I think nobody could be happier than we are."

THE END

NOTES

CHAPTER I

Note the indication as to the time of the story given in the opening paragraph. Look up the words " intermittent " and " occasional "; see whether they have any meaning that justifies the author in using them to modify " person."

Note the changes in the point of view in this first paragraph, from that of the author to that of the peasants, as indicated both by the words and by the thought. Do the changes destroy the unity of the paragraph? Why?

33, 1. Winnowing machine,— flail. Look up in the dictionary. What does their work now? What further hint as to the date of the story?

34, 1. Speak the devil fair. Try to win his favor by courtesy and gifts. The villagers, already shown as ignorant and superstitious, attribute to Silas "the evil eye"— the power to harm by his mere glance.

2. Primitive wants. The struggle to get the bare necessities of life.

3. Illuminated by any enthusiastic religious faith. In those days the Wesleys and Whitefield had preached to the masses, and new zeal in religious matters had been roused. But this revival had evidently not touched the secluded little village of Raveloe.

Notice the comparisons George Eliot uses to make her point clear (page 34). This is a favorite method with her of explaining a subject. She is especially given to using analogy in accounting for mental states.

35, 1. No great park or manor house. Evidently no noble families lived near Raveloe. Only two classes are found here —the small landowners, as Squire Cass, the Osgoods, and the Lammeters, and the workers. The village is typical of English rural life.

2. Could farm badly quite at their ease. During the wars with Napoleon the price of grain and all farm products was so high that the farmers could leave half their lands untilled and still thrive. Naturally, the landowners favored war of which they had all the benefits and none of the losses.

Note how the description of Marner's personality, given by snatches before, is here (page 36) presented as a whole, with the stress laid on his greatest peculiarity, the cataleptic fits.

36, 1. Rainbow. In England the name of the tavern is indicated by the signboard hanging before the door.

2. Unexampled eyes. Look up this adjective and criticise its use here.

Note the change (page 37) in the point of view, from author to villager.

39, 1. A narrow religious sect. One of the many dissenting branches, of which there rose a multitude at the time of the Puritans, and later, the Wesleys. Any one not conforming to the doctrines of the church of England is called a dissenter.

Note the peculiarities of this sect as described here and in Chapter II.

40, 1. David and Jonathan. *I Samuel, XVIII.*

45, 1. Drawing lots was a means used by the children of Israel at God's command, during their wanderings, to discover the secret sinner. Hence the little community believed it to be God's chosen way.

Note the effect (page 46) upon Silas of the two fold blow. He never thinks of questioning the decision; his faith in the justice of God is as completely shattered as is his faith in the fidelity of friends.

CHAPTER II

48, 1. Made various by learning. Look up "various"; explain its significance here.

The picture of the dissenting chapel here given (page 49) is a faithful presentation of the worship of the various sects of that day.

49, 1. Amulet. A magic charm against evil.

Note the analogy used at the last of the paragraph on page 49.

Why is Raveloe so acceptable to Silas?

50, 1. His conception of God is so narrow that it is really the image of a malignant deity, ruling in Lantern Yard, from whom he will escape, by fleeing, as the ancients did, beyond this deity's territory.

2. **Frustrated belief.** Apparently his faith in God has been betrayed and is therefore in vain.

3. **The tale of Mrs. Osgood's table-linen.** The sum total, the complete amount. "Tale" meant "tally" or "reckoning," from *tellan,* to count. Cf.— Milton in *L'Allegro.*

> "Every shepherd tells his tale
> Under the hawthorn in the dale."

51, 1. Look up the working of the hand loom in the encyclopedia that you may have a clear idea of Silas' work.

Note the beginning of his love for gold (pages 51 and 52). The novelty of the gold, waking no painful memories, its beauty, its separation from the human world which had so hurt him — all combine to center the great need of his nature, something to love, upon the gold.

Note (page 54) that in spite of his love for gold he is unwilling to make it by false means, and that his honesty is another means of widening the breach between himself and the already fearful villagers.

Note the analogy (page 55) used to show how his love for gold grew.

56, 1. In the days of King Alfred. When a gold chain might be stretched across the street and left unguarded, without fear of thieves.

58, 1. The brownish web. The linen before bleaching is a light brown.

Had it not been for his gold, what loss would his character have suffered?

CHAPTER III

In this chapter the development of the second plot begins — that centering about Godfrey Cass.

60, 1. The fall of prices, which would naturally come with the close of the war, and to prevent which the corn laws of 1815 were passed, shutting out foreign grains unless English grains were bringing a high price in the markets.

61, 1. Orts. Scraps.

Compare page 62 with the description of Christmas at Coverley Hall as given in the *Spectator.* Note the level, mental and moral, of Raveloe social life.

62, 1. Chines. Something like our spareribs, the back bone, with other parts fast to it. Used also in the *De Coverley Papers.*

Note how the talk of the villagers (page 62) is used to

bring out the character of the two men, before we actually see them. Compare with the manner in which Silas is introduced.

65, 1. Distrain. To seize and hold property as claim for damages, loss, or money due.

What is the weakness in each character (pages 65–67)? Which is the more forceful character?

67, 1. Creep up her sleeve. Win her favor. A bit of rustic slang.

69, 1. Equally disinclined to dig and to beg. What was the feeling among the gentry toward earning one's living?

2. The sword hanging over him. As in the old story, a sword hung over the head of Damocles at the feast, suspended by a single hair, ready to fall without warning, bringing death.

71, 1. Rain cats and dogs. In the old fable cats controlled the rain, dogs the winds.

2. Crooked sixpence. Supposed to bring luck.

Note the analysis of social conditions at the time (page 72), conditions which George Eliot had ample opportunity to study in her own youth.

What is the secret of Nancy's attraction for Godfrey?

Note how the author uses the same means of presenting Godfrey's past (pages 74 and 75) as an explanation of his present condition, that she used in presenting Silas.

CHAPTER IV

Note how carefully the location of Marner's Cottage is described, as preparation for the events to follow.

Note the revelation of the gross evil of Dunstan's character here, and throughout the chapter. Not a good trait is presented. Why?

82, 1. Notice the minute description of the whip; it is to serve a purpose elsewhere.

84, 1. The latch string. A leathern or stout twine string run through the latch hole by means of which the door could be opened from without; or kept locked, were the latch string in. The expression "the latch string is out for you," signified "enter and make yourself at home — a welcome guest."

85, 1. Jack. A device for turning the spit.

Trace the development of crime in Dunstan.

86, 1. An inference that flatters a desire. What was the inference? What desire did it flatter?

CHAPTER V

Why is such stress laid (page 88) on Silas' feeling of security?

What effect (page 89) has his love for gold had upon his character?

Explain why, when he discovered his loss he " instinctively " got into the seat of his loom (page 93).

Note how eager he is to fix the blame on a human thief (page 93). Why?

CHAPTER VI

This chapter ranks, deservedly, among the finest examples of humorous character study in English.

Note the clear picture, yet drawn with so few lines, of the different members of the " Rainbow group "— the land-lord, Mr. Snell, " a man of neutral disposition accustomed to stand aloof from human differences as those of beings who were all alike in need of liquor "; his cousin, Bob Lundy, the deliberate, exasperating, yet good-natured, butcher; the ar-gumentative farrier, Dowlas; Mr. Macey and his " put upon " deputy, Mr. Tookey; the musical wheelwright and joker, Ben Winthrop; and Jem Rodney, the poaching mole catcher. Here we have before us all types of English peasants.

97, 1. Farrier. A blacksmith who is also a veterinary.

98, 1. Parish clerk. Leading in the responses in the Church service.

107, 1. Afore the queen's heads went out on the shillings. Money coined during the reign of a sovereign, bears that sovereign's image on it, hence, since the days of Queen Anne.

Note the analogy (page 110) by which the landlord proves both parties right.

What is the effect of the long words in the last sentence?

CHAPTER VII

How has Chapter VI prepared for the opening scene of this chapter?

113, 1. Strapped for a madman. The old method of treat-ing insanity was either to strap the patient fast and starve him into quiet or to beat him into harmlessness.

Here for the first time since his coming to Raveloe, Silas knows the feeling of human companionship (pages 113 and 114).

Note the low level of intelligence, the inability of the villagers to reason, or to go beyond mere outside appearance.

117, 1. Nolo episcopari. In the service for the consecration of bishops the candidate refuses the office as a mere matter of form in these words. Hence it has come to signify refusing for the sake of appearances, what one fully expects to accept later on.

CHAPTER VIII

So high is the respect for the Squire that no one dreams of connecting Dunstan with the robbery, bad as they all know him to be.

Note the level of village intelligence as shown by the growth of belief in the peddler's guilt.

Why does Silas cling to the belief that the peddler is the culprit?

129, 1. She might come. Who? What has kept her away before?

What is the Squire's character? How has it influenced the character of his sons?

CHAPTER IX

The two plots at the Stone Pit and at the Red House, have been brought in contact, though unconsciously to both, by Dunstan Cass. It now remains to develop the Red House Plot.

134, 1. Prices 'ud run down like a jack. A jack was an instrument used to turn the spit in roasting meats before an open fire. It was sometimes fitted with a mechanical device like clock-work, to keep it turning, which was, however, very crude and apt to run down at unexpected moments.

What has been the effect of the Squire's business methods upon his property? Why is he so adverse to the idea of peace (page 134)?

136, 1. My property's got no entail. I am not bound to leave it to you, but am free to disinherit you if I choose.

138, 1. His own errant weakness. Look up "errant" and explain the passage.

Analyze the last paragraph (page 83), indicating topic sentence and means of development. What purpose does it serve?

CHAPTER X

144, 1. **Mural monument and venerable tankards.** A tablet in the church, and silver drinking vessels handed down for generations — sure signs of an old respectable family.

146, 1. **No phantasm of delight.** Look up "phantasm" and substitute a Saxon synonym. What is the result?

147, 1. **Pigs' pettitoes.** Pigs' feet. Compare Christmas at Coverley Hall.

Study the character of Mr. Macey as shown in this interview (page 148).

149, 1. **Does the cussing of a Ash Wednesday.** Referring to the commination service and penitential office read on Ash Wednesday in the Church of England, when curses are pronounced on various sins.

151, 1. **Dolly Winthrop,** a simple, ignorant, yet noble character, of the same type as Dinah Morris, though far lower intellectually. She works out what is, after all, the best philosophy — to trust God's goodness, when we cannot know it.

155, 1. **I.H.S.** Symbolic letters, used in Church insignia, and given many meanings, among them that these are the initials of the words appearing to Constantine the Great in his vision of the cross.— *In Hoc Signo.* In this sign you shall conquer.

158, 1. **Them above.** Even Dolly thinks rather of several Gods than of one; her deity, like Silas', was a local one.

He is not yet ready to respond to kindness, for the common tie has not yet been found to unite him with his fellow men (page 161).

162, 1. **The Athanasian Creed,** composed by St. Athanasius to ward against the Arian heresy. It sets forth the doctrines of the Apostle's creed, so fully qualified as to make misunderstanding impossible.

164, 1. **Pillions.** Cushions placed behind the saddle, where the women rode, holding fast to the men. The close of this chapter shows clearly Godfrey's fatal weakness — his desire to take the course most acceptable to himself, least likely to cause him trouble. It shows, too, how nature may be made use of to reflect the mood of the hero — Silas, in his bitter despair, would have been out of place in a brilliant summer scene; but the hard winter typifies his state of mind, while the Christmas and New Year season are symbolic of the new blessing to come to him.

CHAPTER XI

How has the appearance of Nancy Lammeter been prepared for? Collect all the references to her, and show how they bear out this description of her.

The scene of country society here presented deserves to stand beside the scene at the Rainbow, the two presenting a perfect picture of English social life and customs in the rural districts, in the early nineteenth century.

166, 1. Joseph. A long coat, answering the purpose of our overcoats or storm coats.

Note how the time is again indicated by the change of fashion from the turban headdress and full skirt, to the extreme of the first empire styles as represented by the Miss Gunns (page 169).

171, 1. Let Gilbert's future wife be whom she might. Criticise the grammatical construction.

172, 1. Dame Tedman's. In old days, every village had its dame school, where some old dame, who had no other means of support, received a few pence weekly for taking care of the children at her home during a part of the day, and teaching them their letters with possibly a little of the rudiments of arithmetic. Irving describes just such a school in his account of Mistress Delap's School, in the Life of Goldsmith.

Note how Priscilla is made to serve (pages 173 and 174), not only in looks but in character, as a foil for Nancy, and yet is possessed of many of the same qualities which make Nancy so lovable. Does Nancy's desire to do what is right go to extremes? Why?

178, 1. Unique. In that this was the finest of Raveloe parlors — the only one of its kind.

What light is here thrown on the character of Squire Cass (page 179)?

179, 1. Silver snuff-box. It was a mark of special friendliness to invite one to take snuff with you, from your box.

180, 1. A deal about my pigtail. The fashion of wearing the hair in a queue had not yet entirely gone out.

181, 1. Bate. Old form for abate, lessen.

Solomon Macey (page 185) seems to be of the same type as Scott's last of the minstrels; in the previous century almost every village boasted what Solomon's brother would call a "musicianer" who went from place to place wherever his services were in demand, but this class, too, was dying out.

186, 1. Sir Roger DeCoverley. A country dance much like our reel.

188, 1. The charter of Raveloe seemed to be renewed by the ceremony. The little village is so conservative that even social functions proceed according to well established order and each repetition fixes them more firmly in the minds of the people as right and proper, giving stability to the village life.

189, 1. Springe. Colloquial for light, lively, quick.

Note the shrewd judgment of the villagers in their estimate of Godfrey's character and the added force it has coming from those who saw his daily life (page 190).

Note how Nancy's firmness is contrasted with Godfrey's reckless desire to gratify himself, whether right or wrong (page 193).

CHAPTER XII

What references have been made to Godfrey's wife before this? Why is this an especially good place to introduce her? What is her character?

Note that the isolation of the Raveloe world is so complete that no one dreams of Godfrey's having a wife no further off than Batherly.

The Raveloe jest about New Year's good luck has prepared Silas to see in the child a direct gift from Providence and to give him a motive for keeping her.

At what points in his life have the seizures occurred before this?

The child wakens memories, not of his sorrow at Lantern Yard, but of the happy days.

What is the purpose of this?

CHAPTER XIII

The scene is brought back sharply to the Red House. Why? How is Silas' entry made dramatic?

211, 1. Felt the cry as if some fibre were drawn tight within him. What is his feeling, love for the child, or fear of recognition? Why?

214, 1. Take the child to the parish. Deliver her to be cared for in the poor house. Has Godfrey any love for her?

CHAPTER XIV

Note how Silas' reward begins from the very first of his unselfish action.

Silas feels that the child has been sent by the same Power that permitted the loss of his gold; though he does not realize it, he is beginning to believe once more in a Power ruling over men's lives for good as well as for ill.

220, 1. **Scrat and fend.** Colloquial — work hard, care and do for others.

2. **Moithered.** Colloquial — perplexed, bothered.

221, 1. **Leeching.** The old cure for any ill was blood-letting by the use of leeches. Hence one who filled this office was called a leech — thus the term came to be equivalent to doctor.

224, 1. **'Noculation.** Innoculation was the predecessor of our vaccination, only more dangerous, as the patient was given the disease though in mild form.

232, 1. **Aberration.** Look up in the dictionary and criticise its use here.

234, 1. **Vicariously.** One who bears a penalty for another, does so vicariously — in his stead. A vicar stands between us and God, acting as his interpreter to us, as our medium of communication, in the church, with him.

Note the effect upon Silas' life in the village, of his care for the child (pages 234–236).

The close of this chapter states the real theme of the book "and a little child shall lead them."

CHAPTER XV

Note how this short chapter sums up the character of Godfrey.

238, 1. **That famous ring.** Told of in a French fairy tale, Le Prince Cher, to be found in *Contes de Fées*, a collection of French tales.

239, 1. **A father's duty.** What is his conception of fatherhood and its duties? To what does he look forward especially?

CHAPTER XVI

The story presents admirable illustrations of accelerated and retarded action. The actual time for the action in each part is short — in part one, a few months; in part two, one day, and then about a week later on. All the intervening years are told of in a few pages at the first of each part.

241, 1. **Eligible.** Suitable, proper.

2. **Ratepayer.** Taxpayer.

What change has come to Nancy? Why? What significance in the fact that Godfrey is not known as squire?

Compare the change in Godfrey with that in Silas.

How does Eppie show that surroundings are a stronger influence than inheritance?

How has Godfrey Cass "done his duty as a father" by Eppie?

251, 1. A consciousness of unity. Silas begins to realize that life is in the hands of a mighty power, shaping that life to certain definite ends, and that every event has a place in this plan though we may not understand it.

What is the analogy by which Dolly works out her explanation of Silas' past wrongs?

Note the evidence of Eppie's character in her desire to include the furze bush in her garden. Whence has she gotten this wealth of affection?

What significance in the fact that by Godfrey's act the Stone Pits are running dry?

Note how the character of Eppie, and the change in Silas are developed in this chapter.

CHAPTER XVII

This develops the character of Nancy as the previous chapter did of Eppie and Silas.

265, 1. Poor rate. Tax for supporting work houses etc.

269, 1. Mant's Bible. Published at Oxford 1814, fully annotated.

270, 1. Rumination. Turning over and over, in the mind, a perplexing question.

Why does Nancy judge Godfrey more leniently than herself? Why did she refuse to adopt a child; show where else in her life her strong sense of duty as she understands it has influenced her acts.

277, 1. The aspect of a retribution. Godfrey, however, still prefers the easiest way; it is easier to remain childless and suffer this punishment, than to run the risk of losing Nancy. He persists in what his conscience says is wrong, for the sake of having what he wants most.

CHAPTER XVIII

281, 1. My gold handled hunting whip. Note how carefully the author has prepared for this by her comment on Dunstan's borrowing the whip with Godfrey's name cut deep in the handle. Where else has she laid stress on matters trivial in themselves, but important in the working out of the story?

282, 1. Its been "I will" and "I won't" with me all my life. Compare with the Squire's comments on Godfrey's character.

283, 1. An error that was not simply futile. The fullness of his punishments lies in the fact that by his sins he lost exactly what he had hoped to gain.

284, 1. I wasn't worth doing wrong for — nothing is in this world. A lesson Godfrey has had to learn through bitter suffering; but a part of Nancy's nature.

2. Nothing is so good as it seems beforehand. Nancy has suffered for Godfrey's sin.

Godfrey always trusting things will turn out his way, still believes he can make things right at a stroke, incidentally getting the child he has long wished to claim.

CHAPTER XIX

This chapter is full of dramatic action. The scene is quiet yet surcharged with strong feeling. The greatest of human passions, unselfish love, fights its fight and wins its victory.

286, 1. The excitement had not passed away. The whole paragraph is an excellent illustration of her power to analyze emotions and feelings. Compare with the study of Silas' sense of security or of his feelings after his loss.

2. Keenness of susceptibility makes external stimulus intolerable. When the whole nature is keyed up to such a pitch that the ordinary calls of life seem irksome, the mind is tuned for higher things.

3. Beauty born of murmuring sound. From Wordsworth's "Three Years She Grew in Sun and Shower."

287, 1. On the table — lay the recovered gold. Compare with the earlier scenes, suggested by this, and note the growth in Marner's character, a growth noticed even by himself — the development of the human loving side of his nature.

2. Our life is wonderful. Compare this with Dolly Winthrop's talk with him as to God's wisdom and love.

Note how dramatically the arrival of Godfrey is prepared for by Silas' words just before Godfrey enters (page 288).

288, 1. Beholden. Colloquial — obliged, indebted.

289, 1. I should ha' been bad off without my work. Compare with the case of Dr. Manette in *A Tale of Two Cities*.

**292, 1. Words — that fall gratingly on susceptible feelings. What words has Godfrey spoken that could hurt Silas?

2. **I won't stand in your way.** Compare the weaver with the gentleman at this crisis.

296, 1. The privileges of respectability. Here speaks the English feeling of class distinction — the voice of the privileged gentry who regard the peasants as but little better than animals with not much more power to feel.

Godfrey learns that repentance can come too late; that " When a man turns a blessing from his door it falls to them as take it in," and thus is made to feel the full bitterness of his punishment.

CHAPTER XX

Godfrey has learned his lesson that " there's debts we can't pay like money debts, by paying extra for the years that have slipped by." But he has this consolation that the shadow between himself and Nancy is at last lifted, and perfect understanding and sympathy take its place.

CHAPTER XXI

305, 1. My old country. To the simple minded peasants the city lay in a different land; it had nothing in common with their home; and Silas feels the same about it.

Dolly Winthrop and Silas have found the secret of true faith — they have " light enough to trusten by," even when they cannot know.

CONCLUSION

The story is rounded out to completeness by Eppie's union with Aaron. She is one of the villagers now, and Godfrey's last hope of claiming her is gone. He must bear the consequence of his sin. But for Silas the evening of life is brighter than its morning, his unselfish love has received its reward.

ANALYSIS OF " SILAS MARNER "

CHAPTER I

How are time and place indicated? What is the value of this method? Compare with introductions in Ivanhoe and

A Tale of Two Cities. Which of the three seems to you most vivid, and why?

How is Marner introduced? The purpose of so presenting him? What is your attitude toward him? Why?

What is the point of view in the introduction? In the description of Marner? How does the author pass from one point of view to the other, and how is it shown?

Explain in your own words and by original illustrations the propitiatory fear which was the most conspicuous feature in the village attitude toward Silas; especially that section beginning " A shadowy conception of power."

Give from memory a full description of Raveloe, emphasizing its most striking feature and showing how this helps to understand the attitude of the village toward Silas.

Why is description of Lantern Yard and Silas' trouble not given as introduction? Show exactly what has been the result on him of this trouble. Take each feature of his life at Raveloe, show its contrast with Lantern Yard, and, using the man's character as key, point out the inevitableness of the change. Put yourself in his place. What then?

CHAPTER II

Give in your own words and with original illustrations the truth which opens this chapter. How is Marner's character explained in the second paragraph? How does this correspond with his actions on coming to Raveloe?

Take all that has been given of description of Raveloe, so far, and from it write a graphic description of the village.

What made the gold attract him? How does such love as this differ from that of the ordinary miser? What is the significance of the fact that he refuses to make money from his knowledge of herbs? Of the attitude of the villagers toward this refusal? Why is the episode of the broken pot dwelt on?

Write a careful analysis of Marner's character at the end of his fifteen years in Raveloe? Has the action of the story, so far, been fast or slow? Effect of this? Is more attention given to character study, or to incidents as in Ivanhoe?

CHAPTER III

How does the description of Raveloe compare with those given before? Any trace of humor in the description?

What is the point of view at first? In the description of

Dunstan? How is the change made evident? Why is village gossip chosen as a medium for explaining Red House affairs? Show how the interview between Godfrey and Dunstan bears out the gossip. Contrast the brothers. Show what in Godfrey's nature has led him into Dunstan's power. What in his home and training aided this? Show how his potential virtues became means of sin, through his one great fault. Compare Dunstan Cass with William Dane.

CHAPTER IV

Characterize Dunstan, taking his strongest trait as your central point. Have you any excuses for him? Explain his attitude toward Godfrey. Show how the suggestion given at the first of the chapter acts on Dunstan after the accident. " Dunstan's mind was as dull as the mind of a possible felon usually is." Defend or attack this, with proof by instances and reasons.

CHAPTER V

Explain and illustrate sentences 3 and 4 of paragraph 1. Describe Silas' mental state at this time. Criticize effect of his loss as natural or unnatural, with reasons. Compare this, in its effects, with Lantern Yard trouble. Show how Silas' acts reveal his nature.

CHAPTER VI

What is the purpose of this chapter? How does it bear out the impressions you had before conceived of the villagers? Show how individuality, and persistency therein, are given to each one. Critics say George Eliot has no humor. Distinguish between wit and humor. Then give your opinion on the statement.

CHAPTER VII

Show how opening of this chapter fits with the preceding. What is effect of previous attitude toward Silas, on his arrival at just this point? Show how his loss becomes, in a way, his gain, by explaining the full effect of his story upon the villagers. Show how the individuality of each one persists.

CHAPTER VIII

How have the Red House and the Stone Pits been connected so far? Effect on the reader of this unconscious connection?

Show wherein the village action is true to life; how Silas' loss may be considered a public benefaction, especially to the sterner sex.

Give illustrations in proof of the statement that association is often mistaken for cause and effect. Explain Godfrey's attitude toward Dunstan's absence. Where do you think the latter is? Effect on such a nature as Godfrey's of suspense?

CHAPTER IX

How do Squire Cass' looks fit his nature? What are his leading traits? How do his sons resemble him? How does this scene help us to understand Godfrey? Why does Godfrey not confess the whole sin now? Show how men of Godfrey's stamp are especially prone to depend on chance. Are they cowards? Why?

CHAPTER X

What significance in the fact that Dunstan's absence is unfelt?

What is Silas' state of mind? The effect on the villagers? Why does no one connect Dunstan's absence with Silas' loss?

Explain Mr. Macey's attitude, and show how it is characteristic of him.

Characterize Dolly Winthrop so as to bring out her leading traits, and show how these appear in her talk with Silas.

How does the Christmas festivity bear out the description of Raveloe already given?

CHAPTER XI

What account of Nancy has previously been given? What new traits are brought out here? Is she the girl you would think Godfrey would find attractive? Why? Compare the scene in the dressing-room with Chapter VI; the Raveloe gentry with the villagers. What have they in common? What is the object in watching the party through the eyes of the villagers?

CHAPTER XII

What makes Chapter XI a good background for this scene? How much of Molly's hatred is just? Has she any love for her child? What part have Silas' trances played in his life so far? What significance in the fact that they have been considered as divine and as infernal visitations? Were you Silas, how would you regard them, and why? Explain and account for his feelings at seeing Eppie.

CHAPTER XIII

What is the effect of the sudden transfer of scene to the Red House? Show how Godfrey's action is natural. What is its worst feature? Why?

CHAPTER XIV

Trace fully, step by step, the effect of Silas' adoption of Eppie on the attitude of the neighbors toward him, and upon his character, his feeling toward mankind, and his attitude toward God. What is the motive power in his life now? Show how this has been present before at the root of all his actions.

CHAPTER XV

Estimate Godfrey's virtue at its real value, with reasons. Give fully what you consider his feelings must be.

CHAPTER XVI

Show how descriptions of Godfrey and of Nancy indicate what has been the development in their characters. What significance in the fact that Godfrey is merely "Mr. Cass" — is he weaker than his father? What maturity would we expect for Eppie, knowing her parentage? Account for the difference. What has worked the change in Silas? What, in the cottage, shows the change? Reasons for the statement that the gods of the hearth should be respected. State in your own words Dolly's solution of the problem of Silas' life. Your opinion of it. Show how it has brought comfort to Silas. What makes it especially fit for him?

CHAPTER XVII

What evidences of Nancy's nature at the Red House? What punishment has come to Godfrey? What significance in the fact that Nancy shares it? Aside from this, what is the character of their life? Show how her attitude toward adopting a child is the natural outcome of her nature. Is she narrow? does she mistake association for cause and effect? Show how selfishness marks Godfrey's whole life,— how it keeps him from understanding Silas' feeling for Eppie. Why does he not tell Nancy the truth when he first suggests adopting Eppie?

CHAPTER XVIII

Explain Godfrey's feeling at the discovery of Dunstan's body. What is his estimate of himself? What has shown him his real self? What has made him so mistaken in Nancy's character? What makes the way in which she takes the news an added bitterness? The justice of this? Shakespeare says: " Even-handed justice commends the ingredients of the poisoned chalice to our own lips, who gave it." Show how this is true of Godfrey.

Why do both he and Nancy ignore Silas' claims?

CHAPTER XIX

Give Silas' explanation of the reason for his loss. Your explanation of the reason. How does this fit Dolly's idea of God's goodness? Effect of Godrey's arrival just at this point? Explain Silas' attitude toward the offer. Eppie's course of action. Its justice.

CHAPTER XX

Show how Godfrey's punishment fits his crime. How does he receive it? Account for his recognition of its justice. Is Eppie in any way punished for her father's sin?

CHAPTER XXI

The reason for this new trial of Silas' faith? Its result? Dolly's explanation of it?

CONCLUSION

Compare it with introduction. What part does this play in Godfrey's punishment? Significance of the village gossip at this last scene. Fitness of this as a last glimpse of Silas.

DESCRIPTION

General directions — Aim to make your picture as vivid as possible, but avoid narration. Use vivid, graphic words; avoid general terms. Keep the central point in your picture prominent and subordinate other details to it. Let the setting be vividly told, and in harmony with the facts of the story. In short, make your pictures word copies of possible illustrations for the text. For example:

1. The Church trial at Lantern Yard.
    (a) The interior of the Chapel.
        (1) Night — the candles heighten the gloom by their feeble light.
        (2) Description of place as shown by dim light.
    (b) People.
        (1) Groups.
            (a) Authorities.
            (b) William Dane near Sarah.
            (c) Speculators — other members of the community.
            (d) Marner.

Other topics for such treatment are:

1. The hut near the Stone Pits.
2. The broken jug.
3. The miser.
4. The brothers (during the quarrel).
5. The bargain.
6. Wildfire's death.
7. The thief.
8. The discovery.
9. At the Rainbow.
10. An attempt at consolation.
11. The New Year's Dance. (Various scenes.)
12. The discovery of Eppie.
13. Marner at the Red House.
14. Godfrey beside his wife's body.
15. The secret disclosed. (Dunstan's skeleton discovered; the group around the Stone Pits.)
16. The Stone Pits (contrasted with 1).
17. Eppie's refusal.

NARRATION

Especial practice in telling imaginary scenes and episodes, in keeping with the story. Use first person where possible.

1. William Dane's story of the trial.
2. Silas' Account of his last interview with Dane just before leaving Lantern Yard.
3. The naughty boy's scare. (Let one of the boys tell of trying to annoy Silas and the result.)
4. How Silas became a miser. (As he told Eppie.)
5. The search for the thief. (As told by one of the Rainbow group.)
6. The story of a bad man. (One of the villagers tells what he knows of Dunsey.)
7. The return to Lantern Yard. (Told by Eppie to Mrs. Winthrop.)
8. Eppie's marriage feast. (Told by one who was present.)

Reproduce the parts of the narrative illustrated by descriptions in first section.

Tell connectedly the stories of the chief characters.

Write character sketches combining description and narration of Godfrey, the Squire, Eppie, Dolly Winthrop, Silas.

EXPOSITION

Exposition is frequently used by the author to throw light on a certain incident or character, or to show results of acts.

1. Explain why Silas made no attempt to clear his name.
2. Explain why William Dane found it so easy to carry out his plan.
3. Explain why Silas chose a place like Raveloe for his home.
4. Explain why he refused to earn money by charms, etc.
5. Explain why, as well as how, he became a miser.
6. Explain why Dunsey hated Godfrey.
7. Explain why Dunsey found Godfrey such an easy victim.
8. Explain the effect on Silas' character of his years of hoarding.
9. Explain the consequences that would have followed Godfrey's revelation to Nancy of Eppie's identity when Silas found her. (Give your own opinion with reasons.)
10. Explain of what Godfrey's punishment consisted.
11. Explain the social life and customs of the time.

12. Explain the intellectual conditions in rural England at this time.

ARGUMENTATION

Choose your side. Draw up a brief, prepare your argument. Support all points by facts.
1. The trial of Marner.
    (a) Prepare brief and argument for the prosecution.
    (b) Brief and argument for the defense.
2. Silas was responsible for his sufferings.
3. Silas was a better man for his trials.
4. Squire Cass was responsible for the sins of his children.
5. Godfrey's sin was worse than Dunstan's.
6. Godfrey's punishment was just.

GENERAL QUESTIONS AND TOPICS FOR WRITTEN WORK

1. The setting of the story (exposition).
    (a) Time — how indicated; value of this means.
    (b) Place — fitness for theme of story.
    (c) Characters — true to life; adapted to the part they play.
2. Presentation of characters (exposition).
    (a) By direct description, and narration of action (give illustrations).
    (b) By presenting opinions of others (illustrate).
    (c) By analysis (illustrate).
    (d) Preparing for characters before they appear (give illustrations).
3. The two main plots — one centering about Silas, the other about Godfrey.
    (a) State each in outline, giving dramatic moments.
    (b) Show how the two plots are interwoven.
        (1) by Dunstan's crime.
        (2) by Godfrey's crime.
        (3) by the child.
4. Prove that no other punishment would have been so fit for Dunstan Cass.
    (a) Consider his character.
    (b) Consider his relations with others.
    (c) Show just what death meant, coming at the moment it did.

5. Discuss English rural life and customs of the last of the 18th and early 19th centuries.
    (a) Occupations.
        (1) of gentry.
        (2) of peasants.
    (b) Home life.
    (c) Social life.
    (d) Dress.
    (e) Education.
    (f) Moral standards.
6. The theme of the story.
    (a) The major theme.
    (b) The theme in the Godfrey Cass plot.
        (1) Quote passages illustrative of each.
7. George Eliot's style.
    (a) Simple or involved and difficult.
    (b) Suited to subject in hand? If so, how?
    (c) Type of sentence most often used.
    (d) Method of preparing for dramatic scenes.
    (e) Method of presenting character.
    (f) Use of contrast as means for emphasis, in scenes and in characters.
    (g) Method of showing relative importance of events, etc.
        (1) Minuteness of treatment for crises (illustrate).
        (2) Hurried action between crises (illustrate).

SILAS MARNER

40

Raymond Reddington

" Touch not this book
for fear of me for I
carry a big jackknife !

Who's afraid of his
darned old jack-
knife?